Rachel Coffman's
REVERBERATIONS

LURLiE APPALACHiAN
PUBLISHING

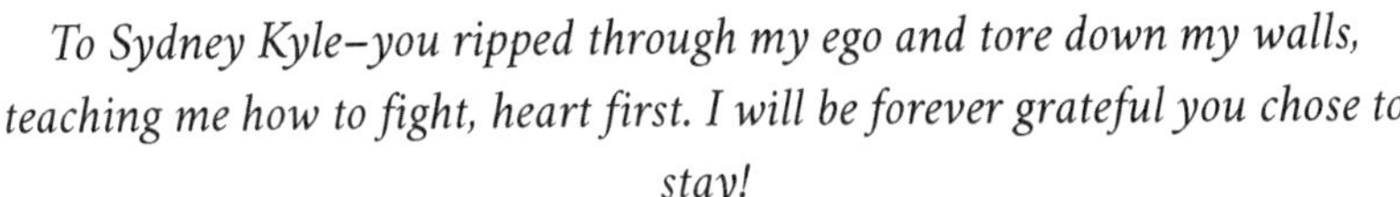

To Sydney Kyle—you ripped through my ego and tore down my walls, teaching me how to fight, heart first. I will be forever grateful you chose to stay!

To Jason—thank you for believing in me and supporting my crazy dreams.

To Mom & Dad—without your unconditional love and solid foundation, I would have never found the courage to be the smart, weird girl.

CONTENTS

CHAPTER 1

Giltine's long, forked tongue glided over the crumbling tombstones, covered in moss and patina, names worn with time. A handful of ghosts still wandered in and out of the unkempt parcel of land, and she knew them all by name. With or without their blessing, she had dived beneath the dirt and tasted their deaths regularly over the decades. It always amused her when a human spirit got disheveled over its husk of physicality, especially when she was there for the end. Obsessed with, and consumed by their deaths, they rarely grasped reality; physical death is but one stage of existence.

The Baltic immigrants who first called her to this land did so because their deaths had been tragic or maudlin. Understanding their fate, they easily transitioned along, but some of these spirits pushed back at fate. Unfamiliar pantheons guided this region of battered fighters, so they coexisted, Norris Lake anchoring them together. The irony was not lost on Giltine.

THE LONG DRIVE down failed to shake off Lexi's dread. She dropped her bags in a pile by the door and hurried to the dock, pushing down the panic threatening to boil over into a full-blown episode. The warmth of the jet ski, and the cold spray on her bare legs, pulled her out of her head and into the moment. Late afternoon wind whipped her long hair around her as she tried to outrun her depression. Eventually, the houses became sparse, and she found herself in parts of the lake only visited by locals and fishermen.

A long breath she didn't realize she was holding escaped at the sudden quiet of the engine as she guided herself into an empty cove. Body gracelessly falling back on the cushioned seat, she propped her shaky legs on the handlebars.

Unable to stop herself, another deluge of tears began, and she thought about taking a deep, cold trip into the Norris Dam. Aiming straight into the tumultuous basin, she visualized solitude and her final goodbye under the frothy, white waters. Maybe the water filling her lungs would finally bring an escape from the hollowness consuming her over the past several years.

The scent of death reminded her of the sound of trees falling. The men, *her* people, damming the river which would damn them all. The business of death was prevalent in rural mountain communities. Misplaced stress fed the animosity over the land spared from flooding; feuds and fighting carved a deep generational scar. The government was the enemy, and the mountain people chose to isolate themselves. She was saddened by the cycle of alcoholism and drugs they often used to cope. As they ravaged their bodies, the Reaper goddess feasted on the inevitable death that followed.

THE CONFLICTING PULL between the desire to live and the desire to die drew Giltine to the broken young lady floating in the lake. When she flicked her tongue, the surprising taste of strong magic varied from the Appalachian folk magic she was used to. She edged closer, realizing Lexi's fate was not yet beckoning for the Reaper, but Giltine thirsted for a change of pace. She decided to keep the girl close, if only to watch her destiny unfold from the ether.

A BONE-CHILLING cold shocked Lexi from her thoughts. Her head swiveled, looking for an intruder in her private moment. Goose-bumps crept across her skin, and all the hairs on her body stood at attention. Fear and dread took control of her facilities, and before her brain caught up to her body, she started the engine and fled back to her rental house.

Comfy pajamas always acted as a security blanket, so she slid into the warm bed and prayed that the spiritual renewal promised by the week's retreat would happen sooner than later.

CHAPTER 2

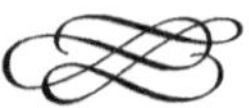

*L*exi's fingers unconsciously caressed the bandage covering the self-inflicted wound on her wrist as she reclined in the large chaise lounge on the deck, which was the selling point when she rented the one-bedroom cabin, because the views of Norris Lake were unparalleled. A wave of emotion gripped her chest, making the air feel heavy as the late-summer humidity settled on her exposed skin. Rubbing her eyes, she cradled her face in her thin hands and let it all go—tears streamed down her face, and she openly sobbed.

The fear of how close she had come to taking her own life clasped its imaginary fingers around her throat. She thought of Kyle and the letter she had written the day before and placed on his kitchen table as she left. The tears of fear, anxiety, and regret fell into her lap. When they finally stopped, and before she could get overwhelmed again, she fought back nausea and went inside.

The quaint cabin felt familiar. The folding glass doors encompassed the entire back side of the house and led to a large back deck which overlooked a short path down a hill to her private dock, and more importantly, a deserted cove of the lake. She flopped onto one of two oversized, brown leather sofas, propped her bare feet on the barnwood coffee table, and stared at the large stone fireplace. She felt a little naked without her cell phone, which she had become much too dependent on over the past several years. Still, it was also liberating knowing she would be free from all obligations. With no TV, her only access to the outside world was a computer alcove in the corner of the room.

Her tense shoulders relaxed a hair at her limited access to the life she so abruptly ran away from the day before. The moment was fleeting, and restlessness crept back in. Lexi got up and paced between the kitchen peninsula and the living room, trying to shake off the ever-present dread. She ran her hand across the rustic cabinets, feeling an innate connection with their careworn vibe. This place had seen life and weathered storms, which created a certain kinship between the two. Just then, she realized that no shades or curtains were on any of the windows facing the lake. A feeling of exposure and vulnerability, both of which she was severely unaccustomed to, sent a small shiver through her. She paused, glaring at the wall of glass, completely aware of the significance of her transparency in contrast to the life of secrecy and lies she had left behind.

She returned to the deck and smiled for the first time since leaving Ohio. The rhythmic fusion between lapping water and earth comforted her battered spirit. There was something in the inevitable sequence she trusted. It was a fluid motion, an absolute which would always be there for her. Even when the storms blew through with their violence and vengeance, those lapping waves would still await her when the worst had passed. She took a deep breath and looked optimistically toward the horizon. But then again, happiness had always eluded her. Lexi hoped whatever magic lured her to the retreat would ensure a better chance.

CHAPTER 3

Sunlight filtered through the white curtains in the master bedroom, slowly rousing Lexi from her sleep. The open window allowed the lapping waves to soothe her out of her dreamland while the cool morning breeze hardened her nipples as she stretched the full length of the king-size bed. She lay there, eyes closed, and thought about the many reasons that brought her to the gorgeous lake.

The breaking point came when she realized she had been crying for hours, every day, for the past two months. She decided she didn't want to face another day. She had a therapist, tried anti-depressants, and spent hours doing yoga and meditation. But the overwhelming feeling of discontent and sadness refused to release its chokehold on her. Again, she touched the bandage on her wrist. She was grateful the unexpected interruption jarred her from her tunnel vision of despair. In that moment, she knew a drastic move must happen to regain control of her life.

Her employer agreed to allow her a leave of absence for several months because of her consistent performance and unmarred attendance. Then, she wrote the letter to Kyle and apologized for leaving so abruptly. There was disappointment that the relationship was over, but it left him no clues to where she was going or how he could contact her. She packed her car, left the note, and headed south to find herself. She laughed at the cliché and pulled herself from the quilted bedding.

The aroma of percolating coffee began its work awakening her senses, and she thought about what adventures she could get into that day. The quiet reflections glimmering beyond the dock called to her, so she grabbed her board and decided to get out in the water and let it wash away her stress.

Tugging at the strings of her suit, she paddled out to the mouth of her cove. The gentle rocking of the water, and the familiar feel of the paddleboard between her legs, reminded her of the clumsy adolescent enveloped in the security of her father's encouragement. Cold water was always cleansing and helped clear the fog of hopelessness. As she paddled, she decided to sit down that afternoon and make a plan, because how can you achieve anything without a plan? A continuous stream of thoughts circulated through her head, making it tough to find her focus and balance, so Lexi remained seated.

The depths of the lake had always fascinated her. She wondered how many people didn't relocate when the government seized the land via eminent domain and flooded the valley. Could she be floating above people's homes? Visualizing a small city residing in the cold, dark abyss below her was unsettling. Although, at the same time, she envied the peaceful stillness of the thought. Eventually, she returned to the dock and sighed as her feet touched the warm planks. The sun was high, and the sky was blue; the morning had aged into afternoon.

Shaking the water out of her hair, Lexi noticed another person on the lake. The kayak was about 200 yards away, swiftly cutting through the water. She assumed he was a local kid, seeing it was not a big tourist section of the lake or time of year. She made a mental note so she wouldn't be surprised to see him again, grabbed her stuff, and headed back toward the house for lunch.

Rocks and brush littered the path to the cabin, stabbing and pinching her tender feet as she fought the harshness of nature. Sunlight peeked through the canopy of trees, creating a lace of light on the gravel, wildflowers, and moss lining the makeshift trail. Stopping momentarily, she tilted her head toward the sun, absorbing its energy. She glanced back at the lake toward the only person she had seen since she had arrived, catching him staring directly at her with eyes full of curiosity. She managed a brief smile and hurried up the hill into the cabin. Once safely inside, she couldn't help but look at the water again. It seemed he wasn't the only curious stranger.

CHAPTER 4

*A*s the jet ski slid onto the community dock at the foot of the retreat property, anxiety churned in Lexi's stomach. She wanted nothing more than to return to her rental and sleep for the rest of the month, but her family's work ethic was strong, and she knew this was the first step toward solace.

A social media ad had initially drawn her to Appalachian Ascension the evening after she'd cut her wrists. Uncertainty had been the blessing that kept her wounds shallow, allowing her to avoid the embarrassment of an ER visit. The thought of her family knowing about her weakness filled her with a deep shame she still carried. Scrolling through all the picture-perfect posts about her friends' idealistic lives, she'd sunk deeper into her depression.

In contrast to the blue sky and weathered mountains, the parakeet-green shade of the lake pulled at her in a way she'd never felt before. It called to a base urge she wouldn't recognize until later, but there had been no hesitation when she found there was still one opening left in the fall session of the women's retreat. She registered that night and was off to Tennessee the next week.

As she looked toward the familiar, well-manicured white house set on the pinnacle of a plot of flat, grass-covered land, the need for change, and a sense of belonging, filled her again. Lexi had never been a religious person, but she was spiritual. The website promised an opportunity to escape to a simpler time when the connection with the land wasn't drowned out by technology; a time when women were strong, fierce, and unafraid to stand tall and take what they needed to survive.

Details were vague, but the intention had been visceral. When she stepped off the wooden planks of the dock ramp, a zap of power tickled at the base of her spine, and the unfamiliar certainty of hope pushed her forward.

A woman stood at the top of the casually winding trail leading to the house. Her gray curls and rosy cheeks bloomed with a welcoming smile as she approached Lexi. Everything about her screamed *confident and approachable*, down to her flowing navy skirt and well-loved Teva sandals. Her fair skin was kissed with a sprinkle of freckles, still pink from the late summer sun. Without a stitch of makeup, she was easily one of the most beautiful women Lexi had ever seen. She waved enthusiastically and greeted Lexi with inviting, sharp eyes.

"We finally meet! I'm guessing you are Lexi, right? Your timing is perfect; everyone has arrived and settled into their rooms, and we have fresh fruit and coffee for breakfast."

Lexi smiled at the woman's distinct dialect, reminding her of days breaking beans with her grandmother on the front porch swing.

"Good morning! You must be Kate. I apologize for being the last person here. I hope I didn't cause a late start."

Kate winked at her and said, "First thing first, I don't want to hear any unnecessary apologies this week. Strong gals don't need to apologize for being human. You are right on time. Now, let's meet the rest of the group and get some food in your belly. Are you ready to work hard this week and open yourself up to a different way of thinking?"

"I am more than ready," Lexi said as Kate grabbed her hand and pulled her toward the feminine chatter spilling from the screen door.

CHAPTER 5

*O*ats in one hand, a journal under her arm, and a tall glass of ice water in her other hand, Lexi wiggled into the swinging chair on the dock. She had been in the waterfront cabin for over a week, and still had not spoken to a single person outside the retreat. Looking at the open journal, pen in her mouth, she thought about the past couple of years and what Kate asked her to write about. Unable to pinpoint when everything started crumbling, she remembered the last time she was out with her friends. Had it really been her 32nd birthday? How could she have gone over two years without seeing her closest friends? But then, she remembered the embarrassment she felt hearing about how sloppy she had gotten at the pub. Unable to remember drinking enough alcohol to get blackout drunk, she was shocked when she woke up with no memory of anything past dinner that night. The next day, Nancy recounted how she had gone off on a tangent, insulting her best friend and even pushing her into a table. Lexi had tried, repeatedly, to apologize and explain that she couldn't remember anything from that night. Unfortunately, it had only been met with unanswered texts and calls, and they hadn't spoken since that night.

Come to think of it, it wasn't long after that she started running into issues with her bank. What a nightmare that had been! She still didn't understand how her bill pay ended up so far out of whack, but she struggled for almost a year to get everything straightened out. Whenever she thought she had it fixed, something would get canceled again, throwing her finances back into chaos.

The bank never would take responsibility for the errors, insisting she made all account changes, but she knew she hadn't. Regardless, she was lucky she still had her apartment in Cincinnati. After several missed rent payments, her landlord alerted her to the mess her auto bill-pay had created. Bills were consistently late because payment dates had changed, while other payments had been canceled. If she hadn't known her landlord personally, who knows what kind of financial mess she would have found herself in.

Amidst all the confusion, she pulled away from everyone, leaving no one to blame for her loneliness but herself.

Lexi gazed at her journal blankly, unable to shake the thoughts that had driven her away from everyone and everything she loved. She sat on the dock of her beautiful lakefront house in a ridiculously comfortable chair, the sun shining on her closed eyes, and she cried again. The familiar tears rolled off her nose, dropping onto the blank page, her incomplete plan to find happiness. She pulled her knees into her chest, dropped her face into her hands, and let the book fall to the floor.

As she wiped her nose on her shirt, trying to shut the floodgates again, she nearly jumped out of her chair when she noticed someone standing next to her. Startled, she jumped up and let out an awkward squeal. "Holy shit, dude, you scared the hell out of me!" she blurted.

"I'm sorry," he hesitated. "It's just... I noticed you were upset and wanted to make sure you were okay. I didn't mean to scare you or make you uncomfortable," he said, "I'll go."

This stranger was the boy she had previously seen on the lake. He looked slightly younger than her but carried himself with the confidence of someone much older. Wisdom and understanding stared back at her through his blue eyes. His manner was casual, almost aloof. Unruly blonde curls tussled in the wind, and his tan body was nearly all muscle. He was a good looking kid, she thought casually.

Realizing she was staring, her cheeks burned.

"No, I'm sorry. I was just...I just didn't know you were standing there, and it startled me," she said. "I didn't mean to..." she trailed off, looking down.

Flashing a big, open smile, he held out his hand. "I'm Todd. I live around here and usually spend my afternoons out there in the water. I didn't mean to barge in on you, but I'm not used to seeing anyone out here and you looked like you might need a friend. Anyway, now we aren't strangers. Keep your head up, and I'm around if you ever get bored or need some company." He grinned and turned to leave, but before he pushed off, he looked back, "You're too beautiful and in too magnificent a location for tears. Have a drink and enjoy the sunset!" he said. Kind laughter faded as he headed back out to the main channel.

Watching him navigate away, Lexi noticed dawn flirting with daylight, and chills rippled across her overexposed arms. Bewilderment held her in her seat as she ran the brief encounter back through her head. How did he notice her crying? She suddenly felt uncomfortable, wondering how long he had been there watching her, but the feeling passed quickly. She smiled, almost laughing, wondering how a young man, barely pushing 30, could seem to have his shit so together.

Oh well, she thought, I'm gonna take him up on one thing: a drink on the dock sounds like the perfect way to end the night. With that, she headed to Kate's for the retreat.

CHAPTER 6

*K*ate quietly went about her pre-dawn rituals to avoid disturbing her sleeping guests. The smell of coffee filled the kitchen as she set out black tea, pastries, and fresh-cut fruit. This had long been her weekday morning routine, giving her mind time to wander as her muscle memory completed the rest of her breakfast duties. The autumn workshop participants would be attentive and thirsty for change, as usual, but she knew many would soon fall back into old traps of habit and fear. It wasn't her job to change people, just offer them a guidebook toward a more rewarding path. Every now and then, hidden gifts would bloom inside one of her students, and that transformation was the fire keeping her going. But even before Lexi Greer rounded the corner and came into view for the first time, Kate knew she was unique.

The air crackled and sparked with magic around Lexi. She suppressed abilities few had ever matched. Only Alva exceeded her, and she was a multi-generational healer. Sadly, the poor girl was locked down tighter than a frog's ass. She had built warded strong-boxes over armed bunkers within below-ground cave systems of emotional armor. Her constipated energy was giving her pain in almost every aspect of her life, and Kate knew it would take more than a one-week retreat to help her. At least Lexi had taken that pivotal first step toward rejuvenation.

Memories flooded Kate as she thought back to her sixteenth birthday when Alva took her out on that rickety johnboat she used to deliver her folk remedies.

They'd left in time to anchor and watch the sunset. The reliable, hand-steered motor shut off, and the smell of gas lingered. That smell always filled Kate with an overpowering urge for freedom.

Once settled, Alva pulled out her worn Altoids tin and started rolling a joint. When she handed it to Kate along with the lighter, the teenager knew something was about to go down because the older lady always told her cannabis wasn't for kids.

"Not too much," said Alva. "You still need a clear head, but this will help keep you in the present. I can feel your urge to get out of this town so strongly, you got me wantin' to leave."

Teenage Kate hit the joint a couple of times and handed it back to the older woman. "Is that what this is about Mama Alva? You gonna try and convince me to stay in this pisshole of a town? Cause that ain't happenin'. As soon as I graduate, I'm outta here, and there ain't nothing nobody can do to stop me."

"Child, you're always talking when you should be listening. I brought you out here because today you turned sixteen. You definitely ain't no woman yet, but you ain't a little girl no more either. You've been sittin' at my feet watching me conjuring up medicine for mountain folks who can't afford to go to them city doctors. You have a blessed gift, but it ain't my job to dictate your future. You gonna leave; I know that, and I ain't gonna stop you. But while you're still here, there are still things you need to learn."

Kate rolled her eyes and flopped onto the bench, unconcerned that Alva had to hold onto both sides of the boat to keep it from tipping. "I ain't never asked to be a witch."

"My lessons ain't about being a witch. They about learning an ancient art passed down from woman to woman for as long as time. All I've taught you is how to identify plants and learn the medicine within 'em. I've taught you how to meditate and hold space for your ancestors. Scared men spent centuries trying to crush that knowledge, killin' us off if they couldn't tame

us. But women are strong; you are strong, little miss Kate. I know you ain't never had no mama to teach you these things. That's all I'm doing."

"You say that, but I know you, tricky lady."

"In my family, sixteen is a girl's first step into womanhood. I was gonna help you take a little spirit journey to talk to your ancestor team, but if you ain't interested, we can always head back to the house."

The rugged, sinewy teenager jerked up, sending the boat rocking again. "What's a spirit journey?" she asked.

"Oh, so now she's interested." Alva smirked and reached behind her and pulled out the old patchwork quilted bag she had carried for as long as Kate had known her. "You ready to shut your mouth, ground yourself, and listen?"

"Yes," Kate huffed.

"Good."

Rummaging through her giant bag, Alva pulled out three items: a tarnished silver locket, a pint of cheap whiskey, and a beech twig. "Women are like trees, strong and beautiful, full of life on the inside. But they can also be fragile to the environment they count on to support them. The potential for motherhood within a woman calls for a different soul state. To know you hold the literal future of humanity inside your body and the power to mold them into the best versions of themselves is a powerful kind of magic. You have to be the root system that can change and weave into a consistent love offered through fluid character growth. This is what it means to be a woman. Once you learn to love and embrace that part of yourself, your power and magic will grow."

Alva handed the locket to Kate and told her to open it. The girl's body instantly relaxed, and a heartfelt smile spread from ear to ear. "I've never seen this," she whispered. "I recognize the picture of my mom on the left, but who is the lady on the right?"

Laughter burst from the older woman, "I thought the red hair would make it obvious, but apparently, I've aged more than I realized. I started babysitting your mama when I was around sixteen, and by the time she'd reached eighteen, we were more like sisters than friends. Did you know she told me she was pregnant before she told your daddy? He still gets sour about that, but that was our bond. She was so happy when she found out you were growing inside her belly; she loved you from that moment until she left this *world. I never imagined the night we brought you into this world would be the last moment I would have with her. She was wearing this locket the night you were born."*

Kate gently cupped the locket in her hand, bringing it to her heart. "I don't have words, Alva. This is the best present I've ever received. Thank you."

"That is your birthday present. Put it in your bra so you don't lose it. This," she said, holding up the whiskey bottle, "is a gift for my mama. That woman loved her a little snort after supper," she laughed, taking a big swig, the rest making ripples on the glass surface of the lake as she emptied the bottle. "The twig is from the beech tree in your backyard. Your mama planted it after she found out she was pregnant with you. I want you to make something for your mama out of it, maybe a ring or a bracelet. Then we'll send it to her through these waters, just like I did with my mama's gift. As you work the twig into something special, I want you to tell her how much you love and miss her and ask her to guide you into womanhood."

Alva lit two candles, one silver and one pink. The silver represented the goddess and female energy, strengthening intuition, telepathy, and clairvoyance. The pink represented unconditional love, helping facilitate relationships and emotional healing.

Kate's fingers weaved the beech twig into a beautiful bracelet for her mom, and when she looked up, she caught Alva watching her with pride and love. "Do you think she'll like it?" Kate asked.

"She will love it. Now, I want you to put on the bracelet, leave your shoes in the boat, and slide into the water."

"What about the locket? It will get wet and ruin the pictures, or even worse, it will get lost."

"Don't worry. I put a charm on the locket so it will never be destroyed and will always find its way back to you. Like I said before, tuck it under your left boob in your bra. That way, it will be connected to your heart. Once you are in the lake, float on your back and wait for your mama to come to you."

Kate did as she was told. The warm lake water kept her afloat as she stared up at the stars shining brightly without light pollution. Alva's melodic chanting helped her slip into a trance, and soon, she was overwhelmed by the smell of honeysuckle. The beech bracelet on her arm began *warming up. She knew immediately when her mom's hand entwined with hers, and she was filled with an unconditional love she'd never experienced.*

When she opened her eyes, she was no longer in the water. Instead, she was sitting across from her mother in a space void of anything but their souls. Her mom's long brown curls reminded her of all the pictures she had treasured since childhood, but photos had not done justice to her amber eyes. Those eyes were a lantern guiding her into the shadows of her past.

"Hello, baby girl," she said. "I see Alva has been teaching you some of our mountain magic. I can't believe it has been sixteen years since I've held you. Your first step into womanhood is a trip into the dark parts you've been avoiding because the best way to overcome pain and fear is to shine a light on them. There are secrets within yourself that I will always be here to help you discover. Are you ready?"

"No. Can't we just be together and talk? I have so many questions," Kate cried.

"Not this time, darlin'. This journey has a specific purpose: to set you on your spiritual path. But keep up the practice with Alva, and you'll have plenty of access to me in the future. Then, once you find your path, start planting seeds for others to find theirs. Now, focus on your third eye, and squeeze my hand if you get scared."

Kate squeezed the tears from her eyes and looked inward. The pain hit her like a hailstorm wrecking a rusted tin roof. Her eyes bulged open as the need to push overwhelmed all her thoughts, and she saw a young, auburn-haired Alva perched between her legs. She was exhausted and felt something wrong in her body, but she ignored it, determined to give birth to a healthy baby. Instinct took over, and she pushed until she felt a sudden release, a gush of fluid, followed by an emptiness.

"It's a girl, and she's en caul," Alva squealed in delight, laying the newborn, amniotic sac still intact, onto her stomach. She gently burst the sac, water drenching the new mom, and removed the membrane. Quickly clearing the baby's airway, a squawk of fury released from the tiny soul.

Kate was aware of a sudden shift toward panic as they laid the baby on her chest, but all she felt was love. Alva was still working on removing the placenta, but the new mama was enveloped in unequivocal happiness. As she slowly faded from blood loss, her last thoughts were pride, acceptance, and complete understanding of her unexpected maternal role from beyond.

Just as abruptly as she was thrown into her mother's memory of her birth, she was pulled back into the void across from her mom. Guilt that had trapped her in an emotional iron maiden for her entire life crumbled. She let out a breath she hadn't realized she was holding and looked to her mother with love and understanding.

"My death wasn't your fault. The universe had other plans for us. I'm sorry you carried all that unnecessary pain for so long. Your immature, stubborn ass wouldn't put Alva's lessons to practice, and this is the first time you've broken through the ether to hear my heart."

Kate laughed at the similarities between her mom and Alva's snarky nature. "Lesson learned, Mama."

"In a couple of years, when you run as far away from this place as you can, don't forget this is where my spirit will be waiting for you to return home. Open yourself to different cultures, people, and ways of living. Never stop learning. Never stop dreaming. You'll make your way home when you finally learn to love this little piece of Appalachian heaven. Talk to me; I'll always be listening and sending you signs. Alva has another present for you from me. I'm taking this special piece you infused yourself into for me. Good-bye, my amazing child. I can't wait for your future to unfold. You will do big things. My love for you will always be your constant; use it as a lantern to discern falsity from the truth when the labyrinth of life distracts you."

KATE RECALLED the insolent teenager she was when Alva pushed her out of the nest. She stifled her laughter, envisioning an adolescent Kate resisting her nature and banging every branch on the tree of enlightenment, flailing like a falling chicken instead of the sparrow she turned into.

As predicted, she ran as far away from Celts Holler as possible. She traveled across Asia, where she was exposed to Eastern medicine, learning the arts of reflexology and Reiki. In Ireland, she found her singing voice and traveled around the UK with a band called Whatever, an opportunity she thought would launch her onto the global scene, but the farthest she got was Sweden before the money ran out and the band split.

There were no regrets. She'd fed her vagabond spirit with experience, food, and freedom. Lovers had come and gone, and lifelong friendships were created. That time across seas blossomed a yearning for the home where she'd been raised and knew her mama's spirit was waiting.

Upon returning to Celts Holler, she saw everything with new eyes—eyes of experience. That was when she finally understood Alva and the lessons she'd been taught as a child. The Appalachian region, which had been such a curse and source of embarrassment for so long, began to make sense. Soon after, Kate began her formal tutelage under Alva and, several years later, bought a piece of property to begin her own legacy.

An ominous energy lay thick in the air. The coffee grounds had warned Kate that something was coming. She'd kept the class size low in expectation, keeping her third eye open. The journey would be life-altering, so she was not surprised at Lexi's arrival. Time to learn would be short, but time to teach would be even shorter. Excited for a new page in her adventure, Kate cleared space for personal meditation before the group's day began.

CHAPTER 7

*B*ubbles erupted from the darkness below Lexi's feet as she kicked the cool water back and forth, thinking about the juxtaposition between wildness and serenity. She actively listened and participated with the group as they were asked to embrace their wildness.

As she listened to the feminine growls and screams, it didn't feel wild to her. Some women stripped, swimming naked in the lake, while others rolled down the grassy hill like children. It was all light-hearted, but none of it made her feel what Kate was guiding her toward. She jumped at the weathered wood squeaking against the foam, keeping them afloat.

"I'm sorry if I startled you," said Kate.

"It's okay, I was just daydreaming. I guess I'm struggling to find my wildness."

Pulling her skirt into a knot, Kate sat beside the younger woman, dipping her bare feet in the familiar waters. "It is probably because your wildness is seated in a much different place than most of the group."

"What do you mean?" asked Lexi.

"Most of the women here have no basic sense of who they truly are, and coming to a place like this gives them permission to experiment, to be heard and seen. Their acts of childlike freedom are a rebellion against their closed, controlled lives at home. Their idea of wildness is pushing against the norm, finally taking the driver's seat in their own lives. But you, Lexi, you are very different. Your wildness lives here," she placed her hand on the soft spot below her breastbone.

"I still have no idea what I came here for," Lexi sighed.

"You're already a successful, independent woman. Your stifling control isn't over your surroundings or the people in your life; your control focuses mostly on that scary part of yourself that yearns for attention. I bet when you lose control of your emotions, it probably surfaces, licking at your awareness. In fact, I bet your temper has even created physical disruption to your environment. But it is such a wild and unfamiliar part of yourself that you've spent a lifetime shoving it back down, ignoring the root cause, and giving it labels like anxiety, panic, and stress. It isn't until you can let go of your fear in those moments and let that part of yourself develop and strengthen that you will find why you've come here."

"How do I break a lifetime of habitual suppression? It's not like I haven't tried to change."

"I think the universe has designated me to be the lantern into your inner shadows. Something inside of you already knows what you need. Let me ask you this: how long did you ponder over resources, time, or money before you decided to make this journey to Norris Lake?"

Thinking back to that original social media ad, she admitted, "None. I saw the ad and went directly to your website to reserve my spot. It was one of the easiest decisions I've ever made."

Kate arched an eyebrow and looked at Lexi with a wicked understanding. "I bet that was probably the first time in your life you let innate wildness and intuition take the driver's seat, wasn't it? Once you learn to harness that part of yourself, you can become who you were meant to be. It took me years of running to accept my life path."

"How did you know this was your calling?" Lexi asked.

"I was an angry kid; lost my mom during my own birth. Alva, my mentor, stepped in and became a kind of surrogate, trying her best to teach me to calm my soul and open myself to the ancient power in these mountains. On my sixteenth birthday, she gave me the three best gifts I'd ever received up until then. She gave me this," she said, pulling the small silver locket tucked under her shirt. "The woman on the right is my mama, and the woman on the left is a young Alva. It had been a gift from my mama, and I was delighted to have another piece of her, no matter how small. Then, she led my first spiritual journey into womanhood, where I met my mom for the first time in the spirit realm. Mom shone a light on a darkness I had carried my whole life. She told me I'd know when it was time to come home. The last, and most precious, gift Alva gave me that night was my good luck talisman. She had been my mother's midwife the night I joined this corporeal world, still en caul. So, in ancient tradition, Alva rubbed a sheet of paper across my newborn head and face, pressing the material of the caul onto the paper. That little piece of my life carries some strong ancestral magic."

"Holy shit, that is one hell of a sixteenth birthday. So, you already knew at sixteen this was your future?"

Kate laughed heartily. "Not even close. Once I graduated from high school, I traveled abroad. In my teenage defiance, I decided I wanted to learn esotericism through an Eastern perspective, so I started in Asia. That's where I acquired several of the skill sets we discussed this week, like Reiki, Tai Chi, reflexology, and acupuncture. I apprenticed under some amazing teachers and learned a lot, but I wasn't practicing the root work of my own magic. And, of course, if you don't actively practice something, you start to lose your expertise. When the opportunity came to go on tour as lead singer of this little band out of Ireland, I headed back west. While touring, I was sexually assaulted, and everything fell apart. The trauma came out in bursts of power I hadn't learned to control, which was terrifying. That led me down a path of too much drinking and drugging. During my lowest moments, all I could think of was coming back home, connecting with my mama and the healing powers of these mountains. It took years of studying under Alva before I was able to release my trauma and develop my own magic. Once I did, I knew I had to share my knowledge with other lost women."

"So, that is how Appalachian Ascension Women's Retreat was born?"

"Basically. It took a ton of work, but I finally allowed myself to reach my true potential. For some folks, allowing themselves to succeed and find genuine happiness is harder than for others." She set her warm hand on Lexi's shoulder and smiled. "How long are you planning on staying at Norris Lake?"

"I don't have a timeline. I knew I wanted to attend your retreat, but I have an open-ended rental contract with the landlord. I've taken a leave of absence at work because I didn't want an external timeline directing me, probably for the first time ever."

"Perfect, finish the workshop with the rest of the women, but once it's over, I would like you to come work with me one-on-one. The exchange of services will not be monetary. I could use your help with the gardens and preparing the property for winter. I would also like you to help me run some errands and do some much-needed foraging before the Holly King blows in his triumphant wintery welcome. In return, I'll help you find why the universe brought you to us, and if we're both lucky, we will each end up with a new friend out of the time together."

Lexi did not hesitate to agree to the unexpected offer. As Kate stood and started to head back toward the group, Lexi asked, "Wait. Who is the Holly King?"

"In old Celtic folklore, the Holly King and the Oak King are in a constant battle for the Wheel of the Year. The Holly King represents the dark half of the year. We can shed our old selves and transform into a better version when he is in charge. You showed up at the perfect time of year if you are looking for transformation. Learn from the trees. They're experts at embracing their beauty, then letting it all go before starting over again each year." She grinned mischievously at Lexi and turned to leave.

CHAPTER 8

*L*exi kicked at stones as she walked along the shore to nowhere. She didn't know where her stroll was leading and didn't care, but realized, after a while, nothing was familiar. Ahead, there was an island in the distance, the undeveloped landscape of the wildlife reserve to her left, and a handful of sparsely scattered houses to her right, some more extravagant than others. It didn't look like very many of the houses were occupied, and she wondered if they were vacation homes until one friendly, well-loved cabin caught her attention.

A paddleboard was propped up against the house and a bike leaned casually against the deck, but the outside shower caught her attention and drew her toward the place. She meandered closer, thinking about how liberating it would be to shower outside, allowing herself the ultimate full exposure.

The faint lull of music drifted from the back door, revealing the presence of an occupant, but Lexi didn't turn away. Staring at the curious house, mesmerized, she noticed a familiar guy approaching the deck: Todd.

Lexi shook her head, and unspoken laughter softened her face, "I guess it was bound to happen, us running into each other again. You know, since we are pretty much the only people on this part of the lake."

"Likely story. We both know you are stalking me," Todd replied casually, cocking one eyebrow. "But since you're here, why don't you tell me your name and have a drink with me?"

Generally, Lexi would have made one of a million excuses for why she couldn't stay, but she surprised herself and said yes. Maybe it was the coolness in the air from the lake breeze, or the fact she had been walking for a minute, but whatever the reason, she couldn't resist the invitation. "Oh, I'm sorry, I'm Lexi. Nice place. I'm guessing you live here year-round since you are still here after Labor Day?"

"Yeah, I've been in this house for a while now. My parents live over in Knoxville, so this place gives me a nice cushion," he said, laughing. "Don't get me wrong, I appreciate my family greatly; they are the reason I have all this, but it's cool to have my own thing going on, you know?"

Todd's bare chest looked even more tanned against the light khaki of his linen pants. He looked like he had just showered, reminding Lexi of what initially drew her toward his place. He plopped down on the sofa next to the outdoor fireplace and motioned Lexi to sit, leaning over to grab a beer from the small refrigerator beside him. "I hope a wheat ale is okay. That's all I have right now."

"Sure, whatever you've got. I have an eclectic palate anyway," Lexi replied, taking a big swig of beer. "Could I maybe get a glass of water, as well? I have been walking for a while today and need to rehydrate, or else I could, quite possibly, chug all your beer."

"Now, we wouldn't want that."

He got up swiftly to get her a glass of ice water. "So, how long will I have the pleasure of calling you neighbor?" he shouted from the kitchen window.

"I'm honestly not sure," Lexi answered as he handed her the glass. "I'll be here at least a couple of months, maybe more if I still feel like hiding from the world."

"Living in the moment?" he asked, noticing she was staring across the rippling water. He didn't push for an answer, instead taking a moment to watch his new friend.

The way her head was turned, he could see the gold in her green eyes, but even more obvious was the worry and distraction pooled in their depths. She was stunning. Though a little older than the girls who usually kept him company, her striking looks were haunting and mysterious, revealing a tortured soul. He immediately felt pulled toward her, knowing their lives had been entwined for a purpose.

He smiled softly, understanding she was obviously *not* living in the moment. "Lexi," he addressed her again.

"Oh, I'm sorry. I keep finding myself zoning out lately. What did you say?" she asked.

"Nothing, just trying to get your attention. So, tell me, Miss Lexi, what brings you to my lakefront all alone?" She could tell by his expression that the question had no judgment, just interest.

"It's a long story, one I am sure that you wouldn't be interested in. Let's just say that I needed some time alone to think." Lexi pulled at the sleeve of her sweatshirt and hoped he wouldn't press further, but knowing he would, she changed the subject. "So, how long did you say you've lived here?"

"I moved here after I graduated college, so I guess several years now. I graduated high school early and finished my master's degree at 25. It didn't feel like it was time for me to start a big career, so I decided to buy this house and live in the present for a couple of years first. You know, figure out who I was and what I wanted before making any major life decisions. My family has done well over the years, so they bought me the house when I graduated, and I work remotely, so I never have to leave the house if I don't want to." He looked up at Lexi with a big grin and added, "Don't think I didn't notice that you avoided giving me any real information about yourself. I gave a little, now you give a little... that's how friendships begin."

Lexi knew he was right, but she wasn't in the market for a new friend. Standing abruptly, she downed the rest of her beer and backed off the deck. "Thanks for the drink, but I'd better get going. I have to get dinner started." She turned and rushed toward the path before he could stop her. Once close to the shore, she turned and waved. "Thanks again, Todd. See you around!"

Navigating the shoreline at night was a little trickier, especially with so many questions fighting for her attention. She managed to stumble back to her dock, where she sat kicking her feet in the water, astonished by how warm the water felt in contrast to the cool evening air. She looked around for anyone watching, took off her clothes, and slid into the dark water.

The lake caressed her naked body as she swam toward the middle of the cove, looking up the hill at the houses surrounding her. They were all empty and dark except the one she had claimed as hers, allowing her to surrender the last bit of self-consciousness she harbored.

She floated on her back, staring up at the moon and replaying the night in her memories. The point of the trip was to let go, let life control her for once instead of the other way around. So why had she been so quick to run from the only guy she'd met since arriving? What would she have said if she had stayed? *I am basically here because my life was on an endless spiral downward, and I was hoping maybe I could find the ladder back up?* Why would she share that with a guy she just met? Maybe because he didn't really know anything about her, he wouldn't judge her? Maybe because if she brought herself to say it aloud, she could figure out why she felt so lost.

The echo of a large animal running through the brush cut her thought short and pulled her back into the present. Knowing she couldn't hide in the stillness of the night forever, she swam back to the dock and headed back to the safety of the cabin. Nothing could be changed now; besides, she wasn't going anywhere anytime soon. If she were supposed to make a friend while she was there, the universe would eventually put him back in her path.

And apparently, they were meant to be because she found herself floating alongside him the next day and accepted his invitation to hang out.

SHE WAS WAITING on the dock when he pulled up in his boat. "You obviously wakeboard," she said, noticing the rack mounted with several boards.

"I do. Maybe I can get you out on the water one of these days. Do you know how?"

"I can ski, but I haven't really tried to get up on a wakeboard."

"Well then, we'll have to resolve that life error as soon as possible." He smiled and helped her board the boat.

It was a short ride to Todd's place and soon, they were sitting on his back deck.

He handed her a drink, "I'm glad you decided to give this friendship another chance. I couldn't believe you ran away from me last time."

She looked up from under her long brown hair, finding his eyes, and then burst out laughing at his mocking look of offense. "You have no idea what you are getting into," she said, shaking her head. "None."

"I had an inkling about what I was getting into the evening I found you crying on your dock," he said coyly, "but I couldn't help but find myself fascinated and intrigued to know why you were so upset. I'd seen you on the lake earlier that morning, and you just sat on your board looking out into the water, almost like you were looking for something that wasn't there. I wondered what you were looking for, or if maybe I could help you find it."

Todd rose from his seat and sauntered over to the fire, poking the embers to feed the flames. He didn't say anything else, just stared at the flames and waited.

Lexi was not used to this kind of exchange. Todd was so genuine and direct, without being intrusive. He looked back at her and smiled, still not saying a word, just waiting for her to decide whether she would trust him or not. That was precisely when Lexi realized they would become friends and wondered if he could help her find what she was looking for.

She finally met his eyes again and took a deep breath. "Todd, I honestly have no idea what I am looking for. I don't even know why I am sad. I'm hoping this women's retreat will give me some answers."

He knelt, handed her another beer, and lightly touched her hand. "Well, luckily, we don't have to figure anything out tonight. How would you like to join me for dinner? I always have more than I need. I never really got the hang of cooking for one, so I'll happily throw a steak on the grill for ya."

Lexi smiled and nodded, taking a big swig of her beer and sitting back in her chair, relaxing a little.

CHAPTER 9

On the last day of the retreat, Lexi sat on the deck waiting for the caffeine to make its way through her system, when she realized one of the significant differences that place had allowed her, something she never felt at home: the freedom to just be. She had always surrounded herself with activity, but never let anyone get too close because she feared loss more than loneliness. It was easier for her to hide from her emotions when she wore the masks everyone expected from her.

On the retreat, she forced herself to lose the security masks and deal with the madness as it came. For the first time since she made the decision to leave, she was comfortable with her actions and under-stood her intuition guided her into the Appalachian Mountains for a reason. In fact, she was proud of the courage she'd shown by finally putting herself before everyone else in her life.

Isn't it funny how the mind works? Therapists always told her meditation would help her find peace and eliminate the stress in her life, but they neglected to inform her that clearing her mind from all thoughts was damn near impossible. The longer Lexi would lay still trying to focus on nothing, the more ideas filled her head. Her attempt to find clarity often left her chastising her failure, frustrated, and disappointed in herself—the roller coaster of emotion rearing its ugly head again.

Kate taught her a different way during the retreat. Stillness wasn't for everyone. Lexi needed mundane physical tasks like working the land or swimming to find her way through panic and fear to mental stillness; that explained why she loved playing sports and working out. She also learned that intelligent women with deep emotion and active problem-solving tendencies never have empty minds. Instead of trying to shut everything off, she needed to treat the process like standing in the middle of traffic, and let the thoughts pass through her consciousness.

The women spent an entire day discussing how the emotional state of worry could trap them. Kate taught them that worry and fear were useful tools to warn us of possible dangers, but their use was fulfilled once that warning was communicated.

That lesson slammed into Lexi. Incessant worry never changed anything and brought no positivity into her life. It had simply become a habit she used to avoid moving forward, and habits could be broken.

As she slid her jet ski into the docking station, she noticed some of the women already packing up their cars. A rush of profound gratitude filled Lexi, knowing she didn't have to leave.

When the group of women held hands on the lakeshore, the cool water grounding them to the present, they said goodbye to the ancestors in appreciation of their lessons. Each woman offered a gift to land by tossing them into the water: tea leaves, fruit from the garden, or various trinkets gathered throughout the week.

Lexi pulled a small yellow flower Kate told her was called a seedbox for the occasion. Chilly goosebumps ran down Lexi's spine as she offered the gift to the lake. Surprisingly, she noticed Kate react and look around at the same moment.

O̲nce̲ e̲ve̲ryone̲ had le̲ft, Lexi and Kate cleaned up the clutter left by the group.

"Why don't you go on and get out of here? I've got this," Kate said.

"I thought chores were part of our bartering system. I don't care to help, it's not like I have anything pressing to do. I really enjoyed this week. I know I've got a lot of growing and work to get where I want to be, but I feel like I have new perspective, and I've given new vocabulary to my inner critic."

"You've made tremendous progress, even more than I expected. But now, I want you to get back into the rhythm of life so you can practice using those skills out in the wild. It's easy to let down those walls when you feel safe, but I want you to get comfortable leaving them down when things get uncomfortable."

"You mean do the work," Lexi said with a laugh.

"Exactly! Besides, I must make a trip to Knoxville, and on to Ashville to deliver products to my vendors and restock on things you and I will need in the coming weeks. Is there anything I can grab you from the city while I'm there?"

"I think I'm okay. The local shops have all the basics, and I'm working on simplicity."

"Smart lady. Do you have a cell phone I can reach you on when I get back?"

"I left my cell phone in Cincinnati because I didn't want my life to follow me here, but I do have a cheap pre-paid I bought on the way down. The lake house also has a landline. I'll leave you both numbers before I head home."

"I'm thinking we'll start once I get back. I also wanted to toss an idea out there, but there is no pressure. Since you are paying rent in your own place, why don't you just move your stuff here once I return? I have plenty of room, and it would save you money."

"I wouldn't want to be a burden," said Lexi.

"Pish posh, you are never a burden. There will be plenty of night lessons as we work, making communication and proximity much easier if you were already here."

"In that case, I'd love to!"

CHAPTER 10

The next few days, Lexi and Todd spent their evenings together with dinner and drinks, usually sitting on the back deck at the house of whomever cooked that night. Lexi learned that Todd had his master's in philosophy, and wanted to return to school, but was unsure where he wanted to take his academic path. This was the main reason he worked remotely from the lake.

He was one of three kids, the middle child, with an older brother and a twin sister, and was very close to his family. As she learned more about him, she realized Todd was not at all typical for his age. He didn't seem to be preoccupied with girls or partying; he was a genuine old soul. His interests were nearly as diverse as hers, and they had found their differentiation to societal norms one of many things they enjoyed about each other.

She was undeniably aroused by his intelligence, and not necessarily in a sexual context. Their conversations stimulated long-dormant places within her, bringing interests and desires she hadn't discussed in years to the surface. Lexi found she could be herself around him and wasn't insecure or conscious of her usual hang-ups. She could be the person she wanted to be with him, not the role she had been cast into back home, which was refreshing. Were these the skills Kate wanted her to embrace in real life?

Looking out the window, she uncorked a nice bottle of chardonnay to breathe. The asparagus and corn were cleaned and prepared for the grill, and she squeezed the last half of the lemon over the scallops she bought at the market earlier that day. She finished wrapping the foil and slid everything into the refrigerator until they were ready to cook.

Miles Davis floated onto the deck, which was lit only by the light from the house, the fire, and several lanterns scattered about. Lexi carried the bottle of wine and two glasses onto the deck, filling one for herself. Sitting down, she covered her bare legs with the blanket. Admiring her surroundings, her smile came easily, and she let her body fall into the rhythm of the music. When she opened her eyes, Todd was sitting in the chair beside her with his full wine glass.

"Nice choice in music," he said smiling. "And, may I say, you look more radiant than ever this evening."

"Thank you," she said blushing. "Dinner is ready to go on the grill whenever you get hungry, and I see you've already found the wine."

The two sat quietly for a moment, just listening to evening noises.

"Can you believe how gorgeous it is tonight? I'm glad you could join me."

"I would never turn down a beautiful woman willing to cook for me! Besides, scallops are my favorite. Did you have a nice afternoon sunbathing? You looked like you were absorbed in your book, so I didn't want to bother you." He had brought another bottle of wine and got up to take it inside to chill.

Lexi watched him walk away, admiring how easy he made things. "I guess I was. I didn't even notice you. Were you in the water? I noticed a couple of boats out there fishing today, but I just couldn't find the energy to do anything but soak up the sun. I think I may have gotten a little too much sun. My shoulders and back are a little tender and I'm freezing, which is usually the tell-tale sign of sunburn." She shivered and pulled the blanket up a little further.

"Yeah, I was out there for a bit, but not too long. I had to run into town this afternoon. Have you put any aloe on? I will happily put it on your back if you want," he laughed and winked at her.

"Actually, do you care? I got my shoulders but can't reach my back very well, and it hurts. Besides, I really don't want to peel and get burned again. Gimme a minute; I'll go grab it."

Much to Todd's surprise, she jumped up and ran into the house, returning with the bottle of aloe.

"Thank you so much!" She handed him the bottle, turned around, and pulled her shirt over her shoulders. Her breath caught, and shivers ran down her body as he slathered the aloe on her back, unsure if it was from the cold gel or from his touch on her bare skin.

"Let me know if I'm hurting you." His fingers lightly touched her skin, and he was surprised by what stirred inside him. As he covered her back with aloe, he was impressed by her muscle tone and found himself wanting to touch more of her but stopped. "There you go. Does that feel any better?" he asked, pulling her shirt back down.

She looked over her shoulder, turned around to face him, and smiled. "Thanks, I do feel better, but still chilly. Will you stoke the fire while I run inside and get the food? The coals should be just about ready."

She stood, causing his arm to brush her leg as she walked into the kitchen, awakening a simmering pulsation. She let out a long breath once inside. She couldn't believe this turn of events and was taken aback by her sudden physical attraction to him. He was so young. Trying not to let her hands shake, she returned to the deck with the uncooked food.

"I'll take that," said Todd. "Since you did all the preparation, the least I can do is cook for you." He took the tray from her, arranged the food on the grill, and walked back to his seat beside her.

She pulled the chaise closer to the fire and wrapped the blanket around her shoulders, exposing her tanned legs.

"You'd be a lot warmer if you'd put some pants on."

"I know, next time I get up. Here's your wine." She handed him his glass as he pulled his chair closer to hers. "So, what did you go into town for?"

"Nothing really, just to pay some bills and take care of some things. But, while I am thinking about it, may I take you somewhere tomorrow?"

She looked up at him inquisitively. "Where?"

"It will be more fun if you don't know until we get there. I promise you will have a good time. You trust me, don't you?" He wanted so badly to touch her, run his fingers through her thick hair. Instead, he stood up to check on the food.

"I trust you, but you have to at least tell me something…like what to wear?" She was flattered and excited he'd made plans for them outside of their new dinner and drinks routine on the deck. Then again, maybe she was reading into it too much. She shivered again.

"Wear something comfortable and bring your lake stuff, how's that? Food's ready. Where are the plates? I'll grab them."

"No, I'll get them. Besides, I really do want to throw on some pants. Rumor is they might help keep me warm."

She handed him the plates through the door and rolled her eyes sheepishly as she walked into her bedroom and shut the door. "Cold water, I need cold water," she said to herself. Leaning over the bathroom sink, she splashed water on her face. What was she thinking? She threw on her white yoga pants, checked herself in the mirror, and softly giggled before she returned for dinner.

When she stepped back onto the deck, Todd couldn't help but stare. The light from the windows cast a glow around her, creating shadows that accentuated her tall, hourglass figure. Her pink cheeks, with a dusting of freckles, were the perfect accent to her flawless skin, even with virtually no makeup. Her smile was scintillating, and he was glad to see it finally make its appearance, cautiously hoping it was because of him. The evening was a stark difference from the first night he met her, although he knew her inner struggle was never too far from the surface.

He stood and pulled out her chair. "Warmer now?"

"Yes, thank you. Everything looks delicious, we make a great team.

I also hear you changed the music. Had I mentioned Harry Connick Jr. was my favorite?"

"Well, your music library was a pretty big giveaway, but he just so happens to be one of my favorites too. Good dinner music."

There was a comfortable moment of silence between them as they ate dinner.

After they finished the first bottle of wine, Todd stood and asked, "Where's your corkscrew? I'm gonna go grab the other bottle of wine."

Lexi stood up to help. "I'll show you. Just let me get these plates."

She put the dirty dishes in the sink, spun around, and ran smack into Todd, nearly causing him to drop the bottle. "Oh shit, I am so sorry!" But as she stepped back, she slipped and fell on her ass in the middle of the kitchen. Embarrassed by her typical clumsy behavior, she just sat on the floor laughing, not sure how to react.

"Graceful," Todd said, laughing with her. "I like it. Now, are you going to sit there all night, or will you show me where that corkscrew is?" He offered her a hand, helped her up, and put his arm around her waist. "Seriously, though, are you okay?"

"Just fucking fabulous," she grimaced. "So now you know my other curse. I am hopelessly clumsy, constantly running into walls and tripping over my own feet. How is it that you seem to know so many of my flaws, yet I haven't been able to find a single chink in your armor? It isn't fair!"

Todd turned her around to face him and tucked her hair behind her ear. "You worry so much about your flaws that you don't seem to realize how exceptional you are. Your flaws are what give you dimension and individuality. It's funny; the things you call flaws are the characteristics that drew me toward you. Perfect is boring. I know you see that in others, so why do you hold yourself to such different standards?" He looked into her eyes, trying to determine what she was thinking or if he had overstepped her comfort boundaries. She was so hard to read—an enigma. He yearned to pull her close to him, feel her embrace.

"You just think that because you've only known me for such a short time," she said, "but you're sweet regardless." She fixed her eyes on him, eventually wrapping her arms around him and leaning into his chest.

He pulled her close with one hand on her back, the other buried in her hair, and she felt safe letting her embarrassment dissolve away.

"A couple more glasses of wine, and you may have to hold me up," she laughed.

"If I'm lucky," he said softly, reluctantly letting her go. "Would you be up for a moonlight boat ride, or do you think it's too chilly? The moon is almost full tonight, and the stars are so much more beautiful once we are away from the light of the house. But we don't have to if you're not into it."

"No, I'd love to. I'm not as cold anymore." She giggled. "I am pretty sure the wine has warmed me up. I'll grab a blanket if you grab the booze."

She flipped out the house lights and put out the lanterns, meeting Todd on the dock.

The moisture in the air was cold on her face, but she barely noticed. They hadn't idled too far out of the cove in case the cold proved to be too much. Todd had spread a blanket on the back of the boat, so they could lie down and look for constellations. They had both finished off a couple more glasses of wine and were feeling the intoxicating effects of both the wine and the sexual tension between them.

"You're a mess," Todd shouted, watching Lexi splash water from the swim platform. He leaned back on the blanket, happily observing every aspect of his surroundings. That was the first time he had seen Lexi drunk, and he loved every minute of it: her playful demeanor, how she seemed to stumble every time a wake rocked the boat, and the way she babbled on about whatever happened to pop in her head without reservation. He was amazed at how intelligent and interesting her capricious mind was, especially when she wasn't monitoring herself as she did when sober. He was fascinated that his intellectual interest and his physical desire for her were equal. Undoubtedly, he had never met anyone like her and knew he probably never would again.

Suddenly, she squealed and jumped up, trying to regain her balance. "I was wrong," she pouted, arms crossed. "Apparently, sitting on the swim platform in clothes is a bad idea."

Todd laughed, seeing she was soaked from the waist down. As she stood there shivering, he couldn't help but be aroused. With the nearly full moon reflecting the water behind her, her wet pants were almost translucent, revealing every curve and muscle. She obviously wasn't wearing a bra under her thin t-shirt, exposing the outline of her full, perky breasts and nipples hard from the chill. He quickly shifted himself to disguise his desire for her.

"What? Why are you looking at me like that?" She suddenly felt self-conscious, looking down to see if she had something on her clothes. The night had been almost surreal, and she had let the evening dictate itself remarkably, relinquishing control of the situation. She felt like a kid, from both the wine and the freedom to be herself around Todd, but as he stared at her, she worried she was acting like a goober. "Seriously, what?"

He hesitated but couldn't stop himself. "You are amazing! You're so goddamn beautiful and smart, and you aren't even aware of it. Do you even realize how sexy that is? Do you have any idea the effect you have on people...on me?"

Her hand was freezing when he leaned forward to take it. He gently pulled her closer, and as he did, she stumbled toward him, losing her balance and landing on the blanket beside him. Laughter echoed off the empty lake as neither could control themselves. She lay back, drenched, laughing uncontrollably as Todd rolled over on his side.

He wondered how she kept surprising him as he ran the back of his hand down the contour of her jawline. Suddenly, he jumped up and held out his hand to help her up, then grabbed the blanket and draped it around Lexi's shoulders. "Let's get you home. You're cold and wet, and I can't have you sick for our adventure tomorrow."

"Wait, I'm not ready for you to go yet. I'm fine." She tried to towel off, desperate to prove she wasn't uncomfortable. She didn't want him to leave, nor for the night to end, not after what he had just said. She was pissed with herself for being so clumsy, always screwing things up at the most inappropriate times.

Feeling her suddenly tense up, Todd took both her hands. "Lexi, relax. I didn't say I was leaving; I just said that we should go back to your place so you can dry off and get warm. I have no intention of letting this moment go either."

As she began to relax, he motored them back to the house. "I will get the fire going again; you go get cleaned up," he said, "unless you would rather chill inside."

"Get the fire going, and we can make that decision later. I'll just be a minute."

When she stepped into the bathroom, the reflection she saw in the mirror was ridiculous, and she immediately understood why Todd had suggested they come back. Her hair was unsightly from the wind blowing it into knots, and her face was a splotchy red from the cold wind. She looked down at her once-white pants and wondered if she could ever wear them again. She was an absolute mess. A shower wasn't a choice but a necessity. She would be surprised if he was still there when she got out of the shower.

The hot water in the shower both warmed her up and irritated her sunburn, but Lexi knew she wouldn't be able to let that sexy man on her deck rub aloe on her again, not if she wanted to keep from doing something she wasn't ready for. Instead, she slipped into her flannel pajama pants, a long-sleeved t-shirt, and some warm socks. She wished she had something sexier to wear but didn't; she hadn't expected to need anything.

After adding a few logs to the fire, Todd lit a lantern and played music, choosing a playlist named "Lexi Mellow." He found another blanket in the closet and laid it on the chaise lounge, deciding to share the chaise with her instead of his previous seat beside her. Surprised at how comfortable it was, Todd laid back, thinking about how the night had guided them instead of the other way around. He quietly offered his thanks and laughed at how Lexi must be internally handling the situation, knowing she was uncomfortable when she didn't have control and proud of her for stepping out of her comfort zone. She was extremely unpredictable, which he found irresistible, so a grin spread across his face when she came out of her bedroom with wet hair and pajamas. Of course, this genuine spirit wouldn't be in some uncomfortable and conventionally "sexy" nightgown. She was totally comfortable and warm in soft pink pants, fuzzy socks, and a green long sleeved t-shirt which hugged her body. He couldn't stop smiling as she walked toward him.

"More wine?" she asked, peeking through the doorway. She noticed that Todd was sitting on the opposite side of her chaise lounge, leaving room for her, which awoke the butterflies in her stomach again. She absolutely needed more wine.

"I will if you are. Do you need my help with anything?"

"No, I'll get it," she said. "Thanks for making things cozy out there."

Walking back toward the deck, she took a deep breath and mentally reminded herself to let the night guide her. She handed Todd his glass of wine and sat beside him as he raised the blanket to make room for her. She settled in, making herself comfortable, and glanced over, only to find him looking back.

"You're warm," she said. "I'm glad you didn't leave while I was showering."

"Why would you ever think that I would leave while you were in the shower?"

"I don't know. I guess I just didn't think you would stay."

As the words came out of her mouth, Todd set down his wine, pulled her closer to him, and wrapped his arm around her. "Lexi, stop. Did you hear anything I said to you on the lake? I'm not going anywhere. I want to be right here with you, the woman who looks breathtaking whether she is a complete mess or fresh from the shower in her pajamas. While we were on the lake, I saw a glimpse of who you are without all the constraints you generally put on yourself. You are so smart, and your mind is wide open, continually challenging me. Don't let your insecurities stifle that, at least not while you are with me. Just let go and be yourself."

Not knowing what to say, Lexi slipped her hands around his arms. Her heart was pounding so hard she was sure he could feel it. Using her fingertips, she unconsciously traced his arm lying across her stomach. "I'm sorry," she finally said. "I'm nervous. I'm not really good at this." She took a big gulp of wine to counter her nerves. "I don't know what to say right now, so I'm just going to enjoy you next to me and not question it." Her breathing slowed, and she nuzzled herself closer to him, wishing his hands would explore more than just her stomach.

CHAPTER 11

The smell of bacon stirred Lexi from her slumber, and she sat straight up in bed. She still wore the clothes she had on the night before but didn't remember going to bed. She jumped up, brushed her teeth and hair, and peeked out of her bedroom.

The blanket she remembered lying under on the deck was on the couch, along with one of the pillows from her bed, and Todd stood in the kitchen humming while he cooked. Her mind immediately ran every possible scenario following her last memory of snuggling with Todd on the chaise. What if he kissed her and she didn't remember it? Had she drank that much wine? Her stomach sank just as he turned around and saw her.

"Good morning, sunshine! Did you sleep well? We fell asleep on the back deck last night, so when your shivering woke me up, I carried you to bed and crashed on the couch. I was up early to go for a run, so I stopped and grabbed some breakfast supplies from the house. I hoped to make you breakfast in bed, but I am apparently too slow."

"Wow, thanks," she said, breathing a sigh of relief. "How long have you been up?" She rubbed her eyes and scanned the kitchen for coffee. The sound of her feet shuffling across the floor got a big smile from the gorgeous, shirtless man in her kitchen making her breakfast. As she collapsed into him, she slid her arms around him and mumbled, "Coffee..."

He laughed, kissed the top of her head, and handed her a cup. "I figured you might need a little pick-me-up this morning. It just finished brewing. Are you still up for our plans today?"

When she didn't take the coffee cup, he sat it on the counter and fully embraced her, pressing her head into his bare chest.

It was exactly what she needed to get her day started. "Of course," she croaked sleepily. "I look forward to finding out where you are taking me. And I guess spending the entire day with you isn't so bad either."

They finished breakfast, cleaned up their mess, and Todd headed back to his house to shower and let her get ready. They planned to meet at his house in a couple of hours.

A Tylenol and blue Powerade later, she decided to take a short walk to clear her head.

THE OVERGROWN PATH across the dirt road had caught Lexi's attention several times since her arrival at the rental. What coaxed her down the path that day was unclear. Something niggled at her curiosity, and the next thing she knew, she was standing at a rusty gate, lurching to one side. The gate was not attached to a fence. The long-neglected cemetery plot wasn't much bigger than the footprint of an Olympic swimming pool, probably a family lot. It would have been easier to go around the gate than maneuver it out of its settled spot in the mud. Instead, she tore at the kudzu, the tangled regulator of sacred land. With a final tug, she toppled through the newly cleared opening, landing on her bare knees. The moment her skin touched the damp earth, everything went black.

.   .   .

A DEAFENING ROAR snapped Lexi into awareness.

SHE SPUN to see that what had once been a view of Norris Lake, was now a homestead with a two-room log cabin anchoring the farmland and barn into its valley plot. Heavy drops of rain pelted her face as she scoured her new surroundings for the source of the thunderous noise. Movement in the valley caught her attention.

A handicapped teen frantically pulled her body from the house's doorway onto the abandoned porch. She was missing both of her legs from the knees down and desperately screamed for help, begging for her mother. The roar closed in, and the girl's shouts became more frantic.

Lexi ran down the hill, also yelling for help, but the valley was deserted. Soon, the roar was joined by loud snaps and pops, mature tree branches breaking violently. No longer able to hear the girl's shrieks, Lexi crouched, covering her ears and face in dread as a catastrophic surge of water rushed to wipe out the entire valley.

Immediately, the cacophony faded into background noise, and Lexi tentatively raised her head. Three ear-piercing cracks of a whip echoed through the mountains. Time slowed, and an ethereal haze tinted everything a sunset yellow color, despite the rain.

Lexi stood. A familiar chill seeped deep into her bones. The air around her felt so dense, she expected to see mustard paint smears as she trailed her hand in front of her. Unlike anything she'd ever experienced, a wave of anguish and loneliness froze her in place at the same moment a woosh of ice-cold air sailed past.

Seeming to ride the wind, a long, cadaverously thin woman with wispy strands of dirty, black hair, dressed in a brilliant white dress rushed by. She reached the legless girl in seconds, but instead of helping the poor thing, she dissipated into a black shadow hovering above.

A huge, almost too-perfect shimmering swan joined the girl on the porch, nuzzling itself under the girl's head, acting as a pillow.

The girl stopped screaming, completely relaxed, and rolled onto her back, seeming to have accepted her fate.

Lexi watched in horror as the shadow reformed her ghastly face and hovered directly over the girl. A black forked tongue flicked over the poor thing's skin, leaving deep blue veins and rotten mucus until the abandoned girl's face lost all color.

With a final dark kiss, the girl in the valley fell limp, her life stolen.

The wave of Tennessee River water, full of demolished land and homes, erased the fertile farmland in front of Lexi, and the ear-splitting sound regained its intensity, jarring her back into awareness.

SHE WRETCHED, rocking on her hands and knees. The annihilation and complete emptiness that seeped through Lexi's emotional barriers was indescribable. Suddenly, she was flooded with unholy guilt for not appreciating how easy her life was in comparison. As she backed through the gate on all fours, she trembled in terror remembering that horrid...thing. She wiped her mouth and her face frantically, trying to wipe away the memory of its black kiss. The kudzu seemingly wrapped itself around her ankles and jerked her down, bringing her back to reality.

What the actual fuck just happened?

GILTINE SMIRKED and resumed her place out of sight in the woods behind her favorite graveyard.

CHAPTER 12

Stunned and shaken, Lexi sat on her bed, confused. She urgently wanted to speak with Kate but had no idea what to say. Besides, she was gone for at least another week. Unable to comprehend what she experienced, she tried to put it in the back of her mind. No solutions would be found then, and she needed to prepare for her date with Todd.

Turning the music up loud, she climbed into the shower. As the warmth comforted her, she slowly loosened her mind, taking back the power worry and fear were trying to suppress, like she was taught. Thoughts of the previous night began to replace the strange incident, sending another kind of jolt through her body, and she smiled. She concentrated on those memories—how Todd spoke to and about her, how his body looked beneath his clothes, how he held her, and how the thought of him made her feel as if she would burst out of her skin.

After she dried off, she pulled on her blue bikini and slipped into a casual, brown sundress and flip-flops. Her skin looked golden in contrast to the brown of her dress, and the length revealed her long and shapely legs, even without heels. She only applied sunscreen moisturizer and lip gloss to her face and tied her hair into a low ponytail to fight the wind. She filled her lake satchel with her necessities, flung it over her shoulder, and headed out the door to Todd's.

Sun reflected off her sunglasses, and a gentle breeze caressed her face as she approached the house.

He had left the door open and lounged on the sofa inside, listening to Ray LaMontagne and watching for her.

As she entered the room, he stood and greeted her with a warm embrace. "Good Lord, woman," he said, stepping back to get a good look. "Your beauty could stop a hummingbird mid-flight! The gods are definitely smiling upon me this morning."

She rolled her eyes, uncomfortably realizing she couldn't hide behind her hair, and smiled shyly, "You aren't looking so shabby yourself!"

"I try," he joked. "So, are we ready to go?" He took her hand and led her out the front door.

She wasn't shocked to see a dark green Jeep Wrangler in the garage, the same car she would have if she lived in the south. He had taken the soft top off, and it was rolled up in the back, and she was immediately glad she had worn her hair back.

Todd walked around to the passenger side of the Jeep and opened the door, offering her a hand up, which she didn't need, but took anyway. He rushed around to the driver's side, hopped in, and started the engine. Turning to her, he smiled and said, "Buckle up, can't let anything happen to my precious cargo." He laughed at how cheesy he sounded.

On the drive toward their destination, Lexi noticed a picnic basket and a small cooler in the back seat. Asking him where they were going had proved pointless, only generating a mischievous smile. He put his hand on her knee and, from the corner of his eye, delighted in seeing her face brighten with a content grin. He focused on the road ahead, excited by what the day might bring, knowing things may go differently than he had initially planned, especially after the turn last night took.

The winding road finally ended up at a small airport, a little off the beaten track.

Todd pulled up to the hangar and stopped the car. "You ready?" he said, smiling.

"Seriously?" she asked, looking at him with wide-eyed confusion.

They were greeted on the tarmac by a gentleman who led them to a set of scooters, spoke kind words to Todd, and promised to have them set for take-off after lunch.

Todd explained that the trip to the restaurant was a beautiful ride, best seen without the enclosure of a car.

They both put on their helmets, climbed onto their scooters, and she followed him away from the airport.

The roads to the restaurant were as beautiful as Todd had promised, spotted with gold and purple flowers. The experience was only heightened by the aromatic fragrance of sweet alyssum and asters.

Eventually, the winding country road dumped them into an older fishing marina. The quaintness was comforting, and Lexi smiled as each person waved or nodded as they rode by. She slowed after trying to keep up with Todd as he weaved in and out of back roads toward a small public pier and pulled into the parking lot of an attached lake-front diner. She noticed a storm-damaged sign out front, *Mama's Kitchen,* and also surveyed additional damage to one of the front windows from an obviously recent storm.

Lexi climbed off her scooter, pulled her helmet off, and shook out her previously tied-back hair.

Todd was in awe of her natural beauty. The sun shone through her thin brown dress as she briskly walked toward him, awakening a need he struggled to subdue. "Glad to see you kept up," he joked, taking her hand. "Follow me. You're gonna love this place!"

When they reached the entrance, he opened the door for her and guided her in, his hand resting on the small of her back. As soon as he stepped through the doorway, the place came alive with salutations. Obviously, Todd was a regular. He worked his way through the small crowd of locals, shaking hands and laughing with his friends until they reached a small booth in the corner near the bar.

He motioned for her to sit, leaned over the bar, and shouted toward the kitchen, "Mama! Are you back there?"

A short, thin, muscular woman poked her head out of the window and smiled. "I shoulda known it was you out there winding up the place! Where you been, boy? I got a window out there that I'm barely keeping patched up, and I ain't seen you in nearly a month!" Her face was lovely; tired and worn from years of sun and hard work, but her smile expressed her inner youth, and Lexi guessed she was quite feisty for her age.

"Let me get Eddie's lunch done 'cause he's just on a break, and then I'll be out there to help ya." She winked at Todd, suddenly noticing Lexi, raised both eyebrows, and was out of sight.

"I guess you come here a lot. You sure get around," she teased.

"I just happened by here a while back, right after Mama had lost her husband to cancer. The food was crazy good, but it was apparent she needed a little help maintaining the building. So, I stop by occasionally to help her with small projects, and she feeds me well. The guys around the dock do what they can, but they are busy, and most of them have second jobs in the off-season. Besides, I think she likes the company more than the help."

"Does everyone call her Mama?"

"Yeah, I guess she's been feeding these guys for over 30 years, and most of them treat her with the respect they'd show their mothers. Don't let the name fool you, though; she's a firecracker and has the mouth of a sailor!"

Lexi laughed.

Todd took her hands in his and looked across the table at her. "I'm so glad I can share this with you."

Just then, Mama appeared around the corner. "Eddie!" she shouted over the crowd. "Come and get your lunch, boy!"

A tall skinny guy took a bag of carryout from her and nodded as he backed toward the door, "Thanks, Mama. Just put it on my tab and I will settle with you next week."

"Will do, hon. Don't let 'em work you too hard, and good luck on your date tonight!"

The place busted with ooooh's and laughter as the flushed young man left the diner.

"So," Mama said, turning her attention back toward Todd, "who is this lovely young lady?"

"Mama, I would like to introduce you to my friend Lexindra."

"Lexindra, huh?" Mama smiled, shaking Lexi's hand firmly. "My boy Todd has never brought any of his lady friends around here before."

Lexi sensed a bit of parental suspicion in her tone. "Nice to meet you, Mrs... I mean, Mama." Smiling, she looked at Todd and down toward the table, blushing.

"Mama is just fine, hon!" She winked at Todd and asked what she could make them for lunch. "Eddie just brought me a mess of crappie. I'd be happy to fry some up for you-uns."

Todd looked across at Lexi, and she nodded. "Sounds good, Mama! Will you bring us a couple of beers, if you don't mind?"

His friend smiled at him, laughed, and turned toward the bar to get their beers.

The two finished the best lunch Lexi could ever remember eating, and a couple of beers later, they were saying their goodbyes to Mama. She refused to let them pay, making Todd promise to be back soon to help her repair her broken window, and hugged him goodbye.

As Mama hugged Lexi, she leaned in and whispered, "I love that boy like he's my own. If he brought you here, you must be a special girl. Take care of each other."

As Lexi pulled away, she smiled at Mama and touched her arm. "Thanks!"

Mama nodded, and the new couple headed back toward their scooters.

CHAPTER 13

The drive back to the airstrip gave Lexi a moment to take in everything. Had he seriously never brought another girl to Mama's, and if not, why her? Her respect for him had grown even more because of the way he had apparently walked into the old lady's life and filled the empty space with no reservations or expectations. She took a deep breath and watched him gracefully weave his scooter back and forth as they climbed the hill back to the airstrip. She realized this was just the first stop on their adventure, and a tickle raced from her cheeks to her stomach.

Still daydreaming about their next destination, she noticed too late that Todd was stopped ahead of her. She slammed on her brakes but was too late and swerved to miss rear-ending his scooter, and lost her balance.

Todd rushed over and knelt beside her, looking a bit frantic. "Shit, Lexi, are you okay?"

Lexi noticed several other men had rushed toward the commotion. Humiliated, she tried to stand up quickly, not drawing more attention to herself. "Oh my god, Todd, I am so sorry! Is the scooter okay?"

"Who cares about the scooter? Are *you* okay? You're bleeding."

She looked down at her leg and noticed she was bleeding. She smiled at him and shook her head. "I'm fine. There's a first aid kit in my beach bag. I can clean it up and put a bandage on it. It's seriously not a big deal."

She was relieved as the small crowd dispersed but was stunned when Todd whisked her off her feet. "What are you doing? I am fine; you really don't need to carry me."

"You scared me," he said quietly. "You *are* a mess, aren't you?"

"Hence, the first aid kit." She laughed nervously and let him carry her to the hangar.

Todd helped her clean the sizeable scrape from the gravel while Jim got the plane prepared for departure.

"I told you I was a little clumsy," she said.

"A little?" He lifted her bandaged leg and gently kissed it. "Girl, you're definitely going to keep me on my toes, aren't ya?"

"Sorry!"

"Don't be sorry. You know I'm just teasing. Are you sure you're still up for our next stop?" He stood up and looked down at her, hand outstretched to help her up. His adrenaline began to settle, and he relaxed a bit, laughing internally at the fact that he found her clumsiness so endearing. This exasperating creature was anything but dull!

"I'm up for anything you throw my way," she said. "Just make sure it isn't anything valuable."

"I'll make sure anything I want to give you of value is handed deliberately," he said, looking into her eyes with that familiar smirk that made her blush.

Grabbing the picnic basket and cooler, he took her hand and headed toward a single-engine Cessna parked on the tarmac.

An older man approached the opposite side and shook his hand.

"Thanks, Jim, you always make me look good. Are we all gassed up and ready to go?" Todd asked.

"Sure are. I assume this is Miss Lexi?" He shook her hand and smiled. "Pleasure to meet you. You have quite a ham on your hands. I offer you my sincere condolences." He waggled his eyebrows at her and slapped Todd on the back. "Let me help you get everything loaded up."

The two men loaded the plane, then Todd helped Lexi into the cockpit and climbed in himself. Goodbyes, nice to meet yous, and thank yous were extended to Jim as the couple buckled in.

CHAPTER 14

*L*exi watched as Todd checked his instruments, preparing to take off. before she knew it, they were in the air.

"Are you going to be this quiet all day?" he said, teasing her. "Because this is just our first leg of the journey. I've planned a whole day of adventure for you. You aren't afraid of flying or anything, are you?"

Lexi looked at him, still confused. "So, this is *your* plane? Are you kidding me?" She shook her head and laughed. "Of course, you have a plane. I mean, this is *so* not what I was expecting! I was thinking maybe lunch or a hike in town, but I was not expecting you to fly me anywhere. Where are you taking me?"

"I got my pilot's license when I was in college, and once I moved here, I found this little airstrip. I started hanging around a lot and got to know Jim and the other guys pretty well. The opportunity to buy a plane just came along, and I couldn't pass it up. Look out your window. Looking down on the world from this vantage point gives you a different perspective on life. You can appreciate your surroundings, realizing that each part creates a beautiful whole."

Lexi was looking out the window to her right as they flew along over the massive body of water. The shades of green reflecting from the lake ranged from deep forest green to an almost-jade color. Listening to Todd talk about flying made her see everything a little differently.

She turned to look at him, feeling somehow safe. "You are right, it is an amazing view."

"Do you know the history behind Norris Lake?"

"I know the government seized the land and built the dam to create electricity for the region."

"The Tennessee Valley Authority, mostly referred to as the TVA around here, was established in the middle of the Great Depression as a part of President Franklin D. Roosevelt's New Deal. And you're right, they purchased 125,000 acres of property through eminent domain for the Norris Dam project. The goal was to bring electricity and modern conveniences to impoverished rural regions across the south. I believe the intention was good because the annual flooding caused by the Tennessee River ravaged the region. That flooding left many small populations of hill folk isolated. But the social cost was significant, leaving scars on more than just the land."

"I can imagine," said Lexi.

"If you look out your window, you'll see the Norris Dam. It was the first dam constructed. Over there," he pointed, "is Norris Marina. That was the quarry where most of the stone was excavated to construct the dam. It is 265 feet high and impounds the Clinch River. They started building in October 1933, and the dam was completed in March 1936. By January 1937, the Norris Reservoir was filled, creating the largest tributary of the Tennessee River."

"I was thinking about the human cost while I was paddleboarding the other day. It was kind of creepy thinking I could have been floating over a dead city."

"They did, in fact, flood a whole town called Loyston. The town was prosperous for the region, consisting of a post office and a handful of thriving small businesses. The businesses in the town, and a few houses even, had electricity. We'll fly over so I can show you; it is still visible from the water, under a mile-wide section of the lake called Loyston Sea. And you are right, it is creepy and sad."

"I wonder how many people lost their homes and land to the project. And where did all those people go?" asked Lexi.

"Don't quote me on this number, but I think it was something like 16,000 people on record. Keep in mind that many of these folks were not landowners, they were renters, sharecroppers, and tenant farmers. Those people didn't receive any payment for the land from which they had been displaced. The TVA relocated people in the five counties surrounding the area, but racism and classism caused a significant loss of the social connections they relied on for support. Many of those people had been on that land for generations; their families were buried there."

"What did they do with those cemeteries?" Lexi asked, thinking of her earlier experience in the small graveyard near her rental.

"It's reported that the TVA investigated more than 69,000 graves, and 20,000 graves were relocated to similar burial places nearby. Think I read somewhere that the fate of the deceased, and their final resting places, were left up to their next of kin. Sadly, that left thousands of graves where no living relatives could be found, so those graves were left in place. I can't help but wonder how many of these cemeteries only relocated the headstones."

The thought sent shivers through Lexi.

"I love this area, and Norris Lake is one of my favorite spots in the world, but I wanted you to know about its history. A lot of sacrifice lies under those waters—lost memories, lost lives, lost hope. Mama can still remember that time. I guess instead of relocating, her family was one of a handful that moved further up the hill, as she would put it. She talks of dark spots on the water, where the land has purged its devastation into the water. As a respected elder in this area, she taught me to give offerings to the ancestors as a sign of my gratitude and recognition of their loss."

Todd took her over the lost city of Loyston, and you really could see the small town from the ariel view. The lake snaked through the mountains, and she sent a mental push of appreciation out to the people who had sacrificed so much to create something so majestic. She thought of the day she'd arrived and the cove where she had felt so much sadness and loss. That must be one of the "dark spots" Mama warned about. Instead of diving into those negative thoughts, she pulled herself back into the present.

She hesitated, flabbergasted by the whole situation. "I can't believe you did all this for me. Things like this just don't happen to me...ever, really, thank you." This time, her hand found his leg, squeezing his knee to show her affection and admiration.

"I can't believe that," he said, looking straight ahead. "I wouldn't have done this for anyone but you. Even before... Well, before last night."

Despite her first instincts, Lexi looked over at him and recognized his sincerity. Not knowing what to say, she turned and looked back out the window.

THE FLIGHT to their next stop in Knoxville was relatively short. Todd landed the plane on a small, private airstrip, surrounded by a giant white and stone house, the Tennessee River, and a gravel path leading to a boathouse.

As Todd was unloading their things from the plane to an old Ford pickup, Lexi asked, "Where are we?"

"This is my parents' house. But don't worry, they aren't home. Just make sure to get all your stuff 'cause we'll head back home from here."

She looked around, a little confused, but made sure she had all her things and climbed into the pickup.

Todd started the truck, and they rattled down a long drive toward the house.

Lexi was a bit overwhelmed by how luxuriously simple his parents' house was as they passed by. It suited what Todd had told her about his family, and she could see that their wealth had given them many opportunities, but no pretension. She tucked a lock of hair behind her ear and felt an easy smile lift some of her anxiety.

The truck stopped near the boat ramp leading to the boathouse, and before she could gather her things, Todd hopped out and came around to open the door for her.

As Lexi looked around, her bewilderment, appreciation, and gratuitous expression made him chuckle. "Not bad, huh?"

"It's beautiful, Todd, just how I pictured it would be."

"I thought that we would spend the rest of the day on the river if you're up for it."

"Are you sure your parents won't mind us taking their boat?"

"Nah, they're cool. I called Dad yesterday and told him we were going to take it out for the day. Grab your bags and follow me."

He unloaded the cooler and the picnic basket from the back of the truck and tossed Lexi her beach bag. She nearly missed it but managed to catch it with everything intact, causing Todd to shake his head and laugh. He headed down the path toward the boathouse, glancing back to ensure she was still behind him and didn't need help.

Todd pulled out his keys and unlocked the door, pulling it open to reveal an extremely well-kept, and rather large, yacht, along with a fairly new runabout. He loaded their stuff onto the smaller boat, jumped aboard, and reached out to help Lexi join him.

"Ready?" he asked excitedly. "Sit here next to me. It might be a little chilly while we are going, but I promise to stop soon so we can warm up."

Lexi smiled and sat next to him. As the engine turned over, the radio came alive with the Zac Brown Band's version of "Chicken Fried." She laughed as the sun poured down on them and the wind whipped through her hair. She watched Todd as he pulled off his shirt, exposing his well-defined physique.

His tan body glistened from the spray as they glided over the water, and he danced to himself, singing along with the radio. Catching her admiring him, he sang every word for her into his sunscreen bottle.

His footloose demeanor was contagious, and she soon found herself dancing in her seat, arms embracing the wind and singing along with him. Goosebumps covered her body, and she knew it wasn't from the chill in the air.

Eventually, Todd slowed the boat and cut off the engine. He looked at the empty shoreline, deciding it was as good a place as any to stop and enjoy the sun for a bit. "Is this good for you? I thought we could just drift for a bit, maybe have a drink or two."

"This is perfect! Absolutely perfect," she said, looking at him through radiant green eyes. His smile delighted her, and she took his hand. "Seriously, Todd, thank you for this. I don't even know what to say, this is all so much."

He cupped her chin, running his thumb down her cheek. "No more than you deserve."

He covertly averted his attention toward the cooler, and Lexi quickly wiped her cheek as a tear escaped unexpectedly. She jumped at the pop as he uncorked the bottle of champagne in his hand.

"Dom? Are you kidding me?"

"Nothing but the best for my lady. Um, I mean for you. I have strawberries, too, and some little deli sandwiches I picked up yesterday if you are hungry." He fumbled for the cooler, trying to cover his prior assumption.

"Your lady?" she teased.

"I didn't mean to assume. I mean, I hope I didn't—"

She cut him off, "I'm fucking with you dude. I would be proud to be *your lady* today. Especially after all the trouble you've gone through on my account. I mean, this had to take some planning. Is this something you do a lot?" The thought erased her smile, but Todd simply burst out in laughter.

"Do you seriously think that?" he blurted out, looking almost hurt.

"Well, I don't know. I mean, you are young, and you have the means..."

"I'm disappointed you would think that about me, but the truth of the matter is I don't really date much. Most of the girls I know either can't hold an intellectual conversation or they are so obsessed with their ambitions that they can only focus on school or their careers. I'm considered either a free ride or a slacker, so I don't waste my time. But you are different. It's like..." he paused to articulate his thoughts. "It's like you really see the man I am, or at least the man I try to be, with no judgments. You're the whole package, Lexi. Highly intelligent, reflective, talented, overtly beautiful and completely unaware of it, and on top of that, you ooze such earthy sexuality."

"You forgot clumsy, emotionally damaged, scared..."

"Don't!" he snapped. "I hate it when you do that. Let me tell you how I see you without your nasty inner voice disapproving. Yes, you are ridiculously clumsy, but that only gives me another excuse to be able to take care of you. And maybe you are emotionally scarred, but who isn't? And as far as being frightened, this scares me too, Lexi. But instead of running away from that fear, I want to lean into it until I understand what I'm afraid of, hopefully eliminating the fear altogether. Hell, when I started planning all of this, I only wanted to spoil you a little and keep a smile on your face; maybe help you heal a little. But last night changed things. The longer I've been with you, and the more you unmask, the more I've seen how special you are and how much I want you. It was all a little overwhelming, and I worried that I shouldn't have crossed that boundary. But when you woke up this morning and sleepily stumbled into my arms, I knew I was willing to take that chance."

He stopped and turned toward the sun reflecting off the water. When he turned back, she was sitting quietly, looking at his feet, tears streaming down her face. "Oh hell, Lexi, I am so sorry. I didn't mean to hurt your feelings. This isn't going at all how I'd hoped."

She looked up at him, wholly vulnerable, and said, "These aren't tears of anger or hurt, and things are going much better than you think. I really do wish I could see myself through your eyes."

"I can teach you," he said, pulling her up and into his embrace, "if you want me to."

She looked up, and their eyes locked.

He wiped the tears from her face with his finger and leaned into her.

She felt his warm breath and soft lips as they met hers. Her fingers entwined in his curly hair as she hungrily pulled him closer, and his grip around her waist tightened as she almost lost control of her balance. Todd's kiss was passionate and entrancing, full of desire and need, and when he finally pulled away to look at her, she was speechless.

"Damn, girl!" he said, breathing heavily. "You are so much more than I was expecting."

He wanted more, but he knew he had to get control of himself and slow things down. He didn't want to take the chance of rushing her, so he turned, grabbed two plastic champagne glasses, and filled them to the top. As he handed her a drink, he looked into her eyes, hoping his intentions were clear, and pulled her head into his chest. "I'm pretty sure that deserves a toast."

"To taking chances," she whispered.

"To taking chances!"

CHAPTER 15

*P*ulling into the marina, they were greeted by a young man who helped them unload the boat and directed Todd toward his Jeep, which had been picked up and driven back to the marina.

Todd handed the kid the keys to the boat, shook his hand, and thanked him graciously as the kid began filling the boat with gas, preparing to return it to his parents' house.

As Todd and Lexi walked to the car holding hands, Lexi stopped and turned to him, "I just wanted to tell you how much this meant to me and how incredibly special you've made me feel today. I have never been spoiled so extravagantly, and I want you to know how truly grateful I am."

He drew her close and kissed her. "I assure you, the pleasure was all mine! But I hope you don't think the day is over. Please tell me you'll join me for dinner," he said as he helped her into the Jeep.

"I was hoping," she smiled. "Your place or mine?"

"I figured you would be more comfortable at your place if that's cool?"

"Sure, just tell me when to be ready."

He dropped Lexi off at her rental and told her he would be back in a couple of hours and bring everything they needed for tonight. "So, relax, and I'll see you soon!"

She waved, smiling as he pulled out of the drive. Walking into the house, her whole body tingled with excitement. Her head was still spinning from the day, and she found herself already missing him.

Lexi poured a glass of wine and started the shower. Looking in the steamy mirror, she saw someone she almost didn't recognize. Had it really been that long since she felt relaxed and happy? Alone, she had time to question things, and doubt slowly tried to needle back into her mind, but she quickly shut it out.

She showered and shaved again, allowing her imagination only a moment to visualize the possibilities of the evening. She casually walked naked through the house to get another glass of wine, something she would have never done a month ago. Wanting to look good tonight, she dried and curled her hair, even putting on a little makeup. She looked through her closet until she found what she was looking for. The fabric from the green spaghetti strap dress felt soft on her skin, and she was pleased by the way it hugged her curves without being tight or too revealing.

The music echoed loudly throughout the house, so she could sing without hearing whether she was off-key or not. Dancing around the kitchen, she held her wine glass in one hand and sang into a wooden spoon she held in the other.

Todd was standing in the doorway watching her, trying to stifle his laughter.

She spun around, bursting out the chorus when she saw him, and screamed.

"Shit, Todd, you scared the hell out of me!"

Todd just stood there, mouth agape, staring at her. "I'm...wow..." he trailed off, unable to take his eyes off her.

"What? Are you okay?" Lexi tried to hide the fact that she was horrified he had busted her dancing and singing like an idiot, but she was startled by his reaction. "Seriously, what's wrong?"

He had always thought Lexi was beautiful, but it had never occurred to him that he had never seen her after she had made an effort. Wine glass and spoon still in hand, she stood in front of him in a slinky green dress that fell well above the knees of her long, lean legs. Her hair was curled, making the blonde, sun-bleached highlights more evident, and she had even put on a little make-up, bringing out the yellow in her green eyes. He literally had to catch his breath before speaking. "You look good, *really* good," he finally got out.

The trouble on her face lifted, and she laughed, "And I'll be here all week, folks!"

"You did all this for me?" he said, looking her up and down.

"No, I have a date after you leave," she said sarcastically. "It isn't much. I just wanted to look nice tonight. I'm glad you like it."

"Hard not to! I'll bet even the boats trolling by the house noticed."

It amazed her how pretty he made her feel, and she walked back into the kitchen with an extra sashay in her step as he followed her. "Wine?" she offered.

"Absolutely!" he whispered as his lips delicately brushed across the back of her neck, causing her to gasp and shutter, which he enjoyed tremendously. "I was thinking about taking you out for dinner tonight, but now I don't want to share you with anyone. So, I'll let you decide what we should do."

She shivered again as his breath met her neck as he spoke. "What was the question again?"

"Should we go out, or should we stay in?"

"Oh," she mumbled, just before she realized she had not been paying attention and had poured half the bottle of wine all over the counter. "Shit," she complained as she stepped back onto Todd to avoid the spill.

"Was that my fault?" he said, smiling sheepishly, keeping her from falling again.

Lexi shook her head and rolled her eyes. "Very funny!" She dumped some of the wine from his overly full glass and handed it to him, tossing a towel on the wet counter. "I guess I'll get that later," she said as he took her hand and pulled her onto the back deck.

"So, since this is your night, which will it be? Should we go out for the evening, or would you like to stay in?"

"Well, it *is* a full moon," she said, gazing at the shimmering light on the water, "so there may be a lot of crazies out tonight. On the other hand, I have a feeling you could cause trouble all on your own if we stay in."

"I promise to be a perfect gentleman if that's what you want."

"And what if I don't?"

"A guy can only hope."

"Well, if I do decide to take my chances alone with you tonight, what are we gonna eat?"

"The universal plan B," he said, grinning. "Pizza!"

They both laughed and Todd moved behind her, wrapping his arms around her slender waist. She smelled so good. He hoped she would trust him and want to stay in.

They swayed back and forth to the music as they observed the quiet evening. The movement of her hips against his body was delicious torture, and he ached to explore every part of her, so before she felt his boner, he stepped back and turned to go in the house.

"Should I call for pizza?" he asked, walking toward the phone.

She grinned. "Yeah. I want you all to myself tonight, too."

As he called to order the pizza, she topped off their glasses and walked back onto the deck. He brought her a blanket and threw a couple of logs into the fire pit, getting a comfortable fire going, and settled down next to her to wait for the pizza to arrive.

"What are you thinking about?" he asked.

"Honestly?"

"I would be hurt if you ever felt like you couldn't be honest with me," he answered, turning her around to face him.

"Well, actually, I'm a little nervous. It seems like my world has turned upside down in the last several weeks, stirring up ideas and emotions that have long been dormant in my life. And while it is all so exhilarating and intoxicating, the pragmatist in me can't help but wonder what happens when it all comes to an end." As the words escaped her lips, she looked up to find Todd smiling sincerely.

"I know you're scared, Lexi. Honestly, I'm shocked at how open you've been to this. I've been waiting for you to shut down or run away, but you haven't. I don't know if it's me that's kept you from falling back into old habits or if you're starting to let yourself open up and trust not only me, but yourself. I sense you haven't trusted yourself for a long time." Todd brushed a hair out of her face and tucked it behind her ear. "I don't know what the future holds, but I do know if it's anything like the present, I look forward to it and don't want to think about an end. Please don't start doubting yourself again, not just when you've started to make forward progress."

"How do you always know just what to say?" She smiled, leaning into his touch.

"Trust me, I don't always know what to say, but for some reason, I just seem to get lucky with you."

"I don't think it's luck. I think you, somehow, know what I need to hear without me even telling you. I've never been around someone who has been so in tune with me. It's like you hear my thoughts by just watching me, paying close attention to my movements and expressions. Sometimes I think you know things about me that I haven't even figured out yet."

"Of that, I am sure!" he said. "But I plan to keep telling you each beautiful thing I observe, and eventually, you'll see the same person I see."

"Looks like the pizza's here," Lexi said as a knock sounded at the front door. "I'll get it."

"No, let me. My treat, remember?" Todd pulled the money out of his wallet as he walked toward his door, paid for the pizza, and turned to carry it out to the back deck.

"Dinner is served!"

CHAPTER 16

*A*fter dinner, Todd suggested they walk down to the dock, so Lexi grabbed a jacket, and they headed away from the house.

The couple held hands as they strolled along the path, the full moon lighting their way.

Lexi was still shocked that none of the houses in this direction seemed to be occupied. "Todd, is there seriously no one else who lives out here during the offseason? How could anyone have a house in this beautiful place and not spend all their time here?"

"A couple of other people live closer to the marina. There's also an older couple who lives year-round a couple of coves in that direction," he pointed the opposite way. "Mr. and Mrs. Rothfield. I sometimes help them prepare and clean up from any big storms; they're awesome. He is a retired cop, and she used to work for a publishing company. There is another house around the corner occupied most of the year, but most of our part of the lake is pretty empty in the winter."

"I just can't imagine having this place and being able to leave. Hell, I don't know how I am going to be able to." She really didn't want to think about having to leave Tennessee. Instead, she just looked to the ground and shivered.

"Come here," he said, squeezing her hand. "I'm not letting you go anywhere."

The two sat on the damp wooden platform, staring out toward the horizon, not saying a word, just holding hands and enjoying being near one another. Lexi was leaning on his shoulder and could feel the rhythm of his breathing and his heart's steady beat. She felt safe with his arms wrapped around her. At that moment, she realized she, undeniably, trusted him and didn't want to hold back any longer.

Pulling away from his embrace, she turned to face him. "I trust you," she whispered, gently kissing his lips, "with my heart and any other part of me you want to explore."

In response, he kissed her neck and slid the straps of her dress from her shoulders. He felt her body quiver at his touch and expertly moved his lips from her neck to her bare shoulder. His hand traced the silhouette of her figure, lingering on her breast, and she softly moaned. He no longer tried to hide his arousal and pulled her into him, kissing her lustfully.

Her body responded immediately. She fumbled to unbutton his shirt, to have his skin on hers.

Jerking off his shirt, he laid it on the dock beside her jacket and gently pushed her on top of them. He sat over her, surveying every inch of her body, thinking of how much he had wanted this moment when she suddenly tensed.

"What was that?" she said, sitting up and looking over her shoulder.

"What was what?" asked Todd.

"I heard something behind us. I heard someone moving."

"It was probably just an animal. There's nobody out here, Lexi. Just you and me."

"No, it didn't sound like just an animal. Not unless it was a massive one."

Then they heard another movement in the brush, followed by footsteps crunching on the ground next to where they lay. They both jumped to their feet, only to see a fleeting shadow of someone running just out of sight.

"Oh my god, Todd, someone was watching us," Lexi gasped. "What the hell kind of person would invade someone's privacy like that?"

Todd bent down to grab their discarded items of clothing and shook them off, "Calm down, it was probably just a teenager from town who happened along and was gettin' off spying on a beautiful woman."

"We are in the middle of nowhere. Who the hell would *happen along* this place? That is flat-out creepy," she said.

"It's okay; a mood killer, for sure, but we're fine. Let's just head back up to the house where we know we won't have an audience," he said, touching her arm. "Seriously, sweetheart, they've gone, and we're fine."

Lexi stood there looking at the dark stillness enveloping the trees and shook her head. "You're right. That just really freaked me out." She looked up at his bare chest, cocked her head to the side, and ran her fingers over his muscular body. "Beat you there," she laughed and took off running back toward the lights of her deck.

"Oh no you don't!" yelled Todd as he took off after her, surprised at her speed.

Both were slightly out of breath and laughing when they got up to the deck. Todd had almost caught up with Lexi, but barely.

She grinned at his apparent astonishment. "What? Embarrassed that you underestimated me?"

"Embarrassed? No. Impressed? Absolutely. Who would've ever guessed a klutz like you had so much speed? You can't walk without falling down, but you run faster than most of the guys I know."

She turned and flipped her hair mockingly as she started up the stairs to the deck. "I'm gonna bet there are a lot of things about me that will leave you speechless, Mr. Novak," she teased as he chased her through the door.

"And I can't wait to find out about each and every one of them," he said, playfully pushing her toward the couch.

Lexi settled into the oversized couch and looked out toward the night sky. Todd sat down next to her and handed her a cold beer, which she chugged while he laughed at her.

"What? Athleticism like that leaves a girl thirsty."

"I guess," he joked.

"I'm still a little weirded out by that person in the woods. What if they are still out there watching us? I mean, they can see right in here!"

"I guess we could turn down the lights. That way, we can see out, but no one else can really see in," he said, playing with her hair. "Besides, the moon is full tonight, giving us just enough light."

As Todd walked through the house turning off all the lights, Lexi followed him with expectant eyes. She was full of nervous anticipation when he pulled her to her feet, locking on her eyes as he drew her close and kissed her. She clutched his taut back as he slid a steady hand up her dress and between her thighs.

He let out a guttural moan when he realized she wasn't wearing panties, and she felt the sudden firmness of his erection. His fingers titillated her sex, guiding her hips in rhythm with his exploration while she worked determinedly to get him out of his pants. Just as she thought her shaking legs would give out from beneath her, he stopped and pulled the green dress over her head, tossing it on the floor, exposing her naked body to the moonlit night. He wrapped his arm around her and swiftly placed her on the couch, her flawless body waiting for his touch. Gently he grazed his teeth across her firm nipples, kissing his way below her stomach until her body pulsed with pleasure and she begged him for more.

As she lured him back toward her, he found her lips again and entered her, unable to contain his inhibitions. She gasped and cried out his name, pleased with how much he had to offer.

They had sex for hours with mutual desperation and need. Each pleasing the other in ways they had never before experienced.

Unbridled words of desire fell from Lexi's lips as she completely let herself lose control and get lost in him.

Todd growled as he ingested every part of her sexuality, releasing the tension that had been hovering between them.

The world seemed to stand still until they both exploded multiple times and lay on the floor exhausted, dripping with sweat, and confidently embraced in one another's arms. They remained silent, still trying to absorb the past couple of hours, when Todd rolled onto his side smiling at her. Her body still glistened with sweat as she opened her eyes to meet his.

"Hey you," she said.

"Hey," he said, and his smile widened. He put his head on her chest, and she absentmindedly played with his hair. "Lexi?"

"Yeah?"

"I honestly didn't know sex could be so... I don't even know how to put into words what just happened between us. But I do know that I have never felt so in tune with anyone in my life as I did just then." He started to say more, but his voice cracked, and he stopped and looked up at her again, tears in his eyes.

She saw Todd's vulnerability for the first time since they had met. She reached up to wipe the tear from his face. "It felt the same for me," she reassured.

"Really? I know this is all so much, so soon. I don't want you to feel any pressure from me, and I definitely don't want you to get scared and pull away." He paused, looking away, and then quickly back to her. "My god, woman, you have turned my world inside out, and I'm a little unsure how to handle myself right now."

"Welcome to my world," she laughed and touched his cheek. "It's okay not to know what to say. Like you keep telling me, just be honest with me, and I'll be honest with you. Otherwise, the relationship we've built this far will most likely fall apart or, even worse, turn into something neither of us wants anymore."

"And you promise my honesty won't send you running out the door?"

"Well, since this is my house..." she chuckled. "But no, I think I am beyond the point of running, and I really do want to know what is going on inside that mind of yours."

"Okay, I really want to tell you, but first, I need a glass of water. You?"

"Please," she said.

He jumped up and strolled across the room into the kitchen, utterly comfortable with his body.

A shiver ran through Lexi as she watched him get them a drink. She was still shocked that such a gorgeous, intelligent, and confident man was naked in her kitchen and wanted *her*. She wasn't afraid of anything he wanted to say to her because she had never been more genuine about fully and unabashedly trusting him.

She stood up as he started back toward her. "Do you want to get something on and sit on the deck, or would you rather go to bed?"

"I definitely don't want you to put anything on! The view from here is breathtaking," he said, handing her a glass, "but I will do whichever you please."

"Well then let me slip on my robe, and let's sit out on the deck for a bit. It's just so nice out tonight. Then maybe we can recreate our last performance before we go to sleep."

"Um, absolutely!" he said eagerly as she went into the bedroom.

CHAPTER 17

*T*odd slipped on his boxers and walked out into the chilly night. The embers from their earlier fire were still hot, so he tossed on another log and got the fire going again. He was full of unfamiliar emotions making his stomach feel a bit queasy. Never had he met someone who completed him in so many ways. He had dated girls who were lots of fun, girls with whom he was sexually compatible, and even girls who could hold intellectual conversations, but with each one, something had been missing. He never even considered getting serious with anyone, even with the few he had dated casually for years. Yet, here he was, imagining an actual future with a woman he had known for less than a couple of months. She was the girl he thought could never exist, and so much more. Dare he believe his soulmate?

Staring into the night, he thought he saw movement out of the corner of his eye. Not wanting to scare Lexi more than she already was, he didn't say anything. Instead, he walked down the stairs and into the trees below to get a better look, confident it was merely his imagination.

"Hey, whatcha doing?" Lexi asked, walking outside in a short, silky black robe that she was pulling tighter, looking worried.

"Nothing, sweet girl, just burning off some nervous energy. Is there anything you don't look sexy in?" he said, changing the subject.

"Flattery will get you everywhere."

"You mean there are places I haven't seen yet?" he said, and they both laughed.

He walked back up the stairs and started to settle in beside her on the chaise but stopped, getting up to turn the lights off before he sat back down.

"Did you see something out there? Why'd you turn off the lights?" she asked.

"You said you wanted to see the stars," he said, not being entirely deceitful.

"Oh, okay. So, are you going to tell me what's on your mind, or is the moment lost?"

"If you snuggle up to me," he said, getting under the blanket she had brought for them, "I will try and put it into words."

She snuggled in closer and entwined her legs with his, laughing as she felt his excitement. "Happy to see me?"

"Happy I don't have to pull away from you every time that happens anymore," he said, grinning at her and casually sliding his hand between her warm legs.

"Damn," she said, "your hands are cold. But don't even think of moving them."

"Trust me, I never want to move them again," he said under his breath.

He looked over to find her staring, searching for answers, and in her eyes, he saw the one thing he needed at that moment—her trust. He could see she was terrified of the conversation they were getting ready to jump into, but she sincerely trusted him, and that made what he wanted to say a little less scary.

"So," he started, "this afternoon, I told you that I don't date much. The truth of the matter is that I've never been in any long-term rela-tionships. I date, but I've never met anyone I considered getting serious with. Part of me thought maybe my expectations were too high, so I became content that I would probably be single for the greater part of my life. I was happy to be on my own and completely comfortable with my place in the world. Then, late one afternoon, I stumbled upon this emotionally wrecked girl, crying her heart out, completely unaware that life as I knew it was over.

You are everything I never knew I wanted, but still dreamed about. When we were first becoming friends, I hadn't let myself think of you as anything more, but I still couldn't get you out of my mind. Even then, I spent the time I wasn't with you trying to figure out what I could do to put a smile on your face, to help you heal your wounded spirit. But each time we were together, you continued to surprise me. Whether it was your unique perspective on life, or the brilliant ideas and theories you brought to our conversations, I was genuinely drawn to you. It was unexpected and maddening, but there seemed to be a gravitational pull that landed me in your company each night. Your character is genuine and honest. Even when you were brutally blunt or sarcastic, your intentions were never hurtful.

As the weeks went on, I became acutely aware of your sexual vibe, which you are blatantly unaware of, and began to want you as more than just a friend. I was worried that it was obvious, and the possibility of losing you to the friend zone terrified me. But I still couldn't stay away. Last night I let my emotions get the better of me, especially as you danced out on the water with no cares in the world. That was when I realized I had to take the chance or regret it for the rest of my life. When you showed interest back, it literally took every ounce of willpower I had not to throw you down and have my way with you at that moment. But I also knew you were drunk, and I'd never taken advantage of that situation. I was so worried you would push me away once you had sobered up that I barely slept at all last night. That's why I was up before dawn this morning. I had to go for a run and clear my head. Needless to say, when you stumbled into the kitchen and wrapped your arms around me, my heart flipped." He stopped and glanced over to make sure she was still following him. Disheartened when he noticed she was looking away from him. "Dammit, I'm sorry. Never mind. I knew this was too much, too soon. Forget everything I just said. Shit." He looked in the other direction, trying to hide his tears but unable to control his unsteady breath.

He sat there in silence, trying to decide if he should get up and leave when he felt her hand turning his face toward hers.

She had obviously been trying to hide her tears and keep her emotions under control too. Grabbing the back of his neck, she kissed him deeply, with no reservations. "Please finish. I'm not freaking out. I'm really not, I want you to finish." This time instead of looking away, she nuzzled her face into his chest, unable to stop the waterworks.

Todd pulled her toward him, letting go of his own emotions. "I don't want you to leave. I can't let you go, not when I finally found you. Today made me realize that I... Lexi, I think..." He stopped, and she looked up at him. "Lexi, I am falling in love with you," he said, sputtering before she could stop him. "I'm scared and confused, but after that mind-bending sex, I need to be honest. I have no other choice but to be honest with myself. I don't care how crazy it is or how long we've been in each other's lives. I can see a future with you."

She didn't say anything, just looked at him with her tear-steaked face.

"Please say something," he whispered.

Instead, Lexi straddled his lap, dropped her robe as the fire flickered behind her, and smiled. "Make love to me again."

Their sex was slow, deliberate, and even more earth-shattering than their previous escapade, and just before he climaxed, she leaned down to whisper, "I've fallen for you too, Todd."

Completely enveloped in each other's presence, neither made notice that they were outside, visible to anyone trying to watch.

CHAPTER 18

Sitting on the edge of the rented property, Crystal waited and watched as she had done hundreds of nights before. But this time, things were different—Lexi was different. This one wasn't like the guy she'd left at home. The way he touched her and looked into her eyes sent waves of rage throughout Crystal's crouching body. She couldn't really hear their conversation anymore, only the occasional moan or cry of pleasure, but after almost being caught earlier, she was afraid to move any closer.

Tiny droplets of blood formed beneath the fingernails on her bare leg as she worked to control her desire and anger through the pain. She watched them fuck for what seemed like hours, not really Lexi's style. In fact, all her usual routines had been entirely out of whack for the last couple of months. It was that son of a bitch who wouldn't leave her alone. Who was he? What was so special about him?

When Crystal saw the man stand and walk toward the kitchen, her frustration grew stronger and her nails dug even deeper into her already scarred leg. He had made *her* his whore! When Lexi got up to leave the room and he started walking toward the back deck, the petite blonde dashed toward the opposite side of the next house, hiding behind an overgrown bush.

No longer able to see them, Crystal's obsession kept her perfectly still. She needed to hear Lexi's voice before she could leave. Instead, the pig began to speak. The horrid words falling from his disgusting pig lips made her physically ill. Still, she swallowed back the sickness to avoid detection.

Unable to control her obsession any longer, Crystal stepped from behind the obstacle between them, allowing Lexi an open line of sight, showing how far she had come to keep her safe from this bullshit again. But instead, she found herself standing unnoticed, watching the woman who was forever hers riding the cock of some fucking man she barely knew. Then, she heard the words she had been longing to hear from Lexi's perfect mouth for years, but they weren't directed toward her.

How could she have betrayed me like this? Crystal thought angrily. She had been the only person emotionally there for Lexi for so many years; she couldn't just stand by and watch the woman she loved cast her off. Quietly, she turned to leave. A red fox was in her path, so she kicked and the stupid animal stormed off. This would *not* be the end; Lexi Greer was hers!

CHAPTER 19

*J*ust as it had been every morning since she arrived in Tennessee, the breeze carried its familiar, earthy scent through Lexi's open window. That morning, however, was significantly different from any other morning she could remember, and she smiled before even opening her eyes.

"Good morning, beautiful," she heard from the opposite side of her bed as she rolled over to face Todd.

"The best morning," she said dreamily, still waking up. "How long have you been up?"

"Not long. I've just been laying here enjoying the cool morning air, trying, unsuccessfully, to motivate myself to make you coffee."

"You mean you haven't made my coffee yet?" she smirked, nuzzling herself against his naked body.

"Well, look who's all cocky this morning. Is it normal for you to take advantage of all the guys who spill their hearts and confess their undying love to you?"

"Of course not. I kick most of them out of bed before I go to sleep."

"Really? So, I guess I am lucky, then?"

"Oh yes, you are terribly lucky!"

She kept her face hidden, and he pushed her away, tickling her until she was forced to jump from the bed. "No fair!" she said, still catching her breath.

"While you're up..." he said, nodding toward the kitchen. His muscles flexed as he stretched his arms behind his head and looked at her expectantly. "Coffee's not going to make itself."

"You are a brave man, Mr. Novak. Brave or crazy, I haven't decided which yet." She scoffed and pulled on her robe as she walked to the bathroom to brush her teeth. When she finished, she walked back into the bedroom, only to find he had already made his way to the kitchen and started the coffee.

She stood leaning against the door frame and considered pinching herself.

He was finding his way around the kitchen as the sun created an artwork of shadows across his back. Todd hummed, and she wondered if he did that often when he was alone.

Her eyes scanned his body, and Lexi asked herself whether staying in bed and having sex all day was out of the question, and blushed when he caught her staring, recognizing her expression.

Laughing, he said, "Busted. I've been thinking the same thing from the moment I woke up this morning." With the coffee percolating, he strolled toward her, his hands grazing the skin at her waist. Moving her out of the doorway, he smacked her ass and said, "My turn to brush my teeth!"

"You are absolutely incorrigible!"

Lexi picked through the kitchen cabinets looking for something she could make for breakfast, but came up empty. She usually just had a cup of coffee or two and a granola bar, but she wasn't sure if that would suffice for Todd. Giving up, she shut the cabinet and went to open the back doors to let the fresh morning air into the house.

As she got closer, she noticed something on the chaise lounge where Todd had professed his feelings the night before. She smiled, thinking he had woken up early and brought her flowers, but when she stepped onto the back deck, she realized it was not flowers. Instead, Lexi found a mutilated black kitten tucked neatly into the blanket they left out last night. An unintentional scream escaped her lips as she cupped her mouth.

At that exact moment, she heard a loud crack echo through the cove and watched a giant Cypress tree split in half, leaving one half still rooted in the ground, while the other splashed into the lake water. The violence and randomness shook something deep inside Lexi.

"Lexi, are you okay?" Todd asked, finding her on the deck. Stopping short, he realized what had upset her. "What the hell is this?"

"I don't know. I went to open the doors and saw something on the chaise. At first, I thought you had left me a gift until I found the little stray cat I'd been feeding. This isn't something that just happens on its own, is it?" She looked at him for answers but saw that he had none.

"It's probably no big deal. Maybe the same teenagers we heard last night came back to mess with us after we had gone to bed."

"Are you serious? No big deal? Todd, they followed us back up here last night, intentionally killed an animal I had been caring for, and left it for us to find. In my book, that's a huge deal!"

She was, understandably, shaken, so he tried to think of any other possibilities that made more sense. "Now, we don't know that's how it really happened. As you noticed before, there aren't very many occupied houses on the lake right now, so it could have just as easily happened at my place. You know how stupid teenagers can be; maybe they thought leaving it to scare an unsuspecting stranger would be funny. Besides, we don't know that another animal didn't do this."

"Do you really believe that?" she asked.

"I'm just saying we don't know what really happened, so I don't think we should be all freaked out yet."

"I can't help it." She sat down on the deck steps and ran her fingers through her hair. "How will I be able to stay here alone anymore, especially since the whole back half of the house is a big window, giving the world complete access to my life? This is not how this morning was supposed to go."

Todd had never seen her pissed off, and wasn't sure what he should say or do, so he took her hand and waited for her next move.

She squeezed his hand and smiled weakly before standing to go into the house. Cabinets slammed in the kitchen, then she stormed back out, grabbed the mutilated cat, and shoved it, and the blanket, into a large black trash bag.

She threw the trash bag in the dumpster out front and handed him the kitchen cleaner and a rag. "Will you please wipe down the chaise? I'll be damned if I am going to let some idiots ruin this morning for me. That's my favorite spot in the house, and I won't let them have it!" She stormed back into the kitchen and was washing her hands when he peeked around the corner. She couldn't help but laugh at his exaggerated gesture. "I'm sorry," she said. "Did I mentioned I have a temper?"

"You mentioned it, but failed to say you were scary," he teased. "Honestly, though, I'm not afraid to admit it's a little sexy. I like a woman that can take care of herself. Just remind me not to piss you off anytime soon."

He met her at the sink and kissed her as he washed his hands, and to his surprise, she seemed to calm down tremendously. He made a mental note and poured her a cup of coffee. "So, what are the plans for today?"

"Well, I was looking for something to make you for breakfast, but all I found were granola bars. I'm not sure what you usually eat in the morning," she said.

He was amazed that she had calmed down as quickly as she had blown up. "I'm up for anything. I've got some fruit and stuff at my house. Do you wanna head that way?"

"I really need a shower."

"Me too." He smiled impishly. "Why don't you grab your stuff and we can hang out at my house today? I've got a shower big enough for two."

"Two, huh?" she said, pulling him toward her seductively.

"Yeah, but if we don't go now, I have a feeling we'll never get out of here, and I'll never get any breakfast."

"Okay, okay, I'm going. Give me two minutes."

As Lexi walked into the bedroom to get her things together, she thought of his outdoor shower, pausing to push down the anger at their loss of privacy. She wasn't going to dwell on it. A gorgeous man who had professed his love stood in the kitchen, and this time she wasn't terrified of her future. No way was she going to let some stupid teenager ruin that for her.

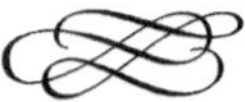

CHAPTER 20

The scent of the innocent animal's death and the sound of the falling tree stirred Giltine's memory. She remembered the men, her own people, damming the river which would damn them all.

The business of death was prevalent in rural mountain communities. Displaced stress fed the animosity over the land spared from flooding. Feuds and fighting carved a deep generational scar. The government was the enemy, and the mountain people chose to isolate themselves. She was saddened by the cycle of alcoholism and drugs often used to cope, and how those in power chewed up and spit out their own people for profit. As they ravaged their own bodies, the Reaper goddess feasted on the inevitable death which followed.

The Reaper's role rarely offered the goddess a way to change human death, for their fates had been set at birth. In the old land, humans had a healthy fear of death, but understood it was an inevitable step into the next state of existence. Modern times, and the growth of overlapping ideologies, had people terrified of aging and death. The extremes they would go through to try and cheat death created a gap between the Reaper goddess and her charges. The beauty of death, and its necessity to balance the physical and ethereal, was rarely embraced anymore.

Giltine sometimes envied her sister, Laima. Laima's role was to bring birth into the physical realm, where she would designate the new soul's fate for that stage in their journey. Those spiritually inclined embraced Laima's help during soul transition, but most feared Giltine and were always trying to ward her away.

The sisters worked together if the soul's transition was tragic or would come with a great burden. Otherwise, her days were spent alone, or with ghosts of mortals who did not recognize or understand her place in the life cycle. It made for a lonely existence that she fought with dark humor and ambivalence.

When she was just a young immortal, an agent of chaos tricked and trapped her in a coffin for seven hellacious years. By the time she escaped, her vivacious beauty had been stripped, and she was left with the dark visage she reluctantly accepted.

She could sense the same chaos trying to manipulate the distraught girl she found floating on the lake. Giltine knew her intended fate and would watch her closely, promising herself Lexi would not fall into the chaotic intention trying to lure her to an untimely death. She slithered close enough to taste and identify the threat, but the girl spooked easily and fled before she could clearly understand the chaos that enveloped her.

An awakening of some kind was building like a thunderstorm, and Giltine hoped she could use it to her benefit. With that arrival, the Reaper goddess would protect the broken mortal from a being determined to fuck with fate.

CHAPTER 21

*C*rystal woke up before the sun, as usual, and looked around the cheap motel room she had rented by the week since she'd arrived. She had been living on nearly nothing to keep her spending low, but quickly realized that to stay close to the woman she loved, she needed to find a way to make some money.

She hadn't had much time to prepare before she left Cincinnati, only knowing Lexi was planning to go somewhere, but unsure where or for how long. She had thrown some clothes, her makeup bag, and a couple of pairs of shoes in her car, realizing that she would have to be waiting for Lexi's departure. Several days before their journey began, Crystal overheard Lexi talking on her cell to someone about payment on a lakefront rental and vacationing alone. That was when Crystal knew she must be prepared to drop everything and go. This was the opportunity she had been waiting for—her chance to get Lexi alone finally, the moment she knew they would fall in love. However, she hadn't planned on being there for over a month, and she didn't have the money to maintain even that pathetic place.

After eating her morning toast, she left to run, thinking of her next move and hoping that an opportunity would present itself. She observed herself in the reflection of each storefront window she passed, disgusted by the person she saw. Although her small frame was nearly all muscle from obsessively working out, Crystal only saw the flaws: the ugly blonde shade of her hair, how the muscle definition in her chest made her look masculine, or how her sad little legs were short and squat. As the ever-present anger began to well up in her chest, she pushed herself harder, trying to run further away from her thoughts.

The sun started to rise as she walked back to the motel. As she let her muscles relax and cool down, she ran across the public posting board she had previously noticed. She scanned the ads, skipping the ones which would put her in the public eye until she saw an ad for what seemed the ideal situation:

Young, responsible student wanted to maintain summer home over the offseason. Must be local and able to regularly perform maintenance on both home and property at owner's request. References are a must. Please call 910-555-5555 or email tandy@indianaemail.com

Crystal pulled down the flyer, hoping that luck would favor her. She first needed to call in some favors and put together some 'references,' which shouldn't be too hard. Rushing back to the room, she showered and called Ms. Tandy, which led to a lunch meeting that afternoon.

She ensured she looked professional, young, stable, and reliable when she walked through the door to meet the homeowner. She explained how she was in college, but after coming home for the summer, she decided to take next year's classes online, and was looking for a little freedom from her mom. She assured her that she had the strength and knowledge to handle nearly any task that would arise, primarily since she had grown up without a father and had dealt with all the household maintenance for her mother.

Crystal offered Ms. Tandy situational examples and her faux references, and by the time lunch was over, she had a job and a new place to stay. Ms. Tandy was so taken by Crystal that she had even offered to let her stay in the garage apartment on the family's property over the winter, and because they were leaving the following day, Crystal would be free to move in very quickly.

Still buzzing from the rush of her lies and recent performance, she lay on the bed, relieved at her new source of income, and happy to be leaving that dump. It often amazed her how stupid people could be when you told them exactly what they wanted to hear. She never really understood the need for truth when you could get whatever you wanted with a manipulated version.

She was free to prepare the perfect situation, allowing her to prove her love to Lexi and ensure their future. Her first step was to eliminate the competition.

CHAPTER 22

For the next couple of days, Todd and Lexi spent almost every minute together, only leaving the house to take a walk or paddleboard. Neither wanted to let the dreamlike euphoria escape, but eventually, reality returns to even the best dreams.

"Fortunately, with reality comes a whole new set of adventures together," Todd reminded Lexi. "Okay, here's the plan," he said as they sat on the back deck of his house. "I'm going to head into town, and you head back to your place to get cleaned up and whatever else you need to do. I still don't know why you are paying to rent that place when you could pack up your stuff and stay here, so think about it again. Please."

"I've already told you I have a place to stay as soon as Kate gets back from her trip. I promise to bring my stuff here and stay until she gets home."

"And I have told you that it is more inconvenient for us to be in two places?" he asked.

Lexi rolled her eyes. "The thought of calling back home makes me sick to my stomach. I left things such a mess, but you're right. I have been here long enough that my family may be worried about me. Ugh, are you sure I need to do this?"

"If this thing between us is going to work, we have to start incorporating ourselves back into the real world. That means facing what you've left behind so we can move forward," Todd said. "But this time, you don't have to face things alone. I'm here for the good and bad of it all, and I promise, if you fall, I'll be here to catch you."

Lexi climbed into his lap and wrapped her arms around his neck.

He held her, understanding how nervous she was about the decisions she faced. Todd felt helpless, but also knew the necessity of facing the pain and hurt she had run away from, and she had to face it alone. He would be there the minute she needed him, and he hoped she wouldn't let fear keep her from letting him be a part of the process.

"Now go; I'll be here when you get back," he said. "Oh, by the way, do you need anything from the store? Do you want me to pick up something special for you?"

She smiled and shook her head. "Would you care to get some more coffee? And maybe stuff to make a salad for tonight?"

"Anything in particular?"

"No, whatever you like. I'm just craving fresh veggies."

Todd kissed her softly and squeezed her hand as he jumped up to leave.

Once he was out the door, the magnitude of what she was facing punched her in the gut, and her breathing quickened. She locked up at Todd's and headed back toward her rental, thoughts rushing through her mind. The responsible thing to do was email her parents, but did she really want to give them Kate's number? If she gave them her phone number, she knew they would call as soon as they got the email. Was she ready to explain why she had left so abruptly, not to mention why she wasn't coming home yet? What was she going to tell work? Should she tell them she would be gone indefinitely? What if this whole thing with Todd fell apart? Was the start of a new life in Tennessee worth losing her job over?

Then, there was Kyle. She knew he deserved more than an email saying goodbye. He was a good guy, but things never seemed to work in their favor. He always seemed to pull away any time they began to get close. She never felt like he trusted her, and she never really understood why. The whole relationship had been a constant struggle, a rollercoaster of affection and distance. At least there were no regrets about ending things with him, just how it had ended.

When Lexi walked into her place, she instantly got a creepy feeling, like someone had been there while she was gone. The atmosphere reminded her too much of her life in Cincinnati. She looked around, and everything seemed to be where they had left it, but chills still shot through her. *It only makes sense I feel anxious*, she thought, looking at the chaise and remembering that poor cat she found last time she was there.

"Let's just do what I came here to do," she said out loud.

Eventually, she sat down at the computer she hadn't used since her arrival. She ran her fingers through her wet hair and stared at the blank email she had addressed to her mom. Thoughts of Todd's words ran through her mind, *Just be honest with them. Don't be afraid to let them into your world, Lexi. They are your parents and will love you no matter what you tell them. You can never be truly happy until you start breaking down the walls you've built up around you. Every person needs relationships in their lives, and healthy relationships are open and honest.*

With that, her fingers began typing at a fevered speed:

Mom,

First, I want to apologize to you and Dad. It was never my intention to hurt either of you. I now realize that leaving without explanation was very selfish of me. This email isn't to make excuses for what I have done, but to instead try and explain why I shut down on everyone. Over the last couple of years, I lost myself, and I have been so confused and depressed that I was terrified of my own actions. There always seemed to be something falling apart, whether it was a relationship or an opportunity for personal growth. Even small things like my car getting a flat or my mail getting lost felt like life was out to get me. I started to feel like I was going crazy, becoming paranoid and anxious all the time. I know I should have just come to you, but I was embarrassed that I couldn't get my shit together, so I started shutting everyone out. Eventually, I always found myself alone, even when surrounded by people who cared about me. I would go to work, come home, and cry myself to sleep every night. I was having panic attacks which isolated me even more, and no medicine they put me on seemed to help. Life kept knocking me down, and I was worried about how little I wanted to get back up.

The night before I made the decision to leave was the worst. I had been to work and felt as if everyone was talking about me, even though I knew I had done nothing for them to discuss. When I got home, I was so paranoid that I convinced myself that someone had been in my apartment going through my things. The doorman assured me that he had not let any strangers in that day, and nothing was missing, but it left me fearful for my own sanity. I sat in the bathtub of my apartment crying uncontrollably, seriously contemplating who would miss me if I were dead, wondering if death would be easier for everyone. It was at that moment that I knew I had to go. I wasn't sure where, but I had to get away from Cincinnati and everything in my life because I was afraid of what I might do if I didn't. I knew it wasn't fair to you and everyone who cared about me, but it felt like a life-or-death decision at that moment. So, I rented a lakefront house in Tennessee and left.

Even though I should have talked to you and explained everything, I am sure that leaving Ohio was the best thing I could have ever done. The time I have spent here has literally been life-altering, Mom! I started to feel free, and the heaviness that had weighed me down for the last couple of years began to lift slowly. I began to feel like myself again and didn't wake up every morning wishing I could stay in bed all day. As I began to let myself heal and forgive myself for such self-hatred, something remarkable happened: I started trusting myself again. I hadn't realized how long it had been since I had let myself be happy or even let myself dream. I lived my life in a straitjacket of pain for so long. I began realizing I had built walls around my heart so high, I couldn't find the people I loved anymore. I am genuinely sorry, and I want you to know that I will never let myself get to that place again. I love you, and from now on, I will trust you to love me.

So, I guess you are wondering when I am coming back. That is the tricky part. As I started to find myself again, someone else saw me, as well. Somewhere along the way, I began to make friends and met a man I could possibly have a future with. I think I am finally ready to let someone love me, and for the first time in my memory, I trust myself enough to know I can love him *back. I know it's crazy, and it happened out of the blue, but I'm ready to embrace the craziness of life again. I'm prepared to take the things I want in life instead of feeling sorry for myself because they are always just out of reach. I want to give this a chance to work, so I'm not sure when I will be back. I feel strong, Mom! I have never been this happy. I've found a sense of peace I've never had. I want you guys to meet my new friends, but I need to get some things figured out first. My new information is attached. I saved it as a contact, so you can just add it to your email contact list.*

I love you so much and apologize for the pain I've put you through. Thank you for loving me and always being there, even when I am too stupid to realize it. I will talk to you soon!

Love Always ~ Lexi

Tears dropped onto the keyboard as Lexi typed. She felt relieved. The burden of loneliness, isolation, and desperation was released as Lexi hit send. She also realized she made the decision to find herself a permanent residence in Tennessee, and felt the familiar butterflies in her stomach take flight. As she wiped her blotchy face and blew her nose, she laughed out loud. Again, Todd had pushed her to make the right decision without telling her what to do.

As she got herself together, she wrote an email to Kyle explaining herself with the same freedom, letting go of the hurt and blame. Her apology for breaking up with him via a note on the kitchen table was sincere, and she finished with a promise to answer any questions he still had. Lastly, she emailed her boss explaining that she would not be coming back. She had thought of asking for more time off, but realized she hated her job, and even if things didn't work out in Tennessee, she didn't want to go back to a career that meant nothing to her. It was time for her to follow her dreams and take her new opportunity for everything it was worth.

CHAPTER 23

odd was all smiles as he walked into the grocery store, even if he was a little anxious for Lexi. It was a small local store, so he knew most of the employees and casually stopped to chat with several people as he shopped. Each remarked how there seemed to be something different about him and asked if he'd gotten a haircut or what he had changed; no one could quite put their finger on the difference. He just shrugged with a big smile, remarking sarcastically that he must have gotten more handsome since the last time he had been in. However, he knew exactly what was different, and he couldn't wait to return home to her.

As he strolled through each aisle trying to decide what he needed and what Lexi would like, he couldn't believe how happy he felt. He had been serious when he asked Lexi to move in with him, and although he would be okay with either decision, he hoped she would. Even the thought of it seemed surreal. Three months before, he would never have imagined how dramatically different his life would soon be. But there he was, grocery shopping for the woman he could see himself spending the rest of his life with.

Chuckling as he turned the corner, he nearly ran over a petite blonde he did not recognize. "Oh shit," he said, making sure she hadn't dropped any of her things. "I wasn't paying attention to what I was doing. I am so sorry."

"It's totally fine," she said. "I guess I wasn't paying attention either. I'm Crys, by the way."

"Well, hello, Crys. My name is Todd. Do you live around here?"

"Actually, I just got into town. I'm staying at the Tandy's place over the winter. Do you know where that is?" she asked.

"Sure, nice place. Are you family?"

"No, I'm a friend of the family. I'll be keeping an eye on the place over the winter. So, are you from around here?"

"Not originally, but I've been here for a couple of years. It's a great town, especially the people. We're all like an extended family. I think you will like it here."

"I can already see a couple of things I like," she said flirtatiously. "Any suggestions on what a girl can do around here for fun?"

"Unfortunately, there's not much to do around here during the offseason. There are a couple of local bars and restaurants. I'd check out O'Brien's; the crowd there is pretty cool, and most of the people are our age. Be sure you also enjoy the weather while you can. The marina out toward the Tandy's is nice," he said, trying to be obtuse to her flirtation.

"Sounds nice," she said smiling and looking up at him sheepishly. "I would love some company tonight. How would you like to give me a tour around town? You could pick me up around 6?"

"Um, I don't think that would be a good idea." He shifted from one foot to the other and tried to phrase his words amiably as to not hurt her feelings. "I actually already have a dinner date with my girlfriend, and we're staying in. I have a bunch of buddies that will be at the bar tonight, though. I'm sure one of them would love to take a beautiful girl like you out."

"Girlfriend?" she snapped out of nowhere. "Maybe you should have thought about your girlfriend before you started hitting on me! Bet she doesn't realize what a fucking dog she's got for a boyfriend."

Todd stood speechless, completely shocked by the turn in the conversation. He looked around for anyone he knew and back at her, still not sure what had just happened. "What?" he asked. "I wasn't hitting on you. I was just trying to be—"

She cut him off and jerked her cart around to the next aisle. "Dick," she mumbled as she walked out of sight.

Still standing in the same spot, he was trying to decide what had just transpired between himself and the blonde stranger. He was sure he had not been inappropriate, but had never seen anyone change their mood or demeanor so drastically with no provocation.

Shaken by the whole thing, Todd quickly finished his shopping and was relieved to see no sign of the girl while he was checking out.

Back at his Jeep, he loaded the groceries and climbed in. As he pulled out of the parking lot, he saw the blonde standing across the street glaring at him.

Her expression was one of genuine hatred, but as soon as she saw him noticing her, she quickly turned and started walking in the other direction. Her reaction in the store had been odd, but Todd was even more baffled by the animosity in her stare. It wasn't just a look of embarrassment; she seemed vengeful, as if he'd killed her dog or something.

Todd re-ran the situation over and over in his mind as he drove home, flustered by the whole thing. By the time he reached his driveway, he was no longer upset by the stranger's reaction. In fact, it only made him realize even more how lucky he was to have Lexi in his life. He just didn't understand some girls, and decided he wouldn't tell Lexi about his encounter. Not because he was trying to keep it from her, but because it was not worth causing her any more stress.

With arms full of groceries, Todd pushed the door open with his foot. He had only been gone for about an hour, so he knew Lexi would not be back yet.

Unloading the groceries onto the kitchen counters, he looked around his place, wondering what it would be like to have someone else around all the time, especially a girl. It would be different, but the thought of waking up to the woman he loved every morning made him feel complete. Thinking of their earlier discussions on the topic, he wasn't sure if he had made it clear that he meant *permanently* when he had asked her to stay with him. He wanted to make a life with her, shape a future together.

With the groceries unloaded, he turned on the stereo and opened the back door to watch for Lexi, then fell onto the couch and closed his eyes. What would he do if she didn't want to stay in Tennessee? He could no longer imagine being without her, and he fidgeted uncomfortably. Was it fair for him to ask her to leave her life? Maybe she would ask him to go back with her to Cincinnati.

As all the possible scenarios rushed through his mind, he heard footsteps enter the house and his eyes shot open.

Lexi was standing next to the couch; her beautiful face was covered in red splotches, and her green eyes were bloodshot from crying. She sat at the end of the sofa and pulled his feet onto her lap, not saying anything.

Nervously he asked, "How'd it go?"

"Well, it didn't go like I thought it would."

"What does that mean? Are you going back?" Todd sat up and looked at her, nearly terrified about what she would say next.

Lexi took Todd's hand. "I'm not sure I fit in Cincinnati anymore. I want to give us a shot and find a permanent place here on the lake."

"I meant it when I said I wanted you to move in with me. I mean, I want you to move to Tennessee permanently. I want you to make a life with me."

"Have you seriously thought about what you are asking? I care deeply for you, but we've only known each other for a short time. I need to figure myself out before we take that kind of step."

"Lexi, I have done nothing but think and worry that you would say no and go back to Ohio. I don't want to live another day without you, so I'll do whatever I need to do to keep you in my life."

Smiling, she shrugged her shoulders. "I guess we need to find me a good realtor then. I can't live at Kate's forever."

"Are you serious?" He jumped up from the couch, pulling her up with him. "You are permanently staying in Tennessee? What changed your mind?"

He picked her up and twirled her around the living room, so relieved she wasn't leaving.

Lexi laughed at his excitement and begged him, in vain, to put her down. When her feet finally found the ground again, she sat back on the couch, tucking her legs beneath her.

"I guess *you* changed my mind. Once I got back to the house and started writing the email to Mom, I realized that I wanted to give us a chance and wasn't ready to leave Norris Lake. Remember, there's still a ton for me to learn from Kate and these mountains. I knew I couldn't go back to the life I'd left behind because I wasn't that person anymore. I told Mom everything and apologized for the way I'd left, and once I started, I couldn't stop. It felt so good to let go of that pain and fear. I emailed work and told them that I wouldn't be coming back. I hated that job anyway. Lastly, I emailed my ex-boyfriend, apologizing for the way I ended things. I guess I finally took the first steps toward putting closure to that part of my life."

CHAPTER 24

Crystal threw all her stuff together and moved into her new apartment above the garage. The Tandy's had offered to help her move in, but not wanting them to see how little stuff she had. She lied, explaining how she needed to help her mom with something that day and couldn't move in until later that week after they had already left for the season.

She stopped by to get the keys to the place and let Mr. Tandy walk her around the property, explaining where everything was and what they expected from her. It seemed easy enough; nothing Crystal couldn't handle. After praising her references' outstanding recommendations, they returned to Indiana, comfortable and confident their property was in good hands.

It didn't take long for Crystal to make herself at home in the main house. The view of the lake was lovely, especially with the estate's privacy. She really couldn't believe how lucky she had been to manipulate her way into this situation and wished it wasn't temporary, but she was there for Lexi and couldn't let luxury distract her.

After the disastrous encounter with Todd at the grocery, she realized he wouldn't be as easy as Kyle to seduce and plant seeds of doubt. He hadn't even been phased by her advances. She chastised herself for the way she lost her temper with him, and wore new abrasions to prove it, knowing she ruined any chance at luring him away from Lexi. The failed attempt left her contemplating her next move.

Earlier that week, she had been by Lexi's house, but no one was home. In fact, they hadn't left Todd's place in a week, so Crystal felt comfortable sneaking in.

She had been able to make a copy of the house key one afternoon while Lexi was paddleboarding. She'd only been in the house one other time, at night, while Lexi was at Todd's. Crystal never took anything, just poked around through her things, making sure to leave everything the way she found it. There wasn't much to offer insight into Lexi's life, at least not like in her apartment back in Cincinnati. The last time she had snuck in, there hadn't even been any activity on her computer; Lexi really had cut herself off from everyone.

Crystal quietly slid her copy of the key into the front door, then walked into the dark kitchen. Things seemed different. There were no dirty dishes, and she didn't see any of Lexi's personal items on the counter. Moving through the living room and into the bedroom, Crystal felt the heat rising from her stomach into her chest. All of Lexi's things were gone! The house had been cleaned and was empty, but Lexi was still in town. What did that mean?

Her anger bubbled just below her skin, but she tried to keep her thoughts under control. She had to find out what was going on. *The computer*, she thought.

Crystal sat down at the computer, relieved Lexi hadn't changed her password since leaving Ohio, pulled up the web history, and noticed Lexi had used her email. She opened her sent items folder and found the newest emails. Crystal cursed aloud as she read Lexi's private correspondence to her mother, slamming her fist into the keyboard.

"You bitch!" she said aloud. "How could you have done this to me? What do you mean you aren't coming back to Cincinnati?"

Unable to control her rage, Crystal ran from the cabin toward her car parked several houses down. She shrieked hysterically through her tears, not caring about being heard. By the time her apartment came into view through her windshield, her skin was torn so badly she had to go into the main house to try and find a first aid kit to stop the bleeding.

She fell asleep that night curled in a ball on the bathroom floor, covered in her own blood and tears.

CHAPTER 25

*K*ate arrived back home to find her house empty. She called Lexi and left a message that she was back in town, so she could bring her stuff by whenever she'd like.

The next morning, a familiar green Jeep dropped off the young lady with her luggage.

"Well, well, well, look at you, my friend. Your energy reads like a completely different woman. I'm assuming not all of that is from the week you spent in retreat," said Kate.

"To be fair, without the week I spent learning from you, this new version of Lexi, who is giving this a chance, would never have even had the courage to try."

"Let's go put your things away so you can spill the beans on you and the handsome Mr. Novak."

Lexi blushed, giggling as Kate stayed on her heels, following her into her new room.

Kate was spouting off questions almost faster than Lexi could answer them. By the time she finished unpacking, Lexi had her caught up about her new relationship with Todd.

"Sounds to me like that boy has fallen head-over-heels for you. I've known him for years, and he rarely lets a girl stay the night at his place, much less offer to move them in."

"*Gawd*, it feels unreal. And there is no way I am ready to move in with him. I mean, maybe someday, but I need to find my own footing first. However, this leads me to the next big announcement. I've decided to stay in Tennessee, so I hope you don't mind me being here until I can find my own place."

Kate squealed like a teenage girl. "I knew it! I knew something big was coming our way, and I couldn't be more thrilled that it was you."

"What do you mean you knew something was coming? How did you know?"

"I have what some people would call the gift of sight. That means my intuition about the future is much stronger than ordinary folk. The first sign came in the form of coffee grounds, which I learned to interpret while studying under Alva. I also read tarot cards and look toward nature for answers. Occasionally, if the energy is strong enough, I will see glimpses of the future in my mind's eye. You see, there are two types of folks that conjure: those who openly embrace their intuitive nature and mentor under a skilled practitioner, and then there are natural witches."

"How can you tell the difference?" asked Lexi.

"Folks like me, meaning those with the inclination, but not the natural gifts, spend years studying and working with nature to create magic. Without guidance or mentorship, our powers would never bloom. Then, there are folks like you, natural witches, who are filled up with magic that is going to come out one way or another. Things that would take me years to master would generally only take you weeks to embody."

"Wait, what? You think I am a natural witch? There is nothing magical about me."

"Do you remember our ancestral ceremony on the last day of the retreat?"

"Yes."

"When you released your gift of gratitude, your body felt a physical response. That's because there were ancestral spirits all around you. In fact, you caught the attention of a dark spirit who has wandered this land for centuries. She is the one who was most touched by your gratitude, and offered a nod in respect, causing the chills you felt when you released the yellow flowers."

"So, not only are you telling me I'm a witch, but that I have also caught the attention of a demon? In what world is that a good thing?"

Years of teaching and traveling to unfamiliar cultures allowed Kate to keep her laughter from bubbling forward. "I'm not saying you brought forth a demon. I am saying there is a dark spirit I am unfamiliar with who found you interesting. Maybe you share an ancestral bond, or maybe she understands the pit of darkness you are emerging from in an intimate manner and is curious. My point is that only a natural witch would have connected with such a powerful spirit. Let me ask you this: since I left town, have you experienced any weird phenomena?"

Lexi's expression must have revealed the truth because Kate cocked an eyebrow and nodded in validation. With a shudder, she proceeded to tell Kate every detail she could remember about her experience in the family cemetery.

"So, you experienced this like a memory?" Kate asked.

"No, it was almost like it was happening in real time. I mean, it felt like I was watching the past as it played out, except for when the dark lady became involved, time seemed to slow down."

"I wonder what triggered the vision. It could have been psychometry, and the land triggered your vision, or it may have been the dark lady trying to communicate. Either way, you could not have experienced that glimpse into the past without having some kind of natural gift."

"We obviously have different definitions of the word 'gift.' Nothing about what I saw felt like a gift. It was terrifying and horribly sad."

"Unfortunately, that is the story much of the land around here offers. It's not all bad, don't get me wrong, but there are spots in this region where anger, fear, and distrust of outsiders have soaked deep into the earth. The family plot you stumbled into was probably host to a family who lost everything to the rising waters that would eventually become Norris Lake. My guess would be the secret you witnessed is what has kept that particular parcel of land sour."

"You mean the dark lady?" asked Lexi.

"No. I'm honestly not exactly sure what the dark lady was, maybe some kind of Reaper or harbinger of death. I'm talking about the girl who was left behind to die. Times were different back then. People were literally starving to death. Maybe her family left her behind because death was the only thing they had left to give her. Maybe they were just cruel people. Either way, something like that leaves scars on the land."

"Do you think the dark lady I saw in my vision is the same dark spirit you noticed at the retreat?"

"I hesitate to assume anything, but the timing gives one pause. Have you tried to communicate with her since then?"

"Um, that would be a hard no; she was terrifying. Besides, I wouldn't even know where to begin trying to communicate with a spirit, much less a scary one."

"It doesn't seem like the spirit is going to wait around for introductions, but I can appreciate your hesitation. I'll make a call to Alva. Maybe she knows more about this spirit, or at least she can explain how she would handle the situation."

"I would appreciate that," admitted Lexi.

CHAPTER 26

*L*exi sat on the deck writing while Todd cleaned up after dinner when she heard a horrible screech. "What the hell was that?"

Todd walked out onto the deck. "I have no idea, but I heard it too."

"Was that a person?" she asked, unable to see anyone over the railing.

"I doubt it, but it sounded awful, didn't it? Maybe it was a catfight; the echo through the coves makes things sound pretty crazy sometimes."

Their heads swiveled at the loud rustle in the woods below, just in time for them to see a brilliant red fox running through the brush, its white tail bobbing through the fall foliage. "That explains it, a fox. Have you ever heard a male red fox's ratchet call? It sounds just like a woman screaming."

"Yeah, I guess. I'm still not used to all the noises out here at night. Did you get everything cleaned up? Need any help?"

"Sure, now you offer," he laughed. He sat down in the chair next to Lexi and looked over to see what she was writing. "What's that?"

"I am trying to make a list of all the stuff I need to get done when I go back home next weekend."

"This is home now, remember?"

"You know what I mean. What am I going to do with my apartment? I guess I could put out an ad in the paper for someone to sublet. And what am I going to do with all my furniture? There isn't room for my whole apartment full of furniture in my room at Kate's. I hadn't really thought about all the details involved in moving; it's pretty overwhelming."

"I told you I would come with you. I can help you load everything and safely get it to Tennessee, then put it in storage until you find your own place."

"I know you want to come with me, but I need to make this trip alone. It will just be for a couple of days, and I will be back, but I need to see my parents on my own. Plus, I need to give Kyle a chance to have some closure, seeing that I pretty much dumped him with a 'Dear John' letter. I promise we will go back together to get the rest of my stuff and meet my family next month."

"Okay, I get it. I just don't like the idea of having to share you," Todd said, looking at her with boyish eyes, "especially with Kyle." He crossed his arms, looking out over the water, pretending to pout.

"Awww, is someone jealous?" She laughed and poked him in the side, knowing how ticklish he was. "I'm going to miss you too."

"So, speaking of family...mine gets back into town this weekend and really want to meet you. Are you cool with going up there Saturday morning to spend the day at their place? I only ask out of formality because Mom isn't going to give us much of a choice," he said with a laugh.

"You've told them about me already? What did they say?"

"They were even more shocked than your parents, I think. I mean, they know me well enough to be as surprised as I was about the whole thing, but they are thrilled I've finally found someone I want to settle down with, and they can't wait to meet you. I'm pumped and have been looking forward to them returning to town. I miss 'em!"

"I would love to go visit your family this weekend, especially if they are as great as you say they are. That reminds me, I meant to ask if you ever called Mama about helping her fix that window?"

"Yeah, I called her, and I'm going to head over there while you're gone. I figured it would give me something to keep me distracted. She asked about you. She literally screamed in my ear when I told her I'd asked you to move in. That offer is still on the table, just to be clear."

"And I'm still not ready. Mama is so sweet. We need to go eat there again soon. Maybe next week before I leave?"

"She would love that!" Todd leaned forward and whispered in Lexi's ear, "Have I mentioned how much I love you?"

"A time or two," she said as she turned to kiss him, "but I wouldn't be opposed if you wanted to prove it to me."

"Oh, I will most definitely prove it to you," he said as he swept Lexi from her chair.

She squealed with delight, wrapping her arms around his strong shoulders as he carried her to the bedroom.

That night, they fell asleep in each other's arms, satisfied and content.

CHAPTER 27

*D*ressed in a pale-blue cotton sundress, Lexi fidgeted in her seat. The drive to his parents' house seemed to be the longest she could remember. No matter how many times Todd reassured her they would love her, she couldn't shake the worries that preoccupied her thoughts. Although she had promised Todd money wouldn't be an issue between them, what if his parents saw things differently? What if they didn't think she was good enough for their son? She checked herself in the mirror again and tucked her hair behind her ear.

"You know, it doesn't matter what you do to your hair, or how many times you put on more lip gloss, there's no way you could possibly get any more beautiful than you already are."

Her internal tirade interrupted, Lexi looked over and smiled weakly. "I think I'm gonna puke. What if they don't like me?"

"Sweetheart, they aren't just going to like you, they're going to love you. You have nothing to be nervous about. You know I wouldn't throw you to the wolves with no warning. My parents love me for exactly who I am, and they have rarely judged my life choices. Besides, you are the best thing that's ever happened to me. Trust me, they will see how happy I am even before I open my mouth."

"I hope you're right," she mumbled.

As they pulled into the long drive, Lexi breathed in and out slowly, trying to keep her nerves in control. The house was even more beautiful than she remembered, and she wasn't surprised to see his parents on the front porch waiting for them.

His mother wasn't a very tall woman, but her posture and confidence commanded attention. Her graying bob was thick and wind-blown, which flattered her tan face. She wore little makeup, and Lexi could see where Todd inherited his beautiful blue eyes. She was dressed in khaki shorts and a white shirt and was barefoot as she excitedly stood and waved toward the Jeep.

His father was several inches taller than Todd and had the same tone, muscular build. He had short brown hair, although peppered with gray like his mother. His eyes were soft and kind, making him very approachable. He was also wearing khaki shorts and was barefoot, but unlike his wife, he wore a long-sleeved, blue button-down. He had been reading as they approached but set down his book to greet his guests.

"Hey guys!" Todd yelled as he jumped out of the Jeep and walked around to open Lexi's door.

"Hey, handsome," his mom shouted back as she walked toward the couple.

His mom greeted him with a big embrace, hesitating to let go of her son. When she finally did, she glanced toward Lexi with a big smile.

Todd grabbed his girlfriend's hand, guiding her toward him. "Mom, this is Lexi. Lexi, this is my mom, Veronica Novak."

"Nice to meet you, Mrs. Novak," Lexi said as she stepped forward to shake her hand.

"Veronica, please. I figure since you have already won my son's heart, there is no need for formalities." As Veronica shook Lexi's hand, Todd's father made his way to the driveway. "And this would be my husband, James."

Lexi smiled and shook his hand. "Nice to meet you, sir."

"And you." James then turned his attention toward his son. "So kid, what good deeds have you done to deserve such a beautiful young lady?"

Lexi looked toward the ground blushing as Todd pulled her into his arms. "I have no idea, Dad, but I can assure you, I have counted my blessings each morning since I found her."

His dad winked at the couple, and his mom smiled, obviously thrilled to see her son's happiness.

"Well, let's not stand here all day," said Veronica. "I've made us a pitcher of spiked strawberry lemonade on the back porch. Oh, and I hope you brought your suits because we won't be able to use the pool very much longer this year. Todd, I need you to look at the pump while you are here. It's been acting funny since we got home. I tried to get the pool guy out here yesterday, but they are backed up until next week. I guess everyone is closing everything down for the season."

"Sure, Mom, I'm gonna grab our stuff. Why don't you show Lexi around, and I'll meet you around back." He gave Lexi a quick squeeze and turned back toward the Jeep.

Veronica reached for Lexi's hand, leading her toward the door.

Her nerves had settled, and she easily chatted with Todd's mom as she showed her around the house. The house seemed huge to Lexi, and was decorated impeccably, although still very warm and personal. Veronica, apparently, loved pictures because they were scattered all about the house.

Veronica showed Lexi photographs of Todd's brother and sister, Caleb and Abby, and she was surprised to see how alike Todd and his twin sister looked. Both shared the same big blue eyes, blonde curly hair, and tan, athletic physiques. Caleb, on the other hand, obviously favored his father. As Veronica took her through each room, she asked about Lexi's family, making casual conversation.

She showed her Todd's old bedroom and told her a couple of funny stories about his childhood. "He really isn't too different now than he was as a kid. He's always been so considerate, going out of his way to help anyone who needed him. He was such a mature kid, but his maturity never seemed to hinder his carefree attitude. Don't get me wrong, though, the three of them together always kept me on my toes, especially Todd and Abby. Those two could spin a situation in their favor before I knew what had happened." His mom laughed to herself, momentarily lost in old memories.

"I really can't wait to meet them," Lexi replied.

"I'm sure it won't be very long. I'm surprised you haven't met Abby yet. She and Todd are close. But then again, he has been keeping pretty busy, hasn't he?" Veronica turned to face Lexi. "I just wanted to say thank you before we get back downstairs with the guys. I've never seen this side of my son. His father and I were beginning to wonder if he would ever find love. He's always had such high expectations, and no matter how much his sister and I encouraged him to be more open, he was never willing to settle. I'm glad he ignored us and finally found someone who makes him so absolutely happy."

The blood rushed to Lexi's face, and she wished her body wouldn't always give her emotions away. "He's a great guy," she said quietly. "I hope you know that I will never take him for granted."

Veronica took her hand and looked at her sincerely. "I know you won't, and I also know that you must be a pretty special person to have captured Todd's heart." She looked away for a moment, then turned to go. "Okay, enough of that, I'm guessing the guys are starting to miss us by now, and we can't have that. Shall we head out back?"

"Sure. Todd's already told me all about your strawberry lemonade. I need to make sure I have the recipe before I leave, if you don't mind."

Todd changed into swim trunks and was fiddling with the pool filter while his dad cooled his feet in the water.

"Yeah, here it is," Todd said, looking up at his father. "Something is jamming up the filter. I told you it wasn't the pump."

"I'm glad we've got you around," James said to his son. "Your mother jumps to the worst possible scenario, and I don't know enough to be able to convince her otherwise. So, you think you've got it fixed?"

"Yeah, I think it will be fine now. Have Mom call the pool guy back Monday and reschedule. He won't need to come out until you are ready to close it down." Todd finished up in the pool, wrapped a towel around his waist, and helped his father up.

"Will do. Have a seat and I'll pour us some lemonade." James walked to the patio table Veronica had set up in the shade and came back with two drinks, handing one to his son. "Here you go. Tell me, son, how are things going?"

"Great, Dad. Lexi is heading to Cincinnati next weekend to pick up some of her things and wrap up some unfinished business. I'm going to go see Mama and help her fix a couple of things around the marina. She's been on my ass because I haven't been around much lately. I think she misses the company."

"She's really moving to Tennessee, huh? That's a pretty big step. You sure you're ready for that?"

"Without hesitation, Dad. I love her. I know it's all happened so fast, but she's the one, and I can't stand the thought of losing her."

"Well, she's a beautiful girl and seems very genuine. I'll have to admit, I've never seen you so happy. Your mom is elated that you have finally found someone to settle down with. I'm happy for you, too, I just want to make sure you understand what you are getting into. I mean, this is the first girl I've seen you serious about. It's my job as a dad to worry about you."

Todd smacked his dad playfully on the back. "Thanks Dad, but I know exactly what I am getting into. There's no reason for you to worry."

"That's good enough for me. I'm looking forward to getting to know her. What does your sister have to say about all of this? I think your mom talked to her while we were gone, but she only briefly mentioned that you had been spending some time with a girl who was staying down the lake from you. But, as I said, we only talked to her briefly. She's due back in town soon, isn't she?"

"Yeah, she should be home this weekend. I called her when I started realizing I wanted Lexi to be more than just a friend. You know Abby. She told me to get my head out of my ass and take a chance. She about shit when I told her I'd asked Lexi to move in. Seriously, her reaction was classic. I can't wait for them to meet; I know they will love each other!"

From the corner of his eye, Todd caught his mom and Lexi coming out of the back door and pouring drinks. He turned and stood to acknowledge their presence, noticing Lexi had relaxed significantly. He pulled another chair over and waited for them to sit before reclaiming his own seat next to his girlfriend.

Conversation flowed smoothly as his parents asked the usual questions, and as the morning turned into afternoon, Lexi began to feel comfortable and opened up. As he watched her laugh with his family and having a good time, his feelings for her grew even more profound, and his happiness became infectious.

CHAPTER 28

The afternoon heat convinced Lexi to change into her bikini top and shorts, and she and Todd were walking around the property, enjoying the serenity of the sparse lake views.

He was pointing out all the significant places from his past: the spot where he first kissed a girl, the rock his brother broke his arm falling from, the place he spent his high school nights by the bonfire. With each story, Lexi was learning so much more about the man she loved, and she found herself hanging on his every word.

They had talked about their families before, but watching him with his parents and hearing all their old stories further convinced her that he was the man she wanted to spend the rest of her life with. Todd was a man who knew how to treat those he loved, and she was taken by the uninhibited way he showed his affection.

"Can we sit for a minute?" she asked.

"Sure, what's up?"

"Nothing, I just want to enjoy you for a little longer before we go in for dinner. I really like your parents; it's been great watching you with them."

"I told you they were cool. Mom and Dad adore you too. They both cornered me today to tell me I better not mess this up," he joked.

"Can I ask you a question?"

Todd looked at her and smiled sadly, already knowing what she was going to ask. "You are going to ask about my brother, aren't you?"

"I won't if you don't want to talk about it."

"No, it's fine. Nobody really talks about it too much, but it's a part of who I am, and I want you to know everything there is to know about me."

"Are you sure?"

"Yes."

"Well, I noticed that he was several years older than you and Abby, and I also noticed there weren't any recent pictures of him. What happened?"

"Well, Caleb was a sophomore in college when I was a freshman in high school. He and I were remarkably close, considering the age gap. I idolized him, and he humored me. Anyway, he had gone away to school that year and had met a girl. When he came home for summer break, he told Mom and Dad he was in love and wanted to marry her. No one had met her, and my parents weren't thrilled he was talking about marriage before he was finished with school. That summer, my parents stayed pissed, and Caleb pulled away from everyone, spending all his time either visiting or on the phone with his girlfriend. We went from being a typical, happy family to severely dysfunctional in one summer. To make things worse, this girl refused to meet my family and convinced Caleb we were all out to sabotage their relation-ship. Mom and Dad were fighting, and Caleb had all but checked out on everyone. Poor Abby didn't understand what was happening, so I spent most of the summer caring for her. It was a mess.

Regardless, Caleb went back to school fall semester with a ring. He proposed to her at the beginning of the school year, and she accepted, so Caleb pretty much quit coming home to visit. I'm not 100% sure exactly what happened in the next couple of months, but according to his friends, Caleb caught his fiancé in bed with some guy from her biology class. Instead of dumping her ass, I guess he spent the next month trying everything to get her back. Apparently, she would confess her love and make Caleb her world for a week and then turn around and completely shun and humiliate him in front of all his friends the next week. Eventually, he failed out of school, so Mom and Dad made him come back home until he got himself together.

Lexi, when he came back home, he was a stranger to all of us. Caleb had always been an outgoing and good-looking guy. When he came home, he was thirty pounds thinner and looked hopeless. My parents were shocked by his appearance and put him in counseling, but nothing seemed to help. He just stayed in his room all day and would explode if Abby or I tried to talk to him."

Todd was looking at the ground, poking at the shoreline with a stick. His voice was low, and Lexi was afraid to say anything, so she slid closer and put her hand on his leg. She could feel he was shaking as she touched him, and it alarmed her, but she worked hard to keep her composure.

Todd took a deep breath and went on. "Mom and Dad were obviously entirely focused on Caleb, so again, Abby and I were pretty much left to fend for ourselves. I guess that's why she and I are so close; we kind of grew up relying on each other that year. We were so young that we didn't understand why Caleb couldn't just snap out of it, and we both started hating him for how much he was hurting everyone in the family.

One night, I was out messing around on the property when I heard a horrible argument. I snuck up, hid behind the big rock just beyond where you and I turned around earlier, and saw my brother and the girl who had obviously broken his heart. He was crumpled on the ground, crying uncontrollably, and she was apologizing for killing his baby, although the tone in her voice was not very apologetic. I watched as he reached for her, and she let him kiss her and almost undress her before she pushed him away, laughing at him, calling him pathetic. She told him the main reason she had gone through with the abortion was because the thought of having his kid inside her made her sick. She also claimed she wouldn't be back again and told him everyone would be better off if he would just disappear." Todd stopped talking, his emotions causing the words to stick in his throat.

He looked up at Lexi, tears spilling down his cheeks. The moment was so intense that Lexi swiped her own tears quickly away, wondering how she had not seen this coming. It amazed her how he could seem so carefree and content with so much pain in his past.

Todd buried his face in Lexi's lap and sobbed hard, painful tears until he was able to regain control.

"Todd, if you want to stop..."

"No, I want to keep going. How can I tell you to face the demons of your past if I am afraid to face my own?" he said, his breathing slowing a little. "So, there I am crouching behind the big rock, seeing my brother in a way I wish I had never seen. Part of me was disgusted with him for being so weak, and part wanted to kick that bitch's ass, but mostly, I was shocked by what I had just heard. I didn't know what to do or how to feel, so I just ran to the house and locked myself in my room.

The next morning, I remember my mom coming into my room, asking me if I had seen my brother. As soon as the words left her lips, I knew something was terribly wrong. I jumped out of bed and ran out the back door, down to the firepit where I had last seen him. My mom was right behind me, yelling at me, confused about my actions, when suddenly, I heard her scream. Jesus Lexi, the sound that came from my mom, was worse than anything I've ever heard in my life, and I just froze. Several feet in front of me lay my brother's limp body, surrounded by red-stained pea gravel. All I could do was fall to my knees and vomit. I couldn't back away from what I had seen. I couldn't even move to comfort my mom. I was frozen, staring at my brother's dead body, knowing he had taken his own life, understanding that if I had just stayed and talked to him, he would still be alive. His eyes were open and looking in my direction, completely empty.

The rest is kind of a blur, but Dad and Abby must have heard all the commotion and found us. I remember Abby pulling me away because I could not control my limbs. She was crying in my ear and kept asking why over and over. Police questioned all of us, and I had to explain everything I'd seen the night before with my parents sitting in the room with me. I knew they would blame me, but instead, they explained that my brother had been talking about suicide since he'd come back home.

The funeral was tough because the girlfriend showed up and my mom lunged at her, making a scene. Of course, they escorted the girl out, and my parents ended up taking out a restraining order in case she tried to come back around. During this process, we found out she had never even been pregnant. She had been holding that over my brother's head, trying to get money from him, and when she found out that he hadn't received his inheritance yet and didn't have any money, she told him she had aborted the baby. My parents were a mess by the end, but they still tried to be there for Abby and me.

School was hard that year, but at least Abby and I dealt with it together. Our friends tried for a while, but everyone was afraid to say the wrong thing, and I guess it was just easier to stay away. If it hadn't been for my sister, I am pretty sure I wouldn't be the same person I am now. We would talk for hours, and it was Abby that helped me realize I hadn't killed my brother. Although she was the younger twin, she was my rock; I owe so much to her.

Eventually, things started to get back to normal. My parents managed to keep their marriage together, and our family slowly began to heal. In the long run, I guess family tragedy either breaks or bonds a family. We're lucky. We learned to trust and rely on each other instead of pushing each other away. I guess that's why we don't have many secrets; we've been forced to depend on each other throughout the years."

Lexi brushed the tears from his swollen eyes and kissed him. Her heart broke for him, and she suddenly understood why he had approached her that first night on the dock. Her respect and love for him grew tremendously, and she wished her touch could soothe his pain.

"Todd, I am so sorry. I wouldn't have asked you to relive everything if I had known." Suddenly, Lexi was a little embarrassed about how she had handled things in Cincinnati. She worried Todd would think she was weak if he had known the whole truth about why she'd left.

Sensing her unease, he grabbed her hand. "I'm glad you asked. I guess I knew it would come up this weekend. In fact, I was probably hoping it would. There was a part of me that wondered if you were scared because I had never been in a serious relationship, maybe thought that I was a flake who would bail on you once I got bored. I've never let myself love anyone because I was afraid it would tear me down like it had Caleb. The first week I met you, though, I knew you would never intentionally hurt me, and that's when I started to trust you with my heart. God, Lexi, I love you so much. I am glad I finally found someone outside of my family to talk to about it."

"You mean you haven't talked about Caleb to anyone outside your family?"

"My friends knew the basics of what had happened, but I've never told anyone the details."

"Wow. Thank you for trusting me. I love you," Lexi whispered, kissing Todd's hands.

CHAPTER 29

eronica had the table set and had dinner ready when Todd and Lexi walked in from outside. She could tell immediately that something had happened while they were gone, and as soon as Lexi looked at her, she knew Todd had told her about Caleb. She quickly turned away, trying to stop the tears before they came.

It had been ten years since Caleb's death, and Todd had finally talked to someone about it—finally. Her heart pounded inside her chest, and she wanted nothing more than to grab this beautiful creature who had finally reached her son.

"So, how was the walk?" she asked, trying to be casual.

"Mom, I'm pretty sure by your reaction just now that you know how the walk went," Todd said, laughing at how poorly she hid her emotions.

Veronica turned around slowly, and as soon as her eyes met his, the attempt to stop her tears was pointless. She rushed across the kitchen and embraced her son, and he held her close to him. "Oh, Todd."

Watching the private moment between Todd and his mom brought tears to Lexi's eyes, which she didn't bother to try and hide.

Once they let go, Veronica turned to Lexi and opened her arms for a hug, which Lexi happily obliged. "I've prayed for you to come into our lives," Veronica whispered. "I don't know what got you here, but I will forever be grateful!"

As James walked into the kitchen, he looked at everyone with a confused expression. "Um, what did I miss?"

"Nothing," said Todd. "I think Mom just realized that Lexi is truly a part of the family now."

Both women laughed and wiped the tears from their faces while James looked at them, still lost. "I'll explain later," Veronica said as she kissed her husband, "but it's time to eat right now. I'm starved!"

DINNER WAS AMAZING, and Lexi was awestruck with how well Veronica could cook. For some reason, she assumed they would have someone on staff who cooked for them. Just another thing she had gotten wrong when it came to Todd's family.

Helping clean up after dinner, she spoke a little more about the walk to the lake earlier that day. She made sure only to answer questions Veronica asked directly, not wanting to betray Todd's trust. However, it was blatant to Lexi how hard it had been for him to unfurrow that event to her, and it only validated how much he cared for her.

As the night ended, his parents didn't seem surprised that Todd wanted to get back to his place. Veronica had given Lexi her secret recipe for her spiked strawberry lemonade, and shared a couple of other things she knew her son would appreciate. They planned on lunch once Lexi was back from Cincinnati, and she hugged them goodbye.

James also hugged the couple goodbye, and both parents stood arm in arm as they waved. The night had surpassed anything everyone had expected; that is, everyone except Todd.

CHAPTER 30

Roughly ten minutes into the drive home, Lexi was asleep on the passenger side of the Jeep. She looked so peaceful; it caused a deliciously warm ache in Todd's chest. The silence of the night gave him a moment to reflect on the day, and he had to admit to himself that even he was surprised by how easily he'd been able to talk to Lexi about Caleb's death. If there had been any reservations about his feelings for her, they were all eliminated.

Remembering the look on his mom's face when they walked into the kitchen brought sudden and fierce waves of grief and relief. He knew there was a reason he waited for love, and as the fascinating woman next to him whimpered in her sleep, he felt completely full.

Before heading home, Todd pulled into a gas station just outside of town to fill up. Not wanting to wake Lexi, he quietly opened the door and slid out to pump the gas. After filling up, he went in to pay, leaving her alone in the car.

She jumped awake at the sound of a car horn and the loud jeering coming from what sounded like a bar. Looking around for Todd, momentarily confused, she noticed a blonde across the street. It seemed she was the cause of the ruckus, so Lexi sleepily watched as the girl shamelessly flirted with a group of guys standing outside.

Realizing Todd had stopped for gas, she turned her attention back to the bar and the familiar girl. Lexi couldn't quite put her finger on how she knew her, but she was sure they had met before. It was something about her mannerisms and face, but she couldn't think of anyone with a blonde pixie cut.

"Hey, sleepyhead."

Lexi jerked around as Todd climbed back into the Jeep. "Oh hey. Sorry, I fell asleep on you. Why didn't you wake me up?"

"You looked so content. Besides, it was a nice drive. Who were you checking out so intensely?"

"Nobody, there was a girl across the street that looked so familiar, but I can't put my finger on why or how I would know her. No big deal."

"Maybe she was at the retreat? Since you are awake, can I get you anything while we're here?"

"Just get me home. This has been one hell of a day, and I am ready to crawl into bed."

"Did that nap maybe give you a second wind?" he said as they started toward the house again.

"Is that all you think about?" she teased.

"What? I thought that you might want to sit up and talk."

"Really, after everything we've been through today, you still want to talk?"

Todd growled under his breath and smirked, still watching the road ahead until they pulled into the driveway.

As soon as he cut the engine off, he was at her door, and she wrapped her arms and her legs around his body. He backed her into the side of the Jeep, pinning her arms above her head as she held herself up, linking her legs around his waist.

"You're mine," he said in a deep, gravelly voice as he pulled her closer, moving her backward toward the house.

She laughed as he fumbled to unlock the door, still holding her in his arms until they finally burst into his kitchen, and he kicked it shut behind them.

"Tell me how much you love me," he demanded, dropping her onto the counter.

"I'm here for everything. I don't plan on missing a minute of life with you. When you told me about—"

He swallowed the rest of her words with a kiss, then reluctantly pulled away and walked to look out the window. A sudden stillness enveloped the room as their breathing slowly returned to a rested pace. Neither had words.

Todd stiffened slightly, unsure how to put together his thoughts again.

Acutely aware of the room's silence and unexpected mood change, Lexi asked, "What's on your mind, handsome?"

Todd hesitated, afraid his emotions would get the better of him. "Nothing, just thinking."

"Really? Because you're acting like something's bothering you." She jumped from the counter and wrapped her arms around him, resting her cheek on his back. "Seriously, Todd, what's up?"

He looked back at her, and she could tell he was upset.

Her eyes darted back and forth, trying to figure out what was going on.

"I love you," he said.

"I know you do, and I love you."

"Lexi, I can't lose you, which frightens me. I guess on the way home, everything just kind of hit me. Sometimes I have a hard time controlling my desire for you, and I'm afraid of what might happen if I give in to that intensity. I don't know what I would do if I ever did anything that scared you away."

"I trust you, Todd."

"I'm not sure I trust myself."

"Today was phenomenal, and you really don't need to worry. Your intensity is refreshing. I don't want you to feel like you ever need to monitor your feelings around me. I know you won't hurt me."

"Really? You aren't afraid of all of this anymore?" he asked.

"I know it's crazy, but I'm not. The trust you showed me this afternoon erased any hesitation I might have been harboring." She gently turned him to face her and took his face in her hands. "Is that all that's bothering you? I feel like there's something more."

"Like I said, I can't imagine my life without you anymore, Lexi. I've never felt so out of control of a situation before, and after reliving all that stuff about my brother this afternoon, those fears trouble me."

"I told you I would do anything for you, and I meant it. Out at your parents' this afternoon, you proved to me that there is nothing you wouldn't do for me. You were willing to relive the worst moment in your life just so I could better understand your history. I guess that's when I realized I could see myself spending the rest of my life with you."

"Does that mean you will move in with me?"

"That means if I am going to make my new home on Norris Lake, I need to consider our relationship during the house hunting."

Todd pulled her in for a hug. "Not exactly a yes, but that wasn't a no either. I'll take that as progress."

ednesday afternoon, Mama had just finished cleaning up from the lunch rush when Lexi and Todd walked into the diner. She casually looked up and dropped everything when she realized who it was.

"Get your sweet little ass over here, boy, and give me a hug!"

Todd laughed as he walked toward his friend. "Have you missed me? We wanted to stop by to get some dinner before Lexi heads to Cincinnati this weekend."

"Lexi is leaving you already?" she said, glancing insidiously in the girl's direction. "You haven't even officially moved her in, and you've already run her off?"

"Real funny, lady. You know she's not leaving me. She's just gotta go home so she can get her stuff to girly-up my place."

Lexi playfully swatted at Todd as he dodged her on his way to hug Mama. "Yeah, I'm going to get my pink doilies and lace curtains," she said, rolling her eyes. "Seriously, though, I wish I could be here to help you guys this weekend. I'm sure you could use an extra pair of hands."

"Well, I appreciate the thought anyhow. Todd, I'm telling you, this girl is a keeper. You better not let this one get away or you may be finding my foot up your ass!"

"Ouch! Is that how you treat the people you love?"

"If they acting like dumbasses, then yes. But I'm pretty confident I've trained you to know a good thing when you see it."

"Not only did you teach me to recognize a good thing, but you also taught me how to treat her once I found her."

Lexi laughed nervously and blushed at the old friends' banter.

Noticing this, Todd grabbed her hand and led her to the booth from their first date. Rounding the bar, he grabbed a couple of menus and three beers as Mama finished wiping down the last table. The restaurant was otherwise empty, so she sat next to Todd in the booth. He knew it was probably the first time she had sat down all afternoon, so he wrapped his arm around her shoulder, giving her a loving squeeze and a beer.

Mama turned her focus back to Lexi. "I hear we havin' a girls' day tomorrow before you head off back to Ohio. Kate called me a couple of days back sayin' you had some questions for me. She said you met the dark lady but didn't know how to join her in conversation."

Lexi quietly sat dumbfounded, trying to remember if she and Kate had ever discussed Mama. It took a couple of beats, but when her mental gears finally caught up, she blurted out, "*You* are Alva?"

Mama's petite frame bounced as she laughed at Lexi's reaction. "Alva to some, Mama to others. But yes, I'm the mentor Kate told you about. I felt your latent gifts the first time Todd brought you in here, but I didn't put the puzzle pieces together myself until Kate's call. She said you were staying with her for a while to learn some of the old ways."

"Yes, I've learned much about myself since I arrived. I also have more unanswered questions. Wow, I can't believe I didn't put things together more quickly. I generally have a knack for that kind of thing. But I guess you understand that better than anyone."

Todd's look of confusion set both women into a fit of laughter. "What am I missing?" he asked.

Mama replied, "You haven't missed a thing, sweet boy. It turns out that your sweetheart is not only intelligent and beautiful, but she is gifted, as well. Kate has asked me to join them on Lexi's journey to self-discovery. It took us a minute to reconcile Kate's version of me with yours."

Todd was still confused, but he was content knowing the two women would be spending more time together.

Mama finished her beer and elbowed Todd in the ribs. "Ain't you two something? Reminds me of how Freddie and I used to look at each other when we first got married." She sighed, caught up in an old memory. "So, what can I make you kids for dinner this evening, or are you just in for a beer?"

"Are you sure it isn't a bother?" asked Lexi.

"This is a restaurant darlin', and I love cooking for my kids! Besides, there ain't nobody here, so I can talk and cook at the same time."

Mama threw together another fabulous meal, and she was able to sit and eat with them before the dinner crowd began meandering in. She reminisced about when Freddie proposed to her and told them about their simple wedding in a little chapel in Gatlinburg.

Laughter filled the diner, and Lexi began to understand why Todd and Kate enjoyed Mama's company. Life had handed that one many adventures, and anyone in her company could live vicariously through her stories.

Eventually, the place started filling with hungry patrons and Mama had to make her way back to the kitchen, but not before she had given Todd a list of things she needed to be done over the weekend.

In good form, he gave her a hard time, and they agreed to meet at 9:00 on Saturday morning.

"Lexi, I will be seeing you tomorrow morning. Todd, I love you, darlin'. See you this weekend."

CHAPTER 32

*L*exi awakened to the smell of freshly ground coffee. She slipped on her pajama bottoms, brushed her teeth, and found her way to the kitchen.

Kate and Alva were sitting at the kitchen table talking about a new recipe Kate found.

Lexi poured herself a large cup of coffee, adding sugar and cream, and took the seat across from them. She rubbed the sleep from her eyes and yawned.

"Good morning, Miss Lexi," said Alva.

"Good morning, Mama. Or should I call you Alva?"

"You call me whichever you are more comfortable with. I take from the looks of you that you aren't much of a morning person."

"Yeah, I don't really hit my stride until about 10:00 a.m. Although, I will admit, not having to rush around to get ready for an eight to five corporate workday makes mornings much more pleasurable. I have thoroughly enjoyed drinking my morning coffee on the deck overlooking the undisturbed waters."

"I'm surprised you didn't stay with Todd," said Kate.

"I knew we would be busy today, so I had him bring me home last night. I wanted to wake up with my own things and I wasn't sure how early you guys would be ready to begin."

"I still don't know how I didn't put Lexi and Lexindra together before Kate's call. I'm getting feeble-minded in my old age."

A laugh erupted from Kate. "Feeble-minded, my ass."

Alva aimed a coy glance in her friend's direction. "So, tell me, ladies, what kind of trouble are we getting into on this glorious day?"

"Lexi, tell Alva about your vision."

Lexi proceeded to tell Mama about the vision she'd experienced a couple of weeks ago. She tried to remember everything precisely, curious about the older woman's interpretation. Once she recalled everything, she looked over for guidance.

"This black lady who frightened you so much, what scared you about her the most?"

"Everything, but I guess the two biggest things were how callously she cursed death upon that poor girl, and the devastating emotional emptiness she left in her wake."

"Okay, let's address them issues separately. First, your interpretation of her actions. You saw what she did as callous and a curse, but let's look at the reality of the situation. You said the girl was alone, crying for help, and in the path of destruction. If that were the case, wouldn't it be fair to say her death was imminent?"

"Yes," Lexi conceded.

"Then the dark lady did not instigate, nor curse, the teenager to death. It was simply the girl's time. In fact, if you shift your perspective slightly, it seems the dark lady may have offered the girl a much less painful and traumatic end. Now, the emotional emptiness you felt as the vision concluded, do you think that devastation was due to the dark lady, or could it have been the emotional abandonment the girl felt when she realized her family had left her to die?"

"Shit," said Lexi, "when you put it that way, I guess you could be right."

"In that case, we should probably start today's lesson with perception. Is it fair to say you are still fairly young? You haven't experienced many of life's major lessons like marriage, childbirth, death of a parent?"

Lexi nodded in rapt attention.

"And how long have you been aware of your gifts?"

"I honestly wasn't aware I had any remarkable talents until Kate's retreat. I mean, I knew I was intuitive, but assumed most people were."

"I'm surprised your abilities have laid dormant for so long. I wonder what other latent parts of you this phase of your spiritual path will open, but let's focus on what we already know. Folks with the sight or, in your words, visions, must be very conscious of perspective. Often, the sights and emotions we pick up are a jumbled mix of the people and environment present at that specific moment in time. How you interpret those moments depends greatly on your ability to be objective, because without objectivity, they are merely fodder for misinterpretation. I can tell you from experience that many of my spirit guides don't speak the same language. Some of them only speak through pictures and emotions, so you must learn to dance together to interpret your partner's lead. Here's an example: one of my spirit guides is a druid. Learning his codes for things took some time, and that was with my mammy's familiarity and guidance. If he wanted to warn me that a season of scarcity was comin', he would show me a stump, and if it were going to be a devastating event, he would show me a forest of stumps. Now, I'm using that one because it's a pretty obvious one, but much of our language is more complicated.

Think of it like this, for as long as I can remember, hill folk have been misunderstood and disrespected because of our vernacular or our distrust of outsiders, when in actuality, our Appalachian dialect is one of the oldest living English dialects, very similar to Elizabethan English. Our distrust comes from a proven history of the government coming in and taking our livelihood. Ain't none of it got to do with intelligence or prosperity. In fact, if you look at the shift in society as a whole, our knowledge of the land and blue-collar skillset is beginning to outweigh the traditional college schoolin'. A fancy education don't mean nothin' if you ain't got the understanding of how to grow food, stay healthy, build shelter, and keep industry functioning.

We've all got an innate bias, but successful people know how to put that aside to see the objective truth of a situation. I know the dark lady you speak of; she's been around here as long as I can remember. When I was a young'un,' she used to put a fright into me, too. As I grew and gained experience, I started to realize that part of what made her so terrifying was the places where I encountered her. She's drawn to destruction and ruination, but she's never played an active role in the pending tragedy. I think she is more of a harbinger of fate or a Reaper. If she's trying to communicate with you, then you need to heed the message. Push your fear aside and impartially examine what she is telling you."

"How do I differentiate situational emotion versus intention? How do I learn this language of symbology?" asked Lexi.

Alva pondered the question for a moment, then stood from the table. "That is a great question. Learning the symbology will take time and practice, just like learnin' a new language, but you have both Kate and me to help you figure things out. If all else fails, ask the spirit, offer a gift of gratitude and give them permission to show you. The first step is getting familiar with the land's emotional baggage. Let's pack up a lunch cooler and go out on the boat. I'll take you to a variety of spots on the water so you can get an idea of what you need to filter."

And that's what they did. Kate drove her pontoon while Alva guided them to some of the more emotional places in their vicinity.

The two older women worked with Lexi, teaching her how to open herself up to receive downloads. The layers of emotion gave each place an individual texture, and by the ride home, Lexi was overwhelmed with new information. She was completely spent by the time she got to Todd's that night.

CHAPTER 33

Lexi pulled the sheets over her head, trying to ignore the bothersome alarm. She really didn't want to get out of bed, but she wanted to leave Todd even less. Although it would only be a few days, they hadn't been apart since the first night they'd spent together, and she felt a nagging sense of dread. She knew she needed to tell him about what brought her here before she left so he would have time to think if he still wanted their relationship.

"Get up, sleepyhead! You need to get on the road so you can hurry and get back home to me."

"I don't want to go."

"Then don't. We'll send for your stuff and we can go together later in the month. I don't want you to leave me either, even if it is just for three days."

Throwing the sheets to the side, she pulled herself out of bed and started to shuffle to the bathroom to shower. "That is way too tempting. Unfortunately, I'll get stuck in traffic if I don't get up now."

"So, I still can't persuade you not to leave me, huh?"

"Don't make it sound like that," she said, starting the shower. "You know I don't want to go. But there is something we need to discuss before I leave. If you still want this relationship when I get back, we can start the house-hunting process, and then you'll never be able to get away from me again."

"That sounds ominous. I can't imagine anything that would make me not want this relationship."

By the time Lexi was showered and dressed, Todd had loaded her suitcases into the car and had started breakfast.

She walked into the kitchen and the smell of eggs made her stomach turn. She didn't want to eat, so she sat at the table as he set a plate in front of her.

"What's wrong?" he said.

"It's not that anything is wrong, exactly, but since you opened up about your brother and laid your soul bare for me to see, I knew I couldn't leave without telling you the truth about why I came here. I don't want anything in between us if this is going to have a chance to work."

"Okay, I'm a little freaked out, but I'm listening," he said, wiping the moisture from her cheeks.

"A couple of days before I left everything in Ohio, I had convinced myself that the world would be better off without me. For years, my life had been in a spiral that I could never quite recover from, and I was so broken and exhausted. That day at work, I could feel the malice and contempt from every single person I ran across. Even my friends were snickering about me behind my back. Maybe it wouldn't have triggered me so badly if I understood where the animosity was coming from, but I had absolutely no clue. It broke me."

"I know things had been hard, but I hadn't realized how isolated you felt."

"That's exactly how it felt; like if I was gone, everyone would be relieved. I lay in the bathtub, drinking wine, I don't know how to describe it exactly. It was kinda like my emotions shut off, and it wasn't *my* hand sliding the razor down my wrist. As soon as the blade punctured the skin, the pain woke me up, and I quickly slid into a panic attack."

"So, are you telling me that you are suicidal?"

"I'm telling you that I was desperate and knew I could no longer function in my current state. Once the physical pain snapped me back into reality, I knew I couldn't live like that for one more day, but I wasn't ready to die. That narrow escape catapulted me into this healing journey, but I understand if this changes how you see me, especially with your brother's actions looming over such a significant part of your life."

"Why are you telling me this now? Why didn't you share with me when I told you about Caleb?"

"Because I was weak, terrified I'd lose you. I thought I could just leave that piece of my story out, and no one would ever know."

"So, you don't trust me? You lied to me, Lexi," his disappointed words biting.

"If I didn't trust you, we wouldn't be having this conversation now, would we? It didn't feel like a lie at the time, but after my own reflection, I acknowledged a lie by omission is still a lie. I don't want to start our life together with lies."

"I honestly don't know what to say. I still love you, but I'm not sure if I can take the chance of going through another loss like Caleb."

Lifting her face to look into his eyes, she burst into tears. She knew she'd find a way to fuck this up. She hoped completely letting go of her ego and putting her vulnerability in Todd's hands would be some sort of relief, but it wasn't. Lexi had acute familiarity with anxiety, but the discomfort she felt that morning was a new kind of beast. It was a confusing mixture of fear, dread, and something she couldn't quite put her finger on. She wasn't sure that Todd would be there when she returned, but she still felt steadfast in her decision to make Norris Lake home. And as uncomfortable as it made her, she knew she needed to leave.

"Hello? Have you heard anything I said?"

The snap of Todd's fingers pulled her from her thoughts back into reality. "I'm sorry. What?"

"I said, do you see how unfair it is for you to dump all of this on me without giving us a chance to talk about it?"

"To be honest, yes. I have a nagging feeling this is a moronic decision, and my fear is trying its best to keep me here. I mean, I literally feel physically ill, and it's not just the usual anxiety stuff I'm used to. But I do have to leave today to put to bed my family's concerns, and you need time to process what I've told you. When we get back, I promise we will talk until you are out of words. It'll only be a couple of days."

"Well, I'll be hanging out with the guys tonight, helping Mama tomorrow, then coming home to hang out with Abby. You go home, see your family, pack up the U-Haul we rented with all your favorite things, and drive back home to me. I do love you, Lexi, but my trust is very shaky right now." Todd took her hand, kissed her fingertips, and brushed it across his cheek. He absolutely did not want her to leave but resolved to let her maintain her independence. He hid his own emotions.

"I'm sorry, Todd," Lexi announced with feigned control. "I guess that means I need to get on the road. Walk me to the door?"

Todd followed her to the car, opening the door for her but keeping himself between Lexi and the vehicle.

She walked into his chest, ignoring the pain telling her not to leave.

He breathed deep, memorizing her smell, wanting to envelop every part of her being. Fear, he had come to understand, was an innate part of who she was, and no matter how helpless it made him feel, a quirk he had to accept. He pulled her closer until her strong arms were wrapped around his body.

"I love you," she whispered.

"I love you. I'll miss you while you are gone, so call me once in a while."

"Keep your phone on in case I get lost," she laughed through her tears, "or I get tired while driving. Have fun with your friends and tell them I'm sorry to have kept you away for so long." Her eyes found him, and momentarily, she felt safe again. "I'm gonna miss you. Don't be surprised if you don't hear from me before I make it to Kentucky."

His lips met hers and they kissed goodbye, each hesitating to let go until Lexi finally climbed into her car and rolled down her window. "We'll talk soon, right?"

"Yeah. Please be safe traveling."

After another quick kiss, Lexi pulled out of the drive. Just before she hit the interstate, she noticed a familiar red car parked at the bank, and the blonde from the bar walking in. Where did she know her from? In the rearview mirror, she noticed the vehicle had Ohio tags and wondered if the girl could be someone she'd met in Cincinnati, but she still couldn't put a name to the face. *Small world*, she thought as she pulled out, heading north.

CHAPTER 34

Todd slowly fought his way through the fog of slumber, awoken by firm, aggressive lips. Momentarily, he enjoyed the pleasure that stirred within him, his body reacting of its own accord.

Darkness was thick as he opened his heavy eyelids, alerting him that he was not in familiar surroundings. When he tried to speak, his words were slurred and unrecognizable. The more he fought to stay awake, the more intense the stimulation became, keeping him caught in a dreamlike state.

Working to piece together his thoughts, the last thing he could distinctly remember was being at the bar with Toby playing darts. Where was he?

"Lexi?" he mumbled, his words garbled by the thickness of his tongue.

As the words struggled to escape, the pleasure was swiftly replaced with the searing pain of teeth and force. Screaming, he instinctively tried to push off his aggressor, only to find his hands and feet bound, leaving him in a panicked state of consciousness. Suddenly aware of the gravity of his situation, Todd fought desperately to free himself and identify his surroundings.

"There's no point in struggling," said a female voice at the end of the bed, "you aren't going anywhere."

CHAPTER 35

*L*exi made it to her apartment around 8:00 p.m., only stopping once to grab lunch. She called Todd several hours earlier, fighting off the drowsy boredom of the long drive. He had been in his Jeep, headed to meet Toby at the bar. Knowing she was tired and emotionally exhausted, he sat in the parking lot talking to her for nearly half an hour before she encouraged him to get inside and have a good time. She knew he was looking forward to hanging out with the guys, even though his mood had been soured by their conversation that morning.

Immediately upon arrival in Cincinnati, she called and let her mom know she made it safely. The family tried to get her to come stay with them, but she knew she only had a couple of days to get everything done and wanted to start packing. They were satisfied to come by first thing Saturday morning, and she knew they would be knocking on her door before 9:00 a.m.

When Lexi first entered the apartment, she felt herself drowning in a sudden rush of emotion, but once she got settled and began sifting through her things, she was content and looking forward to her future.

Stopping to get something to drink and sort through the junk mail she hadn't forwarded to Tennessee, she looked at her phone and wondered if Todd would call. It was past midnight, and she still hadn't heard from him, but she was unsure what to expect since they had never been apart before, not to mention, they'd never been on uncertain terms.

She finally gave in and dialed his number. *He must be in bed already,* she thought. Wishing she had caught him before he had fallen asleep, she tossed the mail on the counter, pushed past the boxes in the living room, and headed for her own bed. A smile crept across her face as she realized that would be the last weekend she would sleep in that apartment, and she peacefully drifted to sleep.

A knock at the door served as Lexi's alarm clock the next morning, and she was greeted with hugs and kisses from her family. She allowed her family to hold and comfort her for the first time in ages as she repeatedly apologized for her past behavior.

After the tears dried, Lexi's dad asked where he and her brother should begin loading boxes, while her mother continued to fire off questions about Todd.

She pointed her dad and Brent to the kitchen where she had only packed what they needed at the lake house, and threw them the keys to the U-Haul.

"So, what are you going to do with the apartment?" her mom asked.

"I'm going to put it on the market. Nancy said she knew a good realtor and would make introductions. I don't think it will stay on the market very long, so if you know anyone looking for a place, have them reach out to me directly. As soon as I get back, I'm going to start looking for houses or land to build on."

"Will Todd be moving in with you?" asked her mom.

"I'm hesitant to jump into a mutual financial obligation that quickly. Besides, there is so much to learn from Kate, and living in the same space would make it so much easier. I'm not giving myself a solid timeline, but if I can't find a place and end up having to build, it warrants a discussion."

"Is Todd's house not big enough for the both of you? From what you've told me, it sounds like Todd has done well for himself."

"His family has done well for themselves for several generations. To be honest, I am still getting used to the thought of it all, but they are great people, Mom. You're going to love them!"

"When did you meet his family?" asked her mom with a twinge of jealousy.

"Last week, and only because they just live an hour or so away. Todd wanted to come with me this weekend, but I needed to make this trip alone. I wanted to spend time with you guys. Besides, I need to meet up with Kyle at some point, not to mention lunch with Nancy, and getting my things from work. Things are just too crazy this weekend for me to have to worry about entertaining Todd. This time apart will be a test to see if these emotions are love, or just infatuation and proximity. But I promise we will be back soon, or you could come to see us. He's really dying to meet everyone."

"It seems you have found a place that makes you happy, sweetheart. You literally exude happiness," Lexi's mom said. "I am so thrilled for you—we all are. Whether you and Todd are a summer fling, or true life-partners, I am grateful for the beautiful smile you wear."

They worked most of the morning, keeping Lexi too busy to check if Todd had called, but by lunchtime, she was getting worried she hadn't heard from him. She dialed his number, but there was still no answer. Brushing aside the nagging worry, she left him a message to call her as soon as he got a chance, then headed out to meet Nancy for lunch.

CHAPTER 36

The coffee shop across the street from her apartment was one of the things she would miss about Cincinnati. She always loved going there on Saturday afternoons and watching the intriguing blend of culture and age intermingle effortlessly.

Sitting at her usual table waiting for Nancy, it dawned on her... *Crystal.* She had been the familiar blonde from Ohio Lexi had seen in town in Tennessee. Apparently, Crystal had, once again, changed her appearance, which is why Lexi hadn't recognized her. The coincidence seemed untimely, but the thought was lost as she noticed Nancy walking toward her, a full box in hand.

Lexi rushed over to help, taking her things and putting them on the floor next to their table.

Nancy hugged her. "I am so glad you called. When they told me you had emailed your resignation, I was concerned about you. I understood why you may have wanted to take some time, but I never thought you would quit."

"God, was I that much of a mess?" Lexi felt embarrassed she had been so transparent and was glad she didn't have to face anyone else in the office. "I guess I hadn't realized how unhappy I was."

"Honestly, nobody had any idea until that little redhead in building two started running her mouth, you know, the one in the marketing department? Office gossip spreads faster than a fire in Southern California. I just wish you had told me. There was no reason for you to feel like you needed to leave."

Lexi was totally lost. "What in the world are you talking about?"

"The reason you left work."

"I left work because I was depressed and having panic attacks. I just needed a break from life, so I went to Norris Lake to regroup. What did you hear?"

Nancy looked at her, shocked, instantly ashamed she had believed the rumors. "Oh Lexi, I feel like such an asshole. I just assumed that you left because—"

"Nancy, what is the rumor going around?"

"Well, apparently, the girl in marketing hangs out in the same circles as your girlfriend. She'd overheard that one of the VP's had caught you two having sex in your office, and then the next day you were gone on a leave of absence. Everyone just assumed the partners had forced you to take some time off, at least until things settled down. That, or that you were just too embarrassed to face everyone."

"What? My girlfriend?"

"Yeah, your girlfriend Crystal."

"Are you fucking serious?" Lexi was furious, and she could feel herself inadvertently directing her anger toward Nancy. "I'm sorry, Nancy. I'm not mad at you, but this is unbelievable. When did you hear this?"

"The day before you left, everyone was talking about it. I thought you knew because you were acting so weird. I am so mad at myself for listening to all that bullshit!"

"So that's why I felt like everyone was talking about me," she said, mostly to herself. She turned back to Nancy and asked, "Does everyone really think I'm gay?"

"You aren't?"

"Are you serious? How long have we known each other? What in the world would make everyone think I had a girlfriend?"

"Well, Crystal did have a picture of you on her desk, and she made it pretty obvious that you guys had a thing. Besides, you never talked about your personal life and never brought anyone to company parties. I figured she was just uncomfortable being around since they fired her."

Suddenly, Lexi felt sick to her stomach. "Crystal, you mean the girl that worked under Johnna in IT? Oh my god, then she started working here, and now she's in Tennessee…"

"Lexi, are you okay? You don't look good."

"I'm sorry Nancy, can you excuse me for a minute."

She stood up and walked to the counter. "Excuse me, is Crystal working today?"

"No, she was a no-show a couple of months ago and we haven't seen her since. I'm not shocked, though," the teenager behind the counter casually replied. "That girl had a screw loose."

Lexi rushed back to the table, still in shock. "I'm sorry, Nancy, I've gotta go. I'll call you later and explain." A wave of anger blinded her, so she barely noticed when two of the coffee house's exterior windows shattered.

Nancy just stood staring at her in shock while she grabbed her stuff and ran across the street to her apartment.

"Pick up Todd…pick up the damn phone!" she yelled into her cell as she hurried through traffic.

CHAPTER 37

It was 3:00, and she still hadn't heard from him, so when the phone rang, she jumped to answer. "Hello?"

"Hey, Lexi."

"Oh, hey, Kyle."

"Wow, you always were good at making a guy feel good."

"I'm sorry, I've just been expecting a call, and I am starting to get worried. How are you?"

"I'm good," he said nervously. "I got your message about being in town, so I'm calling you back."

"I had planned on suggesting dinner, but I'm not really feeling up to it," she said.

"That's cool. I already have plans anyway. Listen, Lexi—"

"No, wait. Let me go first. I want to apologize to you for every-thing. I know I didn't handle things between us very well, and it wasn't fair to you. You are a great guy; you deserved more than a goodbye letter. I guess I just wanted you to know that."

"You weren't the only bad guy in the situation," he answered. "I wasn't really honest or fair with you either. There was kind of another girl; nothing serious, but it seemed like every time you and I would start to get close, she would show up and I would get scared of being tied down, so I would back off. I guess it just wasn't meant to be, but I, at least, owe you an apology as well."

"It's all good," she said. "I just needed to call and make sure we were good. Weirdly enough, I actually do feel better knowing there was another girl. I thought it was me."

"No, it was both of us."

"Well, I guess I'll let you get back to your plans. I'm glad you called me back, Kyle, and maybe I'll see ya around."

"I'm seriously glad you're happy, and I hope Tennessee treats you well. See ya around."

CHAPTER 38

$\mathcal{B}$y 5:00, Lexi was more than a little worried, and debated whether to call Todd's parents, eventually deciding she was overreacting, and he was probably still upset with her. She really wished she had Abby's phone number.

She paced the apartment, giving herself time to think about her conversation with Nancy. The more she thought about it, the more things seemed to fall into place. What if Crystal's job at the coffee shop wasn't a coincidence? Why would she have told anyone they were a couple, and where would she have gotten a picture of the two of them together?

Finally, her phone rang. When Todd's name popped up on the screen, she felt a rush of relief. "It's about time, mister. I was starting to get worried!"

"Is this Lexi?"

Her voice caught in her throat as she replied, "Yes, who is this?"

"I know we haven't met yet, but this is Abby, Todd's sister."

"Oh, hey, Abby! I was just thinking about you. I can't wait to meet you; Todd is always talking about you. I take it you made it home safely?"

"Yeah, I got here around noon, but I haven't been able to find my brother. I was hoping you had heard from him, but it sounds like you haven't talked to him today either."

"No, the last time I talked to him was around 6:00 last night." She felt the panic in her voice. "How did you get his phone if you haven't seen him?"

"I went by Mama's a couple of hours ago to give him shit about bailing on Toby last night, and she said she hadn't seen him all day and hadn't been able to get in touch with him. That's really unlike Todd, so I drove up to the house to make sure everything was okay, and no one was home. Toby said the last time he saw him was around 11:00 or so last night, and his Jeep was still in the parking lot when he headed home later that night. I guess Todd was pretty drunk, so Toby just assumed he had pulled a Houdini and taken a cab home. Anyway, I am in the Jeep now, and his cell phone is on the passenger side floor. I'm worried, Lexi!"

Lexi felt her hands shaking as she tried to swallow her fear. She knew she shouldn't have left him but had lost faith in her instincts with everything that had happened in the past several years.

"Okay, Abby, I'll be on the next flight there. Something is wrong. I *knew* something was wrong!" she said through hot, angry tears. "Listen, I can't go into all the details over the phone, but since I've been back here, I have learned some pretty twisted shit, and I'm afraid it may be my fault Todd is gone. Keep an eye out for a red car with Ohio tags, although I can't remember the model. The girl who drives it is probably your height, has blue eyes, built like a well-trained athlete. When I saw her yesterday, she had short blonde hair and was dressed like a tomboy. I think she followed me from Cincinnati to Tennessee, and I think she may be involved somehow. It's a long story and I'll tell you all the details when I get there. Unfortunately, I don't know if she's dangerous or not. Ask around at the bar to see if anyone has any information on her. I'm going to do some digging before my flight and see what I can find out. I am so sorry, Abby, this is all my fault!'"

"Lexi, what are you talking about? How can this be your fault? Who is this girl?"

"Her name is Crystal, she sometimes goes by Crys, but at this point, who the hell knows what she's calling herself? She used to work with me a couple of years ago, and honestly, I hadn't thought about her much since. She worked at the café across the street from my apartment, so I spoke to her fairly regularly, but it wasn't like we were friends. Today, I found out that she'd been spreading rumors about me, about *us*, to her friends, and no one has seen her since I left for the lake. I think the fact that she worked across the street from my place, and is now in Tennessee, isn't a coincidence. I think she may be infatuated with me or something. I think she followed me."

"You mean like a stalker? Do you think she would hurt Todd?"

"I don't know Abby, but I do know that she isn't a very stable person. Call your parents and tell them what's going on and I will call you once I get to the airport. Maybe the two things aren't related, so check places you think Todd would go if he flaked on Mama, but it seems like too many coincidences to me."

"Okay, I'll call Mom and Dad, but they are out of the country this week. Please call me back if you hear anything or find anything else out. See you soon."

"I will, and you do the same."

As Lexi hung up the phone, she collapsed in the middle of her kitchen floor. She sat with her legs crossed, elbows on her knees, and head in her hands. So many thoughts had flooded her consciousness that she struggled to keep them from blurring together. Processing the new information, she tried to incorporate her existing knowledge with her past, which she had once written off as bad luck.

Suddenly, she began to second-guess everything: missed appointments because of flat tires or car troubles, the late bills she'd never received statements for, letters and cards she knew were mailed but never received, the rumors at work, not to mention all the missing phone messages and emails. At that last thought, she sat up and looked around her apartment skeptically.

"Oh my god, she's been in my place. That bitch somehow got into my apartment and let me believe I was losing my mind!"

The lightbulb above her exploded.

Confusion and frustration progressively cleared and were replaced with rage and understanding. Cleaning up the glass, she remembered what Kate had told her about her emotions controlling her physical surroundings during heightened reactions.

After getting online and booking the earliest flight she could, she opened her phone and dialed Kyle.

"Hello?"

"Hey Kyle, I know you have plans, but I need to know something about the girl you saw while we were going out."

"Lexi, there's really no reason for us to go into this. I haven't seen her in a while, it was really no big thing."

"Actually, it might be bigger than you think. What was her name?"

"Why does it matter?"

"Kyle, please!" she nearly shouted into the phone.

"Okay, calm down. Crys, her name was Crys. Why do you care? Aren't you moving to Tennessee with your new boyfriend anyway?" he said with a hint of resentment.

"Oh my god," she gasped into the receiver.

"What? Lexi, what's wrong?" Kyle could hear the alarm in her voice. "Do you know her or something?"

"Yeah, but it seems she knows me a hell of a lot better than I know her," she murmured and then refocused. "When you were seeing her, did you ever go to her place? Do you think you could take me there?"

"I've got plans tonight, maybe tomorrow."

"Please, Kyle, I really need you to take me tonight. I am taking the last flight back to Tennessee later tonight, and I don't have time to track down anyone else that may know her. You know I wouldn't ask you to do this if I had any other choice, please do this for me!" Lexi cringed at the desperation in her voice, but she knew he was her only option, if she was going to find anything out before she had to leave.

Kyle could tell that Lexi was scared and could feel the seething determination in her voice. This was a side of her he had never seen. "Give me a few minutes to cancel my plans, and I will swing by and get you, but you have to tell me what's going on."

"I'll explain everything on the way, I promise. Just…please hurry!" She fought to hold back her sobs of gratitude as she hung up and waited by the window for Kyle to get there.

CHAPTER 39

$\mathcal{L}$exi called Abby to let her know she would be flying into McGhee Tyson Airport around 2:00 a.m. She had planned on renting a car, but Abby insisted that she pick her up.

"Have you been able to find out anything else about this Crystal chick?" asked Abby.

"A little. Apparently, she'd been seeing the same guy I was dating before I left. I don't have any details yet, but he is on his way to pick me up because he knows where she lives. I should know more later. What about you? Have you been to the bar?"

"Toby and I ran by earlier, but no one was really there yet, and the bartender said he remembered her but didn't have any info on her. Mom and Dad called the police, but they said they couldn't do much since he hadn't even been missing for 24 hours yet. It doesn't help that everyone here knows how spontaneous Todd can be, so they are telling us just to stay calm and he will turn up. Dad has been making calls and raising hell, but I don't know how much difference it will make right now."

Lexi heard a horn and saw Kyle's car idling on the street below. "Kyle's here, so I've gotta go. See what else you can find out at the bar tonight. I'm going to get into her apartment tonight, no matter the means. I will see you at the airport if I don't talk to you before." She hung up the phone, grabbed her purse, and headed out the door.

Driving across the river into northern Kentucky, Lexi told Kyle everything she learned earlier in the day. She also brought back to mind several of the situations she'd found herself in earlier that year and explained how she believed Crystal had been involved or had generated them. The more she spoke, the quieter he became, although she hadn't noticed because of her own cranked emotions.

Finally, she finished. Realizing the absence of Kyle's responses, she said, "It makes sense that I'm freaked out, right? I really need you to tell me what you know about her."

"It makes perfect sense that you are freaked out," he said flatly.

THE SMALL HOUSE was just outside Newport, and it seemed empty.

Kyle pulled the car up to the curb across the street and turned off the engine.

Unable to stand the awkward silence any longer, Lexi spoke up again. "So, what can you tell me about her?"

He looked down, fidgeting with his keys, avoiding eye contact. "I met her maybe a week after you and I started going out. I was at a bar, and she came up to me, flirting pretty obviously, so I bought her a drink. We made casual conversation and the more attention I gave her, the braver she got. She wasn't shy to let me know she wanted me to come back to her place, and you and I had just started going out, so I went. She was always very sexually aggressive but needed constant reassurance. Everything about her was erratic and impulsive, but I just assumed it was because she was young. Eventually, you and I started getting more serious, and I tried to break it off with her. That's when I ran into her at the café across the street from your house." His eyes moved from his keys toward the house and back to his keys. "If I had known Lexi... God, why hadn't I just been honest with you?"

"What happened when you ran into her at the coffee house?"

"Well, she asked me why I was there, so I told her I was seeing a girl who lived across the street, and we were supposed to be meeting up for lunch. That's when she snapped. She grabbed my arm and jerked me around to the back alley, screaming and crying. I didn't know what to do. We hadn't been serious at all, so I had no idea where this was coming from. Then, she started asking me who I was seeing, and when I told her, she told me how you had been there with several different guys that month. At first, I thought it was just jealousy, but she knew so many intimate details about you, and I believed her. Once she realized she had planted that seed of doubt, she flipped a switch again and was suddenly all over me. I'm ashamed to say it, but I followed her into the parking garage, and we had sex in her car while you waited for me never to show up. It was kind of always like that. I wouldn't see you in a while, and as soon as I would come back around, she would be there, eager to steer me in the other direction. I'm sorry, Lexi. So sorry."

"Well, sex sells," she said, laughing uncomfortably. "But none of that matters now. Now I just need to get into her house and see if there is anything that can help me figure out where she could be."

"You're going in there?"

"I'm not going to just peek in the windows. What if she's done something to Todd? You said yourself that she doesn't handle rejection well. Plus, she must know by now that Todd and I are together. I can't just sit around and wait."

"Be careful, Lexi. She's dangerous."

Lexi nodded and opened the car door.

The house wasn't located in a neighborhood, but on a side street next to an empty lot. She circled widely around the house, looking for motion detectors or signs of an alarm system, but she didn't notice either.

She pulled an old credit card from her wallet to pop the lock on the back door. Fortunately, the door was old, and years of locking herself out of her parents' house had finally paid off. She inched the door open, sliding through the narrow opening and closing the door behind her.

The room was blanketed by darkness, but the overwhelming smell of rotting trash indicated she had entered through the kitchen. The house seemed even smaller from the inside, and the smell permeated throughout.

Stepping out of the kitchen, across an old furnace grill built into the floor, Lexi stood in a small hallway and could see each room of the cramped space. Choosing to lessen any attention from neighbors, she decided to turn on a nightlight in the bathroom to the right, the only room with no window. As light poured from the room, shadows bounced from furniture and corners, spooking Lexi even more. Although the small amount of light gave her better visibility, she felt more exposed and vulnerable, so she worked quickly.

Straight ahead was a small living room, furnished only with an old couch, recliner, coffee table, and TV. She rummaged through the mail which had been tossed with no regard on the table. She tossed aside past due bills and advertisements, nothing helpful, although she was surprised after seeing the postmark date that the electricity was still on.

She felt beneath the cushions of the couch, disgusted to find a used condom and remnants of food.

To the left was the master bedroom where a king-size waterbed had been crammed, leaving no room for another piece of furniture. She shimmied along the bed frame toward a closet, stepping on what felt like weeks of dirty laundry, until she found a small dresser and hanging clothes. Using her cell phone to give her a little more light, she wasn't surprised to find an eclectic mix of styles, from lavender golf shirts to spiked boots.

Lexi turned back toward the bed and noticed the picture frame leaning on the headboard. The frame was one Lexi had lost months before, legitimizing her suspicions that Crystal had been in her apartment uninvited. She snatched the frame, which held an impressively photoshopped picture portraying Lexi and Crystal as a couple, or at the least, very close friends, and shoved it into her purse. She knew immediately it was the picture Nancy had seen at the office, and understood why everyone assumed they were in a relationship.

Walking out of the bedroom, to the left, was a small room set up as a makeshift office. A computer sat on an old card table disguised with a tablecloth, along with an expensive-looking photography printer, and an answering machine indicating an unheard message.

Lexi grabbed a piece of paper and a pen and hit the flashing message button.

"Crys baby, where the fuck are you? I doctored up some pretty good references and emailed 'em to your lady. Why in the hell you need references sent to an Indiana email for a job in Tennessee? What have you gotten your crazy ass into now? Regardless, the lady called, and I made sure to give you rave reviews. Anyhow, call me when you get back to town…you owe me, and I've been a naughty boy!"

After jotting down all the pertinent information, she hit enter on the computer keyboard, and the screen lit up, taunting her for a password.

She settled into the chair and tried to put herself in Crystal's mindset, trying possible passwords and coming up empty. The more words that failed her admission, the more defeated and angrier she became. How was she going to find Crystal? Time was closing the doors of opportunity, and the pressure finally caused her to lash out at an empty filing cabinet. When she did, a piece of paper with password reminders fell to the floor. The question next to Log In was "Who?". She typed in *Crystal, Crys, Lexi, Lexindra, LexindraGreer, LexiGreer…* none of them let her in. She thought about what else she could be obsessed with and thoughtlessly entered *MyLexi*.

Once she hit enter, Crystal's cyber world exploded onto the screen. Before Lexi let herself celebrate the win, she reminded herself that she had to hurry. Searching through documents, she found the folder named *Finding Lexi* and copied it onto a flash drive lying near the printer without taking the time to look at it. She brought her own but didn't bother digging through her bag to find it.

After a brief once-over of the office, she reminded herself that time was her enemy, and she had to leave. With the photo and flash drive in hand, she slipped out the kitchen door and sprinted back to Kyle's car with her treasure.

CHAPTER 40

Todd's eyes still felt heavy, but he was pretty sure he was alone. The only light he could see was from beneath the door on the opposite side of the room. He was beginning to lose feeling in his feet, which he continuously worked against his restraints. His wrists were bloodied, but his hard work had, at least, given him some margin for movement, although not enough to allow him to free himself.

It had been at least an hour since his captor left him alone. He had heard the distant slam of a door from above, followed by the roar of a car engine, and the sound of wheels throwing gravel.

He had no idea where he was, who had taken him, or why he was being held against his will, but Todd took some comfort in the fact that he could hear when they were coming and going. He closed his eyes and let his body relax, trying to regain his strength for whatever the next several hours had in store for him. He felt the warmth of tears as they streaked toward his ears, and as his mind raced to piece together the puzzle which landed him hostage to a total stranger, he remembered the night he and Lexi had first made love.

EVEN WITH THE windows down and the wind whipping at her face, Crystal still couldn't get her thoughts together. She thought of Todd tied up in the basement of the Tandy estate, and found childish pleasure knowing he was, assuredly, confused and terrified. But as quickly as she relished the satisfaction of his fear, she was nauseated by fear of her own. Why had she not taken the time to think her plan through entirely before she acted? She found herself in a state of panic, unsure of what to do next.

Unable to predict Lexi's new routines, and having to be conscientious of her new living arrangement, Crystal's original plan to win her love came to a crashing halt. She had been unable to see Lexi for over a week, and her compulsion began to replace rationality.

Several nights before, she carelessly parked in the driveway of an empty house only a couple doors from Todd's and had been sneaking around to try and catch a glimpse of the couple. As she stalked around the side of the house, she was able to eavesdrop on a conversation Lexi and her new boyfriend were having on the back deck about Lexi's weekend trip to Cincinnati and Todd's night out with the guys.

She allowed herself to breathe a little more comfortably at the thought of the couple being apart, until they began discussing plans for the future. Unaware that he asked her to move in, her first instinct was to walk around and thrash Todd right in front of Lexi. She was furious with him, but just as furious with herself, for letting things get that far. In fact, it had taken her a good 20 minutes to regain control of herself enough to make it back to the car to leave.

Glancing at the bandages on her arm, she flinched at the pain from infection, remembering just how much damage she unconsciously inflicted on herself once she settled down and stepped into the shower that night. It was then she decided she would drug and take Todd from the bar.

It hadn't been hard to find the drugs she needed from the locals she had made friends with in the weeks prior, and she hadn't needed to worry about being seen since Lexi was out of town. The tricky part would be getting Todd into her car without being noticed, but that had also worked out in her favor.

At the bar, she had been able to slip the drugs into his beer. As they started to take effect, Todd stumbled to his car, and because of his intoxicated state, he accidentally got into the passenger side of his Jeep. When Crystal offered to walk him around to the driver's side, he had been more than willing to accept her offer. He didn't even notice when she helped him into her car. By the time she started the engine, he was unconscious.

Getting him from the car had been a little more challenging, but she managed to drag him down to the basement and tie him up on a small cot she had moved for the occasion.

Unfortunately, she hadn't considered what she was going to do with him. At the thought, fear settled in, and she was forced to take a drive and gather her thoughts. Snapping back into the moment, she realized she had driven back to Todd's house and was a little alarmed to find an unfamiliar car parked in the drive.

Instinctively, she sped up and turned the car back toward the Tandy's. It was suddenly clear to her she was going to use Todd to get all the information about Lexi she could, and she didn't have time to waste. She would attempt to get what she needed through seduction, but if he insisted on being uncooperative, she would take whatever means necessary to get what she needed. The thought of forcing either sex or pain on him stirred her desire to dominate, and she began to see her situation as an opportunity, maybe for even more than she had initially anticipated.

CHAPTER 41

Because of the late flight, Lexi had the aisle all to herself. Unable to settle her bouncing legs, she realized flying instead of driving had been the right decision. Her thought stream kept getting tangled because of the new information, and she found it very hard to focus on anything long enough to make progress. Anxious to be back, and worrying about what she had gotten Todd into gutted her.

She was also pissed that the battery in her laptop died, and she could not download any of the information she had pulled from Crystal's computer. However, she brought her notebook and began making lists and jotting down questions she needed answers to. She always found comfort in organizing her thoughts on paper when she was upset or stressed.

First, she started listing all the places she could remember Todd mentioning he frequently visited, but she knew Abby's knowledge would far surpass her own. Switching gears, she scanned the list of things she knew about Crystal from their brief encounters at work and the coffee shop. Lexi tried to remember any interests Crystal had mentioned, or past jobs and experiences. Sadly, she didn't know much about the girl. It baffled her that someone she knew so little about had inserted herself so thoroughly into her world.

Shifting focus, she recorded all the different personas or fashion trends Crystal had morphed into and out of since their meeting two years before. Lexi had seen her go from long, red curly hair to a Pulp Fiction-inspired black bob. In fact, she didn't even know the girl's natural hair color.

Another list included anything she remembered in Tennessee that hadn't meant much at the time, but looking back, was out of the ordinary, including her two previous sightings of Crystal.

Lists generally kept Lexi's thoughts from dancing in chaos, but that last list caused a panic attack. Once tapped out of any further helpful information, she started scribbling all the things she had learned from Alva and Kate, noting all the useful things she neglected to put into practice.

She hadn't realized she was crying until the flight attendant tapped her on the shoulder, asking if she was all right. Embarrassed, Lexi asked for a tissue and a whiskey neat, which the flight attendant obliged.

She shut her notebook, closed her eyes, and opened herself to spiritual guidance, and was thrust into an unfamiliar world.

She opened her eyes and found herself in a dark void. Her untucked shirt rhythmically caressed her stomach, and she was overwhelmed by the unsteadiness of floating. Before her mind had time to process her situation, she gasped in fear, both relieved and baffled that she could breathe. Lexi heard, and felt, the reverberation of three loud cracks of a whip, and felt a furious, icy whoosh of movement pass her, bringing with it a dim, golden glow that penetrated the murky water.

Several feet away hovered the dark woman. Although she still appeared tall and skeletal, her dress was tattered, and her skin appeared rotted, shifting ever so slightly with the current. But her eyes shone with curiosity, a contrast to the depth of experience and knowledge usually taking center stage.

Trying to remain calm, Lexi opened her mouth to ask the dark lady's name, but the words did not come.

Giltine smiled, revealing razor-sharp fangs and tiny teeth; the quick flick of her forked tongue felt more lecherous than inviting. Her long hair was tinted blue by the glow surrounding her, but chunks of her scalp were missing. She pointed her bony claw-tipped hands toward a stone-carved Celtic cross covered in muddy green algae.

Lexi turned to look and silently screamed as dead bodies littered the scene. Some were bloated and decomposing, while others were skeletal and dismembered, but all were covered in tiny scavenger fish. When a woman with an old blue flowered apron started urgently drifting toward her, she covered her face and readied for impact.

Lexi jerked awake with a shudder. As her heart raced, she grabbed her notebook and documented every detail of the dream she could remember.

The cabin pressure signaled their descent into the Knoxville airport. Lexi pulled herself together as much as she could and downed the whiskey in one gulp. As the plane landed, she grabbed her laptop and small carry-on and headed toward baggage claim to meet Abby.

Turning the corner, she saw Todd's sister checking arrival times and was floored by how much she resembled her brother. Even Abby's facial expressions and the way she carried herself reminded her of him.

Abby recognized Lexi immediately and rushed to embrace her in a warm, familiar hug. As she grabbed Lexi's carry-on, she turned and looked at her brother's girlfriend, "My god, you are as pretty as he said you were! Follow me, I am parked right outside."

Lexi followed Abby's lead, and after tossing her bags in the backseat, the two were on their way back to the lake house. Lexi could feel the weight of sheer exhaustion trying to lull her to sleep as they rode through the darkness, but she was determined to stay focused.

"I was able to download some stuff from Crystal's computer, but the battery on my laptop died and I couldn't look at it on the plane. I spent the whole trip making lists and trying to write down anything I thought pertinent or helpful. I just wish I could have gotten here earlier. I mean, he has already been missing for 24 hours." As Lexi spoke, her voice cracked, so she looked out the window and ran her fingers through her hair.

"Hey, there was nothing you could have done here that Toby and I weren't already doing. From what you've told me so far, it sounds like what you did in Ohio was far more productive. We're going to find him, and he will be okay. Why don't you try and get a little sleep while we're driving so you can have a clear mind when we get home? There isn't anything you can do right now, and I can tell you need to let yourself slow down and regroup. You're here now, so rest, and when you wake up, we will piece everything together and develop our plan of action."

The calmness and confidence in Abby's voice were reassuring, and Lexi closed her eyes, allowing her mind to wander until she fell asleep.

Abby drove the rest of the trip in silence, trying to keep her concentration on the road and off the nagging feeling that her brother was hurt and scared somewhere. She, too, knew that things were definitely not okay, but she also knew she needed Lexi coherent and focused, not running purely on emotion.

Lexi shot up in her seat as the tires from Abby's car switched from pavement to the gravel driveway. For a minute, her eyes darted across her surroundings, her mind fogged with the confusion of sleep. It all cleared, though, as soon as she saw the house.

"What are we doing here? We need to be out there trying to find Todd! I've got to find Todd..." She was overcome with emotion as her words trailed off, leaving her momentarily broken and vulnerable.

"I know this is hard, Lexi, but I need you to calm down. We first need to see what you downloaded from that girl's computer, and then we need to figure out how we want to approach this to best utilize our time. Todd needs us to work together because neither of us can find him alone."

"You don't understand. This is all my fault. He would have never been in this mess if I hadn't been so weak. I would have traded my happiness for his safety, I just didn't know. Why didn't she just come after me?"

Abby walked around to help her out of the car and held her hand while she let Lexi have her moment. She understood how it felt to feel responsible, to be so overwhelmed that each thought blurred together in a tirade of self-degradation. Instead of trying to calm her down, Abby let her unload some of the blame and self-hatred, because until some of that was diffused, Lexi would never be able to focus. She sat next to her and watched as Lexi held her face in her hands and screamed through her tears and shook uncontrollably as she rocked back and forth on the floor.

"That fucking bitch! She has taken everything from me, every goddamn thing! She stole my sanity. She shattered my confidence. She ruined my reputation. Hell, she even had me thinking I would be better off dead. But I can assure you, I will not let her take another motherfucking thing. No, she *cannot* have Todd! If I have to hunt her down and slit her throat myself, I will not let her take one more thing from me!" Abruptly, she jumped to her feet.

Abby watched as Lexi's desperation switched back to boiling determination, hoping she had gotten it all out of her system.

Lexi paced the living room, picking at her fingernails, trying to hold back the tears until she regained control of herself. She looked at Abby and laughed feebly. "Fucking nice first impression I've made."

Abby couldn't help but burst out laughing. She tossed Lexi a box of Kleenex and went to the kitchen to pour some stiff drinks. "Yeah, I'll be honest with ya, it's not exactly what I was expecting either. Here, take this, I think we both need something a little stronger than a beer."

"Thanks. So, now that I've gotten that out of my system…"

"Trust me, I understand how it feels to want to go back and change the past, but at least this time, we still have a chance to change the outcome. This time we have the upper hand. Why don't you go grab the laptop so we can see what you were able to download from this girl's computer? While you do that, I'll tell you what Toby and I were able to find out while you were gone."

Lexi walked to the door where she had dropped her bags and started to hook up the computer. "Okay, I'm listening."

"So, after I last talked to you, Toby and I went around to all of the places I could think where Todd could have been, and no one had seen him since earlier that week. I did talk to this one guy I knew in high school who works at the market downtown. He said he remembered overhearing Todd get into a weird conversation with a girl he didn't recognize. Apparently, the girl was brazenly coming onto Todd, which caught his attention. Anyway, the girl said something about Todd showing her around town, and when Todd said he had plans with his girlfriend, she went batshit on him. The guy said Todd seemed shocked and dumbfounded by the whole thing, tried to apologize, but the girl wouldn't have it and stormed off. Unfortunately, he didn't get a good look at her because she left in the opposite direction, but he said it was pretty fucked up."

"Did he hear a name or anything that could tell us where she would be?"

"Toby said the guy didn't really start paying attention until after the initial introductions, but he would call if he could remember anything else." Abby looked up to make sure Lexi was still listening, and when she saw her nod, she went on. "Anyway, by the time we'd gotten around to all the usual haunts, the regulars were starting to filter into the bar, so we headed that way. Several of Toby's friends remember hanging out with a blonde chick named Crys, and they were confident she was not a local. In fact, she'd slept with a guy named Cal a couple of times, but each time, he'd either taken her out on his boat or they just had sex in his truck somewhere, then he dropped her back off at the bar to get her car. He said he was a little leery about taking her home because there was something a little *off* about her. He said she was controlling and contentious one minute, and needy and clingy the next, but her sexual advances were damn near impossible to turn down. I asked him if he knew anything about where she was staying, and he said when she'd initially gotten into town, she'd been staying in some shit-hole hotel, her words, but she'd recently found a job and a serious lodging upgrade. Cal and Toby hang out, so I told him you would probably want to talk to him when you got back; maybe something you could say would trigger something he had forgotten. The other guys—"

"Oh my god!" Lexi cut her off mid-sentence and stared at the computer screen.

"What?"

"I think I'm gonna be sick." She stood up and ran out the back door, leaning over the railing on the deck.

Abby could hear her puking, but instead of going to help, she rushed over to see what had freaked Lexi out to the point of physical illness. There, on the screen of the laptop, was a picture of Lexi sleeping, obviously in her apartment in Cincinnati. She was only wearing a pair of panties and was blissfully unaware she wasn't alone in her own home. The photo was only the first in a folder of pictures labeled *SOON*.

All were pictures of Lexi in intimate situations, which revealed that not only had this Crys girl been in her apartment, but she had hidden cameras throughout the place. She had somehow been able to get photos of Lexi in the shower, of her sleeping, and even video of Lexi doing things people usually only do alone, in the privacy of their own beds. Abby closed the file when she got to the latter of the pictures, knowing that Lexi should be the only person to review the data in that specific folder.

She felt guilty she had seen any of the images, feeling she had violated an unsaid trust between her and her brother's girlfriend. She sat at the computer, her mouth agape, and immediately realized things were much worse than she thought. When she finally looked up, Lexi was standing in front of her. The two stared at each other for a moment, unsure of what to say. Abby diverted her eyes instinctively, which caused Lexi to laugh nervously.

"So, think I can get some good money from Playboy for those?"

"Holy shit Lexi, I had no idea. I…I don't really know what to say."

"It's okay, I don't either. I just can't believe I had no idea, but I guess we need to look through everything else."

"I'm sorry. If I had known, I wouldn't have looked through them."

"It's not your fault Abby. It's my fault for being so self-absorbed that I wasn't even paying attention to what was going on around me. I wonder how many other people have seen them…" her voice trailed off, and her thoughts wandered. She refocused and said, "I guess it doesn't matter right now. We need to focus on finding Todd, and to do that, we need to finish going through everything on here."

"Would you rather I let you go through everything alone? I can't imagine how invasive all of this is. I don't want to make it any worse."

"No, I need you to do this with me. I want to look at it objectively, and I can't do that alone. I just need to detach my emotions for now and deal with them later. But I do need to know that whatever we find on here won't make things between us uncomfortable and that Todd doesn't need to know all the details until I'm ready to tell him."

"I promise. I more than promise. In fact, when all this is over, I will tell you anything about me you want to know, even though I know that could never compare."

Abby's genuine smile reminded Lexi of Todd, boosting her optimism as she hesitantly sat next to Abby in front of the laptop. Together they began sifting through the pictures and information, hoping to find anything that could help.

CHAPTER 42

It wasn't the sounds surrounding him or the faint glow of light in the room that woke Todd from his uneasy sleep; it was the familiar smell of Lexi's favorite lavender candles. He never thought he would be the kind of guy who would have lit candles at home alone, but that's what he found himself doing after Lexi left. Within a couple of hours, he started missing her, so he lit every candle she had scattered throughout the house, smiling as the smell of her filled the room.

It was one of the first things he noticed about her when they started hanging out. She loved lavender and always subtly smelled of the flower. Once she was staying over every night, he loved how she put on lavender lotion every morning after her shower, and always lit a lavender candle at night right before she settled down for bed. She told him it was something she had done since she was a young girl, something that helped her relax. That was why, when he opened his eyes, he expected to be lying next to the girl he loved, away from the nightmare he had fallen asleep to.

"Good morning, handsome. I was beginning to think I was going to have to wake you."

Todd glanced erratically around the room, trying to focus on where he was and where the female voice was coming from.

The room was sparse. One wall was lined with racks of old vinyl records covered in dust, while the opposite held shelves and organizers full of tools, with an old wooden workbench connecting the two. An old record player sat on the edge of the bench, and the scratchy sounds of an old Allman Brothers album filled the room.

From what Todd could see, it looked as if this space was just off a larger room, and he assumed he was in a basement somewhere. As his eyes adjusted to the soft light, he saw a feminine silhouette in the corner of the room.

"What am I doing here? Who are you?"

As he spoke, she stepped out of the shadows, and he immediately recognized her from their encounter in the market. Her petite, athletic frame looked even more chiseled in the boy shorts and matching bra she wore. Even as he despised her and feared her expectations, he couldn't help but acknowledge that she was attractive.

She sauntered toward him, a lecherous smile and determined eyes surveying her prey.

"What do you want from me? Why am I tied up?" he said.

"I think it is pretty obvious what I want from you, and I thought you might enjoy being tied up. You have been a naughty boy, after all."

As she walked closer, he noticed her legs and upper arms were severely scarred and freshly wounded. Bewildered by her approach, he wondered if she was acting alone, or if the person who marked up her body was involved. He was also confused about how he should handle the situation. What should he say to this girl?

"How did you hurt yourself?" he asked.

She inched closer, taking out the knife hidden in the waistband of her panties. "Sshhhh, the questions are not yours to ask, Todd. How about we play a game?" She ran her sharpened blade from the inside of his ankle to his inner thigh. "You answer my questions, and you get rewarded, or you lie to me, and I punish you." She paused, laughing. "I love this game. I win either way!"

"I don't understand why you are doing this. Is this about money?"

At that question, she nicked his leg, breaking the skin. "I told you, no fucking questions!" To reiterate her point, she jerked the blade swiftly and ripped the side of his shorts with a practiced hand. "Now, tell me, why were you out all alone last night? Where was your girlfriend?"

Todd shifted as much as he could as she ran the blade across his hip bone. His heart was beating feverishly; he was sure she could see his pulse just beneath his skin. He no longer saw her as a victim, not with the way she handled her weapon of choice. It was apparent she was no stranger to dominating the men in her life. With these enlightening observations, Todd tread lightly. "She's out of town for the weekend."

"Good boy! Now for your reward." She moved her hands beneath the fabric still left of his shorts, tracing her finger from his thigh toward his waist.

"Stop! I don't want this!"

"Well, your body seems to think otherwise," she said, increasing her desire to tease him even further.

Todd was disgusted with the way his body turned on him, and no matter how hard he tried to fight it, he could feel the growing firmness she was referring to. No matter the horrid thoughts he tried to inject into his consciousness, the friction from her touch proved a stronger influence.

"When are you expecting Lexi back?"

"How did you know her name was Lexi? Have you been following me?"

Again, she nicked him with her knife, but this time the cut ran deeper.

He flinched at the pain, but to his surprise, his erection only grew.

Tears filled Todd's eyes, amplifying Crystal's arousal. The allure of control and pain started to interfere with her directive, and to keep herself in check, she made a small cut on her own arm to bring back clarity. Crystal didn't understand Todd's tears. They weren't initiated by physical pain, they were tears of heartbreak for the way he was betraying Lexi.

"I won't ask again. When are you expecting Lexi back?"

"She won't be back until the beginning of next week."

She didn't catch the lie, and as his reward, she used the blade to rid him of his boxers, exposing his genitals.

Fear and vulnerability overwhelmed him, and he was suddenly aware that he was at full erection, the opposite of how he felt. Inside, he felt disgusted, dirty, and worried that if he didn't comply with this crazy bitch, he might never make it back to Lexi.

"How did you meet her?"

"The lake; we both paddleboard."

"Paddleboarding, really?" she cooed. "How did you convince her to move in with you?"

Todd wondered why she was asking so many questions about Lexi, which fueled his discomfort. "I know you don't want me to ask questions, but I really need something to drink. It has been since last night."

"Answer my question, and I will get you water."

He tried to phrase his answer as ambiguously as possible so as not to trigger any adverse reactions. "She hasn't moved in with me. She decided she was staying permanently, so she moved in with a friend."

Crystal's relieved smile momentarily diffused her harsh face before she turned to walk out of the room.

CHAPTER 43

It took them several hours to go through all the folders from Crystal's computer. Although still shaken, Lexi was surprised to find her usual modesty did not seem to apply around Abby. She felt exposed and raped of her dignity by what they found, but tremendous gratitude for Abby's presence. Appreciation strengthened by a level of fearlessness, suddenly made her aware that she was willing to die or kill to save the man she loved. It was a freedom she had never felt before.

The files didn't give them any specific information on where they could find Crystal, but they gave them great insight into her routines and motivators. She had kept a meticulous journal of Lexi's every move for the past couple of years, but beyond that, she had recorded her own thoughts and emotions throughout. They may not have been able to find Todd from the computer files, but at least they had some leverage, something that could give them a hand up in Crystal's fucked up little game.

The only lead they had to go on was the message Lexi pulled from Crystal's answering machine, and all they knew was she requested references for a job in Tennessee, and the person she interviewed had an Indiana email.

"So, do you know any businesses or companies in the area that are based out of Indiana? Would your dad be able to get that information?"

"I can't think of any local businesses headquartered in Indiana. There are only a handful of factories nearby, so it shouldn't be too hard to find out. I'll call Dad and get him asking around right away."

Abby stared at the ground, wiping a tear from her chin, and opened her cell phone to call her parents.

Lexi felt overcome by another wave of guilt as she bore the burden of responsibility for Todd's disappearance. It was her fault his family not only had to face the uncertainty of their son's well-being, but they had to relive the pain and loss of Caleb. She walked toward the deck, listening to Abby tearfully explain to her father what they had found on Crystal's computer. As she heard the questions about local business owners in the background, she closed the back door and stood alone, staring into the darkness.

Lexi felt the familiar squeeze of panic and regret in her throat when, out of nowhere, a fierce burst of chills crept down her spine. The familiarity triggered her memory, and she dialed Kate's number. It went straight to voicemail. She left a message explaining what happened and asked if she could rally Mama as soon as possible. She needed their help interpreting her dream from the airplane.

CHAPTER 44

"Why don't you lie down and try to sleep for a few hours? I know you didn't sleep at all last night, and I got a couple of hours in the car on the way here. There's not much we can do until a little later in the morning anyway. We may as well sleep now to make good use of our time. I'll try and doze off for a little bit, too. You take the bedroom, I'll crash on the couch."

Abby couldn't argue; she was exhausted. She walked into her brother's bedroom, shut the door, and laid down on what she knew was Todd's side of the bed. Tears rolled down her cheeks and landed on his pillow. The past 24 hours seemed like days. She willed herself to keep her emotions in check, spending zero time thinking about the possibility of not finding her brother. Left alone with just her thoughts, time kept replaying itself, and she tried to swallow back the dread threatening to suffocate her.

Abby felt uneasy all morning the day before, but attributed it to the pressure of meeting her brother's new girlfriend. She still couldn't believe Todd asked someone to move in with him, much less a girl. For as long as she could remember, he'd sworn off the idea of marriage, content with the occasional tryst.

After everything with Caleb, they both built up nearly impenetrable walls in the romance department, but she still hoped for marriage and kids; Todd simply hadn't. But she saw the spark the first time he mentioned Lexi. It had been evident to her, even if not yet clear to him, things with Lexi were different. She couldn't quite put her finger on what it was, but when he spoke of her, his eyes lit with curiosity and giddiness, and he hadn't compartmentalized her the way he had every other girl he dated. Usually, after the first couple of dates, he dissected them, tearing away the parts he didn't care for or respect. No matter how often Abby tried to redirect his attention, it always fell on the negative characteristics. Once he got to that point in the relationship, it was only a matter of time before he moved on.

He seemed far more forgiving of Lexi's flaws. He was more intrigued by her dark complexities and emotional depth. When Todd spoke of her beauty, his compliments entwined with an appreciation for her intelligence. Over the phone, he got so excited it winded him. The whole situation unfolded so quickly, and what started as friendly fondness and admiration, soon evolved into something far more unfamiliar. He didn't teeter on the fulcrum of uncertainty with Lexi; his affection had been immediate. Once he knew the opportunity for romance was a possibility, he rushed in unconditionally. At first, Abby had been leery of her, unsure of her intent or expectation, but it didn't take long to see Todd was in love. It was her mother's phone call, however, that had put Abby's heart at ease. Veronica had not even waited for the couple to leave the driveway before she had called with an update. She remembered laughing at her mom's clattering recap of the evening. Her mom had babbled, sounding like her son only a couple of weeks before. They both cried when her mom relayed how Todd shared the story of Caleb's death, and just like the rest of the family, she also fell for Lexi.

As her heart filled with affection, it seized with dread. Surely fate could not be so cruel as to bring two damaged souls together, offer them unfaltering happiness, simply to yank it away so abruptly? Even more devastating was the thought of her parents having to mourn the loss of another son. Her entire body shuddered as she pulled her blankets up over her shoulders and fell into a nightmare-fueled sleep.

CHAPTER 45

Crystal begrudgingly fulfilled her promise to Todd, offering him a glass of water, then leaving him naked and humiliated. She'd been excited, not to mention stimulated, by his physical responses to their time together. She also felt a sense of pride and empowerment, having been able to seduce some valuable information from him. Men were pathetic, easily manipulated creatures. She knew he had wanted her all along, so she decided he was worth keeping around to play with for a little while longer.

To win over Lexi, she would have to orchestrate an end to her relationship with Todd. That meant she still needed him. Crystal hadn't yet decided how she would make that happen, but knowing Lexi's scheduled return, she had a little time to come up with a plan. She was finished waiting on the sidelines.

Feeling a little more in control, Crystal showered and headed out to the market to get some supplies and food. She also needed some booze and wondered if alcohol would loosen the boy's tongue even further. She thought of the way her pulse raced when she pierced his skin with the knife, and the way her body hummed from the experience. The power she had over him was lascivious, but as tempted as she was to go back downstairs, she knew part of the game was the waiting. Her thoughts swirled with her desire for Lexi and her lust for power over Todd.

How should Crystal inconspicuously create an exit for the boy, leaving her an opening to step in as the shoulder for Lexi to cry on? The time out of the house would help her clear her mind, and maybe after a drink with her restrained houseguest, the situation would reveal itself. She smirked with satisfaction.

THE WATER TASTED glorious to Todd, helping eliminate some of the cloudiness in his mind. As his head cleared, humiliation clung to him like algae on a boat's waterline. His mind swirled with questions. Who was this person, and why had she been following him? How had he gotten himself into this fucking situation? Why all the questions about Lexi?

Fear pushed him as he battled against his restraints with urgency. He had made progress and could feel the raw skin and blood on his wrists. He'd found a sharp edge on the metal frame of the cot, and it was slow and tedious, but the consistent movement allowed him to fray enough of the rope that he created minimal wiggle room, so he kept working.

He contemplated his approach with this girl. He considered the possibility of convincing her to let him call Lexi under the ruse of breaking things off. If he could get Lexi on the line, he could somehow alert her so she could go for help and protect herself. Could he convince this crazy bitch she won him over? He knew to do so, he had to reciprocate her sexual advances. The thought made him wretch, but he would do whatever necessary to save Lexi. The problem was his sincerity. Hopefully, he could lean into his pain at Lexi's latest admission and manipulate his own emotions.

CHAPTER 46

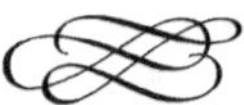

exi shot up to a horrific scream from the bedroom.

She slammed her knee into the coffee table, lurching forward as she tried to get to Abby. Bursting through the door, prepared to defend against an attacker, she found her new friend thrashing against the covers.

Fear twisted Abby's beautiful face as her eyes darted open. She was disoriented and still shaken from her dream, not recognizing her brother's room.

"Abby, are you okay?"

Still wild-eyed, it took Abby a minute to respond. "It was Todd, he was tied up and I couldn't get to him. No matter how hard I screamed and pounded on the glass, he couldn't hear me," she said, chest heaving.

Lexi rushed to the bed and gently put an arm around Abby's shoulders, unconsciously rocking to soothe her. Guilt pierced her heart, but she had spoken to Kate while Abby slept. Mama was on her way to meet Lexi and Kate. She needed to let Abby calm down, discuss separating their searches, and get to Kate's house.

"It was just a nightmare, Abby," she said as she made eye contact. "We will find your brother. I refuse to accept all other options."

"I know. I'm okay now. It all seemed so real. And after Caleb, I just can't stand to feel helpless again."

"It's around 9:00 central time, so will you start making calls in Indiana and sending emails? I'm going to head over to Kate's to talk to Mama. She and Kate have some non-conventional ways to find Todd. Are you hungry at all? I'm not, but I have granola bars or something if you are." Her voice trailed off as she was reminded of Todd and Crystal's encounter at the store.

It wasn't a sizeable town; somebody had to have seen something. They just had to figure out what to ask.

"Actually, why don't you go to the market and see if they have some kind of video footage from that night. Maybe there will be something on there we can use."

"Do you really believe in all that witchy shit? I know how much Todd loves Mama, and she is a good holistic healer, but the rest of that stuff doesn't seem plausible."

"Honestly, when I started Kate's retreat, I would have told you no. But I've had some insane shit happen since I got to Tennessee. Personal experiences, so yes, I do believe there is more to this world than just what we can see," said Lexi.

The girls ran through their next steps, agreeing to meet back at the house. Lexi took Todd's Jeep and headed to Kate's while Abby headed into town.

Mama was already there when Lexi pulled into Kate's driveway. When she walked into the kitchen, both women were busy at work.

The kitchen table was covered in a white tablecloth. In the middle of the table was an old, and very well-loved, Bible with a lit oil lamp and a porcelain bowl of water behind it. To the right were jars of herbs, salt, oil, a black granite mortar and pestle, a white handkerchief, candles, and various other tools Lexi didn't recognize.

Kate was at the stove stirring something in a cast iron pot. "Good morning, sweet girl. Alva and I have already started working to get together some protection satchels and jars to put over this property and Todd's place. I briefly explained to Alva about what you found out in Ohio, but she has questions. Did you bring the things I asked you to?"

Lexi held up a tote bag. "It's all here. Every sharp item I could find at Todd's, a white handkerchief, some of his hair from the brush, and my urine. I'm not going to lie, I'm a little more than worried about what you are going to do with my pee."

Alva laughed and said, "Child, all kinds of gross things are used in conjuring. Just wait until I ask you for toenail clippings. In fact, if you are on your moon cycle, the menstrual blood in the urine will add an even bigger kick." At Lexi's horrified look, she chuckled. "You've got a lot to learn, but first, we need to cleanse your energy and get grounded. I could feel your spirit's chaos before you left Todd's house. You can't conjure with that kind of energy, so let's get out back and clean up some of that before we start. Kate will keep working on the protection magic while we ground and try to interpret your dream. Take your shoes off, grab your handkerchief, and leave the rest of the stuff for Kate to use."

Lexi slipped off her sandals and did as she was told.

A circle of river rock was in the backyard near the lake shore. Inside was another porcelain bowl, a white pitcher, and a handful of other objects.

Mama instructed Lexi to sit in a chair just outside of the circle. "Now, I have filled this bucket with rainwater and rock salt. I want you to soak your feet in the salt water for 15 minutes and repeat this with me."

Lexi put her feet in the ankle-deep water and took the words from Mama.

Together, the two women spoke the words three times. "Goddess, let this heavenly water cleanse my spirit. Let the salt dissolve the black cloud of energy surrounding me. Bring me clarity in my thoughts and words as I work today."

When they finished, Lexi stepped out of the bucket of water and dried her feet on the white towel she was given. Then, she stepped directly into the dew-covered grass and sat in the stone circle. As she tried to settle her spirit, she focused on her breath work and absorbed the music of nature. Eventually, she laid back for a fuller connection to the earth beneath her. After some time, her breathing found a comfortable rhythm, and she slipped into a meditative state.

"Much better," said Mama. "As you lay there, tell me every detail you can remember from your dream of the dark lady."

Lexi repeated her dream, trying not to leave out any details.

"Okay, now tell me which things stood out to you the most."

"There were several things that stood out the most," said Lexi. "First was the stone Celtic cross. Second were the floating dead bodies, especially the lady in the blue flowered apron that came at me. Lastly, the dark lady's appearance was different from the first time I saw her. This time, her skin was rotting and loose on her bones, and she was missing chunks of hair. Her dress was also tattered and falling apart, when before, it had looked like a simple white dress."

"I'm impressed with your attention to detail. Now, let's see if we can figure out what in the Sam Hill all that means." She paused thoughtfully, then said, "Describe the Celtic cross to me."

Lexi remembered back to the dream. "It was big, like 7 or 8 feet tall, and it stood on a pedestal of the same material. It was covered in algae, like it had been in the water for a long time. The murkiness of the water and the algae made it hard to see any details, but I think there may have been a circle in the middle with a trinity knot."

"Did you see any names on it?"

"No."

"Okay, now tell me about the dead bodies. Did they look hostile?"

"No, they seemed sadder than anything else. There were about 25 or so, each with different genders and body types. I did notice that their clothes were from a variety of eras. Like, some were in old sack dresses, others were in more modern dresses, some men were wearing work clothes, and others were in church attire. I think I may have even seen an old Civil War-looking soldier. And then there was the lady that flew at me. She was probably in her 30s, full-figured and pretty enough, but I think her blue-flowered apron was the only piece of clothing that I remember having color."

"Almost done now," said Mama. "The last thing we need to remember is the dark lady herself. Tell me about her."

"Well, I already told you she looked different from last time. This time she looked like a dead, rotting corpse, whereas the time before, she just looked emaciated, but not falling apart. Her hair had been wispy and thin in the cemetery, but she was missing parts of her scalp entirely in the airplane dream, and certain pieces were barely hanging on."

Mama asked Lexi to sit up. "Some of the things you remembered triggered something in my memory, so I'm thinking if I can sit with it and do a little research, I hope to figure it out. I'm thinking maybe the stone cross, and the random dead people, may be from a small family cemetery plot, but I was so young when the water came that I can't remember the details. On the other hand, the lady in the blue dress is very familiar to me. There was a schoolteacher that lived around here. She was such a blessing to the children in the area. She would make house calls and try to find the money for school supplies since some of us couldn't even afford shoes back then. My mammy knew her well. In fact, I remember her doing some of the foraging in exchange for times she needed remedies and such. But I'm gonna have to go through Mammy's journals to see if I can find her name or anything more about her. And from my dealings with non-human spirits like your dark lady, how they portray themselves is, more likely than not, something to do with the intention behind the message. Since she is a tattered mess, I'm thinkin' she was not happy with something about the scene she was showing you.

Let's get up in the kitchen and help Kate finish up the protection jars. And I want you to keep that white handkerchief with you from now until we get this mess handled. Handkerchiefs have caught the sweat and tears of our ancestors. It's used as a gesture of kindness, cleaned the hands of many a kitchen witch, and kept some of our most precious trinkets safe. It holds magic and can keep you safe, but never use another person's handkerchief when conjuring. Replace them after cleaning up an extra nasty project like this one."

CHAPTER 47

The three women spent the rest of the morning conjuring up the protection magic. Afterward, Mama and Kate walked through the rituals of placing them on the properties. They had satchels hanging in the trees around the house, salted all the exterior doors and windows, then buried the protection jars at the four corners of the property.

Lexi was especially fascinated by the protection jars, which did include her urine, toenails, hair from each of them and Todd, dirt from a cow pasture, nine nails, graveyard dirt, red thread, and beet juice. Then, the bottles were sealed with wax and planted upside down in front of the four railroad spikes Kate already had protecting the property. She was grateful for the magical help and knowledge as much as the distraction of conjuring keeping her panic at bay.

They sent her home with four of her own railroad spikes, protection bottles, satchels, and written instructions on the exact rituals of placement. Mama encouraged her to find a safe place to keep everything she learned and written down to go into her book of conjure and rootwork later.

Armed with her spiritual line of defense, she was almost to Todd's when Abby called.

"Hey girl, did you learn any good witchy tricks while you were gone?"

Lexi laughed. "Yes, and you get to help me place them all when I get home. You know, you hear about gross things witches put in their cauldrons in stories and movies, but I now realize where that notion began. I'm almost back to Todd's. Where are you?"

"I actually got a video of Crystal and Todd from the market. The manager was kind enough to let me download what we needed, and I was heading toward the police station. I can swing by and you can come with me if you'd like. You may notice something on the tapes that I missed. Besides, they are going to need to talk to you anyway."

LEXI BEAT Abby back to Todd's, which gave her just enough time to unload the boxes of protection wards and put them next to the sofa.

When Abby arrived, she explained that the video from the market did not have audio, but there was some footage of Crystal and Todd's confrontation. Then, the two headed down to talk to the police.

WHEN THEY ARRIVED at the station with what they considered a possible lead, the police department saw it as an insignificant, brief encounter with a stranger.

"But I know this girl. She's been stalking me for years! How can you tell me this is insignificant?"

"Ladies," said the officer with little interest, "Todd has only been gone for 24 hours. Don't you think you are overreacting a bit? So, you know this girl? We get lots of tourism traffic from Ohio. I don't think it's a stretch to believe someone other than yourself would be traveling down from Cincinnati. We've put out an APB for your brother, so I'm sure he'll show up soon, and you'll realize how foolish this has all been."

Abby stepped in. "Officer Stand, are you aware who my family is?" She hated using her father's money and influence but was tired and desperate.

"Yes, Abby, we know who your father is, and I have also explained to him that we are working to find your brother." He sighed before he went on. "I also know the tragedy your family has suffered in the past, so I understand your worry for your brother. I will keep the video and have someone look at it to see if we can get a clear photo of the girl. Still, we don't have the manpower right now to have guys chasing down someone who has more than likely run out of town for a couple of days and forgotten to check in."

Abby could feel the sting of tears welling up in her eyes, but she pushed them back. She knew he looked familiar. He had been there after Caleb's death, although he had aged over the years. She could see the pity in his eyes, and emotions she pushed down for years began to bubble toward the surface. She remembered the mawkish way everyone regarded her back then, treating her as if she wouldn't understand or be able to handle the magnitude of the situation, how everyone she knew suddenly looked at her with a stranger's eyes.

As the heat climbed up from her chest, she balled her hands into fists. "I am not a fucking child! I know my brother, and I know good and goddamn well that he would not take off without telling us, especially without checking in!" Her fury was outpacing her mind's ability to find words to express her thoughts. "I can assure you, I will be calling in every influence my father has, and if I were you, I would not be caught standing around with my hands in my pockets!"

Lexi was shocked when Abby started yelling at the officer.

Her face was splotched and red, and her eyes were glazed with an unfamiliar emotion. She stood inches from the man's face, belligerently pointing her finger at him. The entire office stopped to stare.

Lexi took her friend's elbow and tried to pull her away, but she shrugged her off and kept ranting.

Soon after, another gentleman came out of an office and intercepted Abby's tirade. He assured them that her brother's disappearance was a top priority in the office and thanked them for the information.

Lexi assumed he must be the sheriff, or someone with more authority, because Abby started to calm down, and the man spoke of Todd's father with more than casual familiarity.

"I assure you, Miss Novak, we will keep you and your family updated on any new information we receive and would appreciate it if you could do the same." His face softened, and he took her hand. "Excuse me for saying, but you two look completely exhausted and on edge. In my years of experience in this job, I've found that clear thoughts and fresh ideas are frequently found on the other side of some much-needed rest. Why don't you go home, try to get more than an hour of sleep, and leave this in our capable hands for the moment? Please don't misunderstand this as a disregard for your concerns. I promise you, an overtired mind can wreak havoc on one's emotions."

This time it was genuine concern, and not pity, Abby saw in the sheriff's face. She smiled weakly and thanked him for his time, and when Lexi took her elbow, she let her lead them toward the door.

CHAPTER 48

*C*rystal descended the stairs with two glasses of whiskey. She only wore a short pink sundress—no underwear, no shoes, no frills. It was a dress she had stolen from Lexi's house when they first arrived, and she hoped the similarities would further stimulate his interest. She found the boy just where she had left him and hungrily admired his hard, lean body.

He lay on the cot, his briefs on the floor beside him, looking more relaxed, not fighting the restraints like before.

She had left the electric lantern lit, allowing her to see his chest's slow, steady rise and fall as he breathed. She was conflicted. On the one hand, she was happy to see his relaxed demeanor, hoping it would make him more pliable. On the other hand, the desire to see him beg as he writhed in pain stirred deep within her.

As she ran her finger down his cheek, he fought not to flinch. "You're finally back," he said.

She cocked an eyebrow. "Well, this is certainly a change in attitude."

"I've had a lot of time to think. Lexi and I got into a big fight before she left," he said coyly.

"Indeed."

"I see you have two drinks. Can I assume one of those is for me?"

She dragged a chair next to the cot, sat down, and kicked her feet up, barely brushing his leg with her toes. "If you are a good little boy. So, tell me, what were you thinking about while I was gone that would elicit such a change in attitude?"

"You."

"What about your precious girlfriend?" she sneered.

"I thought about her too. Unlike you, she would never have the self-confidence or balls to take what she wanted. It occurred to me that I have had more excitement in the last 24 hours with you than I had with her in two months."

"Is that so?" She put the glass to his mouth, tipping it so he would get a good swig of whiskey.

With no food and little fluids in his system, the whiskey was harsh, and he pulled his face as he swallowed.

She laughed. "Not much of a drinker, huh?"

"I could be if I had someone who would drink with me." He ignored the burning in his stomach and smiled in her direction.

"Lexi never was much of a liquor drinker," she mentioned offhandedly.

The comment caught him completely off guard, and he wondered if he heard her right. Did she just say she knew Lexi? The comment sounded like she *really* knew Lexi. He hoped she hadn't noticed his subtle reaction and confusion in his eyes. His mind raced with thoughts, but he tried to focus on the mission at hand.

"Difference between girls and women, I suppose," he said, trying to sound casual.

She tipped the glass even heavier, and he forced himself to drink the amber liquid smoothly. Acutely aware of his lack of control in the situation, he shifted on the table, catching her attention.

Her eyes crawled across his body lecherously. "Oh, I'm certainly no little girl."

"No, you have the touch of a real woman, but how am I supposed to show you how much pleasure you can find as I explore every inch of you if I'm all tied up?"

Her head jerked back toward his gaze, and he saw the suspicion in her eyes. "Don't you worry about touching me. I get off watching you, watching your pain turn into pleasure, watching your curiosity turn into desire. *If* I decide to let you touch me, I'll tell you exactly when and how."

"What does a guy gotta do to be so lucky?"

She, again, poured more whiskey into his mouth, and he fought to keep his thoughts straight. If he could just convince her to untie one hand.

"Let's see," she said, straddling him, "maybe you could answer a few more questions."

"If it gets me inside you, ask away." He could see she wore no panties as her juices created lubrication and her inner thigh gripped his hips, but he worked to center his panic.

His answer aroused her, and she rolled her hips. She rubbed her aching clit over his cock and her complete control of him almost pulled an orgasm out of her. Knowing she could enjoy his body while gaining useful intel filled her with the mighty rush of control. Her ego started to take over, but she reigned it in. "If you want inside me, you need to prove to me you are done with everyone else."

"You mean done with Lexi," he said, fighting the revulsion as he thrust his hips into her.

Her body tensed, and her fingers dug into his hips as she quickened her pace. "With an end comes a new beginning," she said, gently flicking her clit, voice thick with desire.

"Let me prove to you I'm done. Do you want me to call her and end it now?"

"I want you to fuck me now," she said.

Her touch made his skin crawl, but he tried to focus his mind elsewhere.

She peeled off her dress, leaning back and using one hand to present her vagina while aggressively fingering herself into a hard orgasm, intentionally squirting him in the face.

He willed himself to get hard, but his body betrayed him once again. He couldn't stop his mind from thinking about her previous comment about Lexi. Words were easy tools of deception; male physicality was not.

"What the fuck?" she snarled.

"It must be the whiskey on my empty stomach. Let me use my hands, and I promise to make you scream."

Her eyes cleared, and he saw the unfiltered rage behind them, clearly confirming she was capable of anything.

"Are you fucking kidding me?" She swallowed the last of the whiskey while grinding her sex on his face. "Do you think I am some stupid, naïve little bitch? I watched you fuck my girl for hours, and you think I'm going to believe your limp dick is because of a couple of drinks of fucking whiskey? You've got to be shitting me. I should just sit here and suffocate you while I rub another one out."

She slammed the glass of whiskey in her hand to the ground, pulled out the knife from behind her back, and held it to his neck. Tempted, she thought of cutting his throat and ending it right there, but remembered she may still need him. "You think you are so goddamn smooth, don't you? You think a little charm will save you? Why don't you lay here and think about how much I'm going to enjoy raping and killing your precious little Lexi? Maybe I'll drag her out to that pretty little outdoor shower you have, then scour your stink off her before I fuck her in your bed. I'll violate every part of her lavender-scented body until she's worthless and damaged beyond the hope of ever remembering how it felt to be loved by anyone but me. I'm going to make the bitch beg for her life as I take anything I want from her."

The fear Crystal saw in his eyes aroused her masochistic nature, and she was tempted to stay and satiate herself through his torment, but she refused to give him the satisfaction. She grabbed the dress, leaned close to his ear, and whispered, "Your whore will be dead by the end of the night, lake rat."

The last thing he felt was slicing, bone-deep pain, and the sensation of blood rushing from his thigh before she threw the lantern and slammed the door, leaving him in total darkness.

CHAPTER 49

The next time Todd heard the sound of tires pulling out of the driveway, his panic kicked into overdrive. He tugged and pulled at all four restraints, trying to focus on the weakest path of resistance, while turning over the recent conversation in his mind.

As he rewound the experience, several points of awareness steamrolled his previous perception. The mention of lavender when she threatened Lexi, and the scent of the candles earlier could not be a coincidence. This crazy bitch not only knew his girlfriend, but she also knew where he lived. And he wasn't positive, but he swore he saw Lexi in that dress before. His fear tore through the pain, threatening to get away from him. He focused on his anger.

Panic settled into his gut as he tried to remember everything he and Lexi had done together, thinking of each place they had gone, trying furiously to work out where he had seen this girl before. The familiarity haunted him from her first step out of the shadows, but Todd couldn't put his finger on why.

He and Lexi spent a lot of time on the lake; maybe she had seen them on the water. He tried to picture everyone at Mama's diner the two times they visited, but his attention was focused on his beautiful date, oblivious to any other woman in the room.

As he fought through agony and fatigue, he remembered the night he and Lexi first made love, the night they heard someone in the woods. Then he remembered the dead kitten on the deck.

"Lexi had been right," he said to himself, "and I just blew it all off."

The thudding in his temples pulsed more rapidly, and he cursed himself for not following up. Maybe if he had called the cops, he could have avoided this mess. He left Lexi alone in that house. The thought flooded him with guilt, but he shook it off. He had to keep thinking. They had not seen anyone that night.

Fuck, why did she look so familiar? He thought about their trip to his parents' house. Had they stopped anywhere on the way? They stopped for gas, but Lexi didn't get out of the car, and he only ran in and right back out to pay. Then it struck him: *the grocery store*. That is where he had seen her before. A chill shot down his spine when he remembered the glare she gave him when he made eye contact with her on the road. It was a look of unmitigated hatred.

But none of that made any kind of sense. Why was the woman following him, and what game was she playing? Her interest seemed closely tied to Lexi, and he sensed her obvious jealousy, but it seemed off. If she was jealous of Lexi, why did his answers about Lexi appease her? Come to think of it, hadn't almost *all* her questions been about his relationship with Lexi? It still didn't make sense, but regardless of the why, his girl was in danger, and he needed to do whatever was necessary to get to her.

The struggle against the ropes on his ankles was futile, and the more he fought, the more blood puddled in the space between the back of his knees and thighs. It wouldn't be long before the fight caused dizziness from blood loss, so he stilled and focused on his loosened hand.

Todd knew Lexi was not yet due home, but he also knew he had been here at least a day without calling her. She would be alarmed; he wondered if she contacted his parents. He hadn't remembered to give her their number before she left, so she probably had yet to speak with them.

Slowly, an ugly realization began to settle. With her apprehension about going, he knew she would come home early if she reached anyone concerning his whereabouts, leaving her vulnerable.

His thoughts jumped to that first night on the dock. He remembered the feel of her bumpy, chilled skin and the delightful, easy tone in her voice as she rambled. That was the night he realized he loved her. The words may have taken longer to come, but his heart knew. When they returned to her house, and she fell asleep in his arms, he felt content to lay and watch her breathe. His fingertips gently explored the exposed parts of her body: her arms, her neck, her cheek. Lexi slept so peacefully, occasionally letting little moans escape, as she snuggled in closer to him for warmth from the rest of the world. He had been in an intimate part of her world, one not even she had been aware of.

Todd started to learn her body's reaction to his touch that night by merely enveloping himself in her every response. He knew she was sensitive where her jaw met her ear because when he touched her there, she pulled him closer, sliding her leg over his thigh and tilting her hips toward him. A fingernail slightly tickled along the back of her arm soothed her when she tensed or became restless. A caress across her cheek or lips always elicited a faint smile. He'd held her willing body for several hours that night to learn how to please her and make her safe and happy.

When he picked her up to take her to her bed, she had not wanted to let go, pulling him with her as he gently laid down. She had briefly opened her eyes, brows furrowing together in denied desire, so he stayed with her, tracing his fingers across the fabric on her back until she had, once again, settled into sleep. As he pulled the blankets over himself on the couch that night, his heart knew it was home.

A sudden snap and release in tension on his wrist pulled Todd out of his memory. Hope swelled, and he quickened the friction between metal and rope. Thread by thread, the rope frayed, losing its tensile strength until he could free his hand. He rotated his wrist to recirculate the blood, subsiding the numbness. The constant movement had rubbed off a layer of skin, and he was aware of the flesh's rawness, but the elation trumped any pain. He quickly worked to loosen his other hand from its binding, which proved more laborious than he antici-pated. His strength was significantly weakened by the lack of food, water, and blood loss, but his determination had not lost ferocity. He knew it was a matter of life or death, and it wasn't his own life he was worried about. He had to get free to keep Lexi safe. If anything happened to her, he honestly didn't know if he had the willpower to get through another loved one's senseless death.

Finally untying his second hand, he sat up to assess the damage. He had several superficial cuts, not to mention a bruised cock. "Crazy fucking bitch," he said aloud. But it was the gash on his leg that worried him. It bled substantially, and the more he moved, the worse it seemed to get. He looked around, unable to see much of anything, but he could still hear the hum of the record player, which had long quit playing music, but never turned off. It was on a workbench along the wall. About eight feet further was the light from beneath the closed door.

Once free, he swung his legs around and stood up quickly, a much too ambitious move. His knees buckled and he landed on the concrete floor, feeling the skin on his elbow split as it made contact. He pulled himself up and limped toward the workbench, feeling for a lantern or something to help slow down the bleeding from his leg, whichever came first.

When he made it to the workbench, he balanced himself on the splintered wooden surface and edged to the other side of the room, looking for any sign of the door. His hand fell upon some material, so he ripped it with his teeth and tied it above the wound on his leg.

The walls were cold, but his adrenaline kicked in and progress was quick, considering his condition. When he finally made it to the door, he found it locked. He cursed, throwing his body against it, but he was weak. After several attempts, he stopped, holding himself up with one hand, breathing heavily, and fighting dizziness. Once he regained his balance, he returned to the workbench to find a tool to weaken the door's integrity.

He desperately grasped for anything; a hammer or something with a blade would be ideal. His hands fumbled across plastic, knocking over containers of nails and bolts until he felt the metallic edge of a screwdriver.

Back at the door, he used the tool as a lever, trying to break the lock or unhinge it from the door frame. He heard the wood giving way but not breaking free from the carriage. Luckily it wasn't a dead-bolt, so he stepped back and aimed his shoulder again. Since he had dislocated the metal from the wood, when the force of his weight rammed into it, the door finally gave way. Wood from the doorframe splintered, and he fell into another room.

Great, he thought, *more darkness. Where am I?*

He pushed himself from the floor and let the room settle around him. He needed to find a light switch. There was something familiar about the smell and temperature of the room, but he didn't quite recognize it.

Slowly limping forward, hands in front of him, Todd felt for obstacles in his path, and came upon some type of shelving system holding cool, glass bottles. Some were housed in crates, some cradled in curved shelving. Hope bloomed as he realized the room was probably similar to his parents' wine cellar.

Methodically, he made his way to the left, avoiding the shelving, and followed the rows toward what he hoped was the front of the room. Once he'd run out of rows, his fingers found the smooth wooden wall and, eventually, a light switch. The blinding glare from the sudden brightness seemed the equivalent of staring into the sun, and he shielded his eyes until they adjusted.

He looked around, frantically trying to figure out where he was. The cellar was smaller than his father's, and he quickly spotted the exit. Fortunately, there was no keypad lock system. He quietly tried the handle, and for the first time in what seemed like an eternity, luck was on his side.

Afraid his abductor may still be in the house, he climbed the stairs as silently as possible. He slowly stepped his uninjured leg up, dragging the damaged limb behind him. Halfway up the staircase, he needed to steady himself again, almost toppling toward the concrete bottom.

Once at the top, he stepped into what he assumed was some sort of butler's pantry. That part of the house was lit with security lights, so he could see to make his way through to the next room. The kitchen was lined with large picture windows, and the view from the lake was vaguely familiar. It was dark out, but he was unsure how long he had been in the cellar—one day, maybe two? His eyes probed every corner of the room as he stepped in, and he breathed a hesitant sigh of relief when he saw it was empty. He spotted a telephone on the other side of the room and headed toward it.

CHAPTER 50

Crystal sat on the cobblestones, staring up at the huge dam built to create Norris Lake. She didn't know how long she had been gone, but the sun transitioned from late afternoon to dark, and the lake was empty.

She had to stop the car and get better control of herself before she could make any more decisions. She parked, and with her rage spilling over, she punched the window. The pain brought her closer to reason, and with her knuckles still sticky with her own blood, she let her mind wind around the situation at hand. She couldn't believe that pathetic excuse for a man who thought he stood even a chance of outwitting her. Even more disappointing was the fact that, for just a second, she bought into it and thought her plan was working. What was she thinking? Her mom would be so disappointed in her. After all, she'd been the one who had taught her about manipulation and that sometimes the most important part of the con is patience. Then again, that cunt abandoned her with a pedophile stepdad, so who gave a fuck what she thought. She balled her fists together in frustration, then forced herself to release them and calm down enough to think of her next step.

She did not understand the allure of lake life. She hated the sinister deep waters and shoreline muck, she hated watersports, and she hated all the little bitches with their perfect blonde hair and perfect tans sauntering around in bikinis like they're better than everyone else.

When she was around five or six, her mom was working a con on some guy who lost a kid. Crystal had been excited at the promise of going to James Taylor Park, but instead, they ended up following the man to Riverboat Row and walking the ramp to get on one of the riverboats. When her mom pushed her off the ramp, she flailed in panic, trying to keep her head above water, but she couldn't swim. Her mom screamed and made a huge scene for help, then everything went black.

Crystal woke coughing up water as the man they'd be tailing patted her back, reassuring her she would be okay. Her first instinct was to blame her mom, but she already knew the beating she would get, so she kept quiet.

The incident sparked a deathly fear of large bodies of water, so she didn't spend much time on the river at home. None of the people she surrounded herself with in Ohio had boats, and she had no desire to swim in that waterway cesspool anyway. Besides, there weren't as many shadows to find anonymity in on the water, especially at Norris Lake. It was all open air; she didn't even have the cover of a crowd to get lost in.

She jumped a little when a couple cautiously passed behind her, sending a handful of rocks tumbling toward her. "What the fuck?" she grumbled toward them.

"Excuse us," said the timid teenage girl, hurrying past.

Crystal watched them walk toward the dam. They couldn't be more than seventeen, and the boy's arm wrapped around the young girl's waist, hand neatly tucked into the back pocket of her jeans. When she giggled and glanced up at him, he leaned down and gently kissed her forehead. She could not hear their conversation, but the scene made her realize she wasn't far from where she had been the night when she watched Lexi and Todd on the dock.

Todd's house was only a couple of miles down the lake. Knowing Todd wasn't home, and Lexi was out of town, the temptation to touch

Lexi's things and lie where she slept was too overwhelming for Crystal to pass up. She stood up, dusted the sand from her pants, and headed to the car.

As she drove, her excitement grew. She craved the smell of Lexi's sheets and longed to surround herself with her energy. Her smile immediately dropped when she saw Todd's car in the driveway. Her hands grasped the steering wheel so tightly, her fingernails dug into the vinyl. She slowly pulled into one of the empty driveways a couple of houses down and turned off the car.

Lights were on in Todd's house, but Crystal could not see any movement inside. She stepped into the cold night and gently shut her car door. Her heart raced, and part of her knew it was not the smartest idea, but her compulsion would not let her leave without looking.

Deliberately keeping away from the light, she walked toward the back of the house where she knew she would have the best view. It was quiet, except for the low hum of music she was following. *If there is music, someone must be home,* she thought.

As she stepped around the back side of the house, she could see into the kitchen, but no one was inside. Hadn't Todd said Lexi would not be home until the following day? She moved onto the deck in practiced silence and could see someone asleep on the couch. Crystal immediately froze. Now she knew, without question, she needed to walk away; but she couldn't. The urge spiraled out of control, allowing the physical need to pull her forward.

The pictures from her computer flashed through her mind, and she rubbed her hands on her jeans. Tucking herself into a corner next to the glass door adjacent to the couch, she watched the figure move in her sleep. She imagined Lexi in her thin, green pajama shorts and t-shirt, knowing exactly how much room was between the fabric and her skin. Crystal felt the heat jolt throughout her body, and her breath quickened. She continued rubbing her hands, longing to touch and probe.

The figure rolled onto her back, the blanket shifting just enough to bare the skin on her stomach. It was too much. Crystal had rarely been this close to Lexi while she slept. She had watched her on the computer screen, but this thrill of watching the rise and fall of her chest as she breathed contently was unparalleled.

Taken by the moment and unable to control herself, she slowly crept forward, placing her hand on the door handle. *Please let it be open,* she silently prayed, but it wasn't.

She frowned and surveyed her environment for her options until her eyes settled on a barrette sitting on the banister. Her body tingled with anticipation as she gingerly maneuvered the small, pointed end behind the latch, waiting for the click. She concentrated carefully, nimble fingers slowly working the metal, when the figure sat up. Panic shot through Crystal when she was caught looking into the eyes of......*Todd?*

CHAPTER 51

*A*s hard as Lexi and Abby had tried to fight it, Sheriff Whaley was right. There was nothing else they could do, and by 3:00, the girls were unable to resist the inevitable. They had both been awake for well over 24 hours, and it had taken its toll.

After forcing down some food, Lexi showered and tucked herself into bed while Abby took the couch. They figured they would get a little quality sleep, and then start again.

After the scene at the police station, neither of them remembered to secure the house with the protection wards Mama had sent home with her.

Abby heard movement and sat up, rubbing the sleep from her eyes. A bolt of adrenaline rushed through her when she realized someone was on the back deck. "Hey!" she yelled. "What do you think you're doing?"

She kicked her feet, trying to unwrap herself from the blanket, when the figure darted off. Abby jumped from the couch but slammed her shin on the coffee table as she fell over the tangle of cloth at her feet. "Lexi! *Lexi!*"

Throwing the bedroom door open, Lexi burst into the room. "What?" she said breathlessly.

"There was someone at the backdoor! They just ran off. Call the police, I'm going to go after them."

"Wait," she said, but it was too late; Abby had darted out the back door.

Lexi stood, cell phone in hand, as she heard the squeal of tires. She stepped out the front door, only to see taillights and Abby standing in the middle of the road, cursing.

"Yes, 911? I need to report a break-in!"

"What's your location?"

"We're at 627 Mountain View Drive. Listen, I think this may be related to my boyfriend's disappearance."

"Is there a threat to life or property?" the operator said in a bored, even tone.

"No. No, we caught the intruder trying to open the back door, and they got away. They drove off." She looked at Abby. "Did you see the plates?" she asked.

Abby put her hands on her knees, catching her breath, and shook her head. "No, but it was a small, red, older model car."

"We weren't able to get the number from the license plate, but it was a small, older model, red car. I think I know who it belongs to."

"So, they are no longer on the property?"

"No, ma'am. But someone needs to follow her! You need to find her!" Lexi's hands were shaking as she paced the floor.

"Can you describe the person you saw?"

"She was short and athletic with a blonde, pixie cut." She looked to Abby for verification and was met with a nod.

"Ma'am, may I ask your name?"

"We don't have time for all of this," she said sharply into the phone.

"I've already sent a car, so an officer is on the way. Please, ma'am, what is your name?"

"I'm Lexi Greer, and I'm with Abby Novak. We've spent all day looking for my boyfriend, Todd Novak. We think the person who tried to break into our house tonight has him." She felt her shoulders shudder as a wave of sobs hit her.

"Ms. Greer," said the calm voice on the line, "a squad car should be pulling into your driveway now."

Abby ran to the door, and Lexi saw the red and blue lights flashing through the window.

"They are here. Thank you," she said, ending the call and running after Abby.

Lexi and Abby stood outside the front door as the police officer quickly moved toward them.

"Ladies," he said, but before he could get another word out, they both interrupted him, rapidly firing questions. "Slow down. If you come with me, I will update you on what is happening."

Abby turned to him. "What do you mean? What's happened?"

CHAPTER 52

rystal's heart was pounding as she flew through the back roads to the house. As she ran back to her car, it took a minute for her brain to catch up to her eyes. When the girl on the couch sat up, she could have sworn she had been looking at that boy. In a panic, she ran. She had barely pulled out of the driveway before the figure sprinted into the road behind her. Through her rearview mirror, she realized the girl must have been Todd's sister. The resemblance was uncanny and caught her off guard. Between the shock of being seen, the realization she had not been watching Lexi sleep, and seeing a female version of the pig boy, her nerves were wrecked.

Fortunately, that girl had never seen Crystal before, and she no longer fit any recognizable description Lexi could give. But it had been too close. There was no more time to waste.

Crystal had underestimated the *boyfriend*. He was nothing like the last couple; she knew what that meant. It was time to finish this. She already made sure the Tandys had none of her real contact information and no pictures of her. If she left the house with a thorough cleaning, she knew no one would be able to trace her back to them.

She had not made any friends, and only used cash since she had been in town. She had changed her appearance before coming so she could stay hidden from Lexi until she knew her intentions. There wasn't much tying her to the town, and because it was offseason, the house would not be opened again until the spring. Sure, her timeline had moved up, but that was perfectly fine with her; she was done playing cat and mouse with Lexi. It was time to take her girlfriend home.

Crystal slowed at the stop sign, checking before she turned. Suddenly, she heard sirens and saw flashing lights race by her. She didn't move as a wave of nausea punched up from her gut. A minute later, an ambulance flew by. Knowing there were only two more turns before she was at the house, one of only four from that point, she backed up her car, turned off the lights, and sped off in the opposite direction.

CHAPTER 53

*L*exi refused to go anywhere without explanation. She stood at the cruiser, hands on her hips, still breathless from what happened. "We're not going anywhere until you tell me what's going on," she demanded.

The officer's eyes softened, and he calmly stated, "We've located Mr. Novak. They are en route to the hospital as we speak."

"What? You found him? Is he hurt? Why are you taking him to the hospital?"

"Yes, ma'am. Mr. Novak called 911 not long before your call came in. He stated he was injured and did not know his location but had just escaped captivity. Sheriff Whaley called to tell me they had found him as I was pulling into the driveway."

"Oh my god! How bad are his injuries?" she choked out through panicked tears.

"Calm down, Miss Greer, he's okay. According to the Sheriff, he is hurt, but was walking and alert when they arrived at the scene."

"You have to find Crystal!"

"Who's Crystal?"

"The bitch who took him!" Abby yelled in frustration. "The one who peeled out of here right before you showed up. The one who has been stalking Lexi. We brought you the fucking videos, and the sheriff said he would investigate. How do you not know who Crystal is?"

"I'm sorry," said the officer as he started the engine, "they only realized that your call and Mr. Novak's call were related as I was driving over here. Officers are out patrolling now. Now that we have your description of her car, we can narrow our search significantly. If she's in this town, we will find her."

Face swollen and red from tears, Lexi took Abby's hand and collapsed against her friend. "They found him."

BEFORE THE POLICE cruiser came to a complete stop, Lexi swung open the car door and jumped out.

As she ran through the door of the emergency room, a police officer spotted her and escorted her through the maze of hallways and corners, stopping outside of Todd's room. She stepped through the doorway, her heart overflowing with relief, fear, and love. She stood there staring at his battered body, watching a doctor bandage his thigh, when he looked over.

"Lexi," he said lazily, obviously groggy from some kind of pain medication or sedative. "I was so worried about you."

She walked toward him, unable to stop the upsurge of tears. "Why were you worried about me, you silly man?"

"The blonde chick...she knew things about you...said she was going to hurt you," he said, eyes closed, the furrow in his brow relaxing.

She took his hand and touched his bloody palm to her lips, guilt nearly choking the words as she spoke. "I'm so sorry, Todd. She would have never come after..." She looked back at his face, but he had slipped into sleep.

Todd opened his eyes with alarm, immediately scanning the room and processing his location. His sister sat in a chair, head resting on her arms as she slumped over a small table. His mother was on the other side of the table looking down at a book, reading quietly. Lexi was sitting on the other side of his bed, her fingers resting softly on his arm. His breath left him in a rush, vaguely remembering the trip to the hospital.

"Lexi," he croaked, throat dry from sleep.

She shot up. "Todd?"

At the sound of his voice, his mother rushed to his side, laying a warm hand on her son's face. "You're awake," she said softly. "How do you feel?" Veronica handed him a glass of water.

He tried to take the drink, arm meeting resistance from the IV tubes.

He looked at his mom, and she saw the questions in his eyes. "You were pretty dehydrated, honey. They just want to be sure."

Abby stood up as well, sneering at him. "What the fuck, man? I go away for a couple of weeks, and you manage to get your ass kicked by a girl?"

"Abby!" said her mom, mouth agape as she elbowed her daughter in the ribs.

A snort escaped from Todd, followed by laughter. "Give me a break. The bitch drugged me and tied me up."

She tousled his hair and wiped the tears from her cheeks. "Next thing you're gonna tell me is that she had a knife too," she said, nodding toward his leg. Humor fading, she squeezed his shoulder. "I was so scared," she whispered.

"I'm fine, sis," he said. Glancing back at Lexi, he worried about the conflict in her eyes. "I see you met my beautiful Lexi."

Abby laughed, eyes moving between the two. "Not the introduction I was expecting, but yes. I'm looking even more forward to getting to know the relaxed, happy version."

He let his family fuss over him, calling the nurse into the room so she could check his vitals and administer more pain medication. He answered all their questions and reassured them he was fine, just sore and hungry. The nurse left the room to check on any dietary restrictions, and he asked his family for some time alone with Lexi.

Happily obliging, his mother explained they needed to find his father anyway. He was still busy working with the police, offering any resources he had available to find the woman who hurt his son.

After everyone left, Todd focused his puzzled eyes on his girl, brushing a finger across the contour of her chin. "I have never been so happy to see anyone in my life."

Her sad eyes surveyed his injuries, only briefly looking up at his face, then back to the bandage on his leg. "I would never forgive myself if anything happened to you."

His face pulled with confusion, "How in the world can you take any responsibility for an obviously mentally unstable woman who is fixated on me?"

"It's not *you* she's fixated on, Todd. It's me. If I had never come here, this would have never happened." She, unsuccessfully, fought to stop the tears from brimming over.

"What are you talking about?"

"I'm talking about the fact that I thought I could escape my fucked-up world by coming here. I was stupid enough to think I was actually going to get a happy ending, but instead, I just brought all of my troubles into your life, as well."

"Seriously, babe, I'm okay. You're the reason I got out of there. The thought of her coming after you," he shuddered, "pushed me to keep fighting. It gave me the strength to get myself out of that situation. You saved my life!"

She stood up and paced the room. "You don't understand, Todd. You don't know the whole story."

"Stop," he said firmly. "Come here."

Hesitantly, she sat beside him.

He wrapped his arm around her waist and pulled her onto the bed. "Just shut up. I need you in my arms. I don't want to talk about this right now, I just need to feel your body against mine. I need to know this is really happening."

She let him pull her close, knowing she would do anything he needed until he regained his strength. With her neck cradled into the crook of his shoulder, she slowed her breathing, pretending to settle until she felt him slip into the healing hands of sleep.

They were awoken by the deep voice of James Novak.

Todd lifted himself with one arm, wincing slightly as his father engulfed him in a full embrace, tempered by the unapologetic love of a parent castrated by loss.

No longer in control, his father's desperation had undone him. He crushed his son's face with his hands as tears streamed down his face. "After Caleb, I don't think I could have…" he cut himself off and pulled his son close again.

"Sheriff Whaley is here. Do you think you are up to talking?"

"I'm fine, Dad. I figure the sooner I tell them what happened, the more information they will have to find that crazy bitch."

At his response, James looked at Lexi, slightly confused.

She quickly interjected, "Let's let Todd have a chance to tell the police his side of the story."

James nodded, realizing she had not told Todd anything yet. He moved to the door and motioned for Sheriff Whaley to come into the room, stopping him and leaning close, saying something inaudible.

Lexi sat quietly as the sheriff asked questions, allowing Todd to recap the whole story from the night at the bar with his friends until he broke his restraints and found his way to the phone. He intentionally left out some of the intimate details, needing to find the right way and time to share those with his Lexi first. Besides, those were inconsequential to the search anyway.

To Lexi's surprise and relief, Sheriff Whaley did not mention her side of the story to Todd. When they finished their conversation and he headed toward the door to leave, Todd's father asked Lexi to step outside with them.

"Thank you," she whispered.

"I figured this was your story to tell, Lexi," James said, Sheriff Whaley nodding in agreement. "But you have to know this is not your fault. You are as much of a victim of this situation as Todd."

"Sure," she said, avoiding eye contact.

"Look at me," he said with stern, understanding eyes. "This is *not* your fault. Listen, I don't know exactly how you feel, but I do know how it feels to blame yourself for the harm of someone you love. Trust me, nobody knows better than me the temptation to let that guilt eat away at you and separate you from those you love, but you can't let it. You need to understand that you had absolutely no control over this situation. Lexi, you are the best thing to happen to my son. I've seen him become a new man in the wake of your love. Don't let that be damaged by someone you had no knowledge of, much less any control over." He pulled her close to him, kissing the top of her head. "I am as much here for you as I would be for Abby or Todd. There were times I thought I would lose myself in the guilt I harbored over Caleb. The determination and strength of my Veronica kept me from drowning. If you need that lifeboat, remember you have the both of us because we will be forever indebted to you for what you've done for our son. We love you."

Her heart swelled, and she knew she could not speak without her emotions betraying her. She looked at James, his eyes full of pain and understanding, and nodded. "Thank you," was all she was able to get out as the two gentlemen walked away.

Watching them walk down the hall, she knew he, sincerely, understood her pain, but she also knew there was a stark difference in their situations. The Novak family hadn't known how detrimental Caleb's situation was until it was too late. Lexi clearly understood her situation, and she also knew there was something she could do to prevent it.

CHAPTER 54

*L*exi called Mama and Kate as soon as Todd settled back to sleep. Both were relieved he had been found alive but were still wary of Crystal being on the run. Mama asked if the girls had set their protection wards, and Lexi admitted that after the confrontation at the police station, they had forgotten. She promised she would get them set as soon as she had a chance.

"I know this is all new to you, hon, but you cannot wait any longer. Those need to be set directly. You got big powers you ain't learned to control yet, and when gifted folk get emotional, sometimes their magic comes out in crazy ways. There are plenty of varmints in the spiritual world that will follow that power like stink on shit. You have enough problems right now; you don't need some pestering spirit causin' any more chaos than you already have."

"Okay. I'll get them set as soon as possible," said Lexi. "Have you had a chance to think about the dream anymore? Did anything click into place?"

"I reckon I did. I knew that Celtic cross seemed familiar, so I did a little huntin' through Mammy's old stuff and found a picture of the cross in an old cemetery of a family that had all passed. I looked up the family ancestry but didn't find anything that caught my curiosity.

But I also found the name of the schoolteacher with the blue flowered apron, and it turns out she lived in the same holler as the family plot."

"And let me guess," Lexi interrupted, "the house they found Todd in was in the same vicinity."

"Yes, ma'am. Where there's bees, there's honey. I think all them dead bodies you saw must have been because, with no living kin, the TVA never relocated the cemetery. If I were guessing, I'd say your dark lady looked a hot mess because she was none too happy with the way that family's dead were disregarded."

"Wow. I mean, that makes sense, but why would she show me images of things I've never seen?"

"All we can do is guess, but I would say she can only show you the pertinent things she's seen, or maybe she's telling you that if you're gonna stay in our little piece of paradise, you need to get familiar with the land's history."

"Do you have any idea how weird all of this is? I mean, having a stalker kidnap and abuse your boyfriend is... well, beyond fucked up, but communicating with something that has never been alive is a whole different level."

Mama chuckled. "I can imagine it is, but I grew up talkin' to spirits and was taught by generations of women before me, so I sometimes forget not all people were blessed with my education. Trust me, in another year or two, it won't seem so novel to you either, hon."

Lexi wasn't so sure she agreed. "Is there any way we can do a spell or something to locate Crystal?"

"Me and Kate been working on that, but since neither of us knows her, and we don't have anything of hers to use as a compass of sorts, we are coming up blank. I think we're gonna need you here with us to make the connection. But you worry on getting my baby boy healed up and back home. She don't seem like a stupid one, so I'd say she is laying low right now. I doubt she'll be an immediate threat. If she's patient enough to have stayed off your radar this long, I'd say she's smart enough to know too many eyes are looking for her to take any risks."

"This is all so surreal. I'm not sure if I should stay in Tennessee anymore. I brought all this heartache and pain with me and dumped it on you guys. It's not fair to keep everyone in harm's way."

"Now, don't let this girl turn your milk of human kindness into bonnie clabber."

"I don't know what that means," she choked out, caught between tears and laughter.

"It means don't let this Crystal girl turn you sour again. You've put the work in to open your world, and the opportunities followed. Blessings will continue, just as long as you keep strong and don't let her win."

"I am terrified she is going to come back and hurt the people I love."

"I understand, hon. But that is going to happen regardless of where you are. You can't help a bird from flying over your head, but you can keep it from building a nest in your hair. And that's what we're here for, to help you keep that madness out of your life."

Lexi took a long, deep breath and sighed heavily. She knew what Mama was saying, but she was torn.

"I know you're still troubled," said Mama. "So go set them protection wards and enjoy your family while they are here to help you. Once things settle back down a bit, me, you, and Kate will work a cord-cutting to rid you of her emotional attachment. And if that doesn't work, I've got plenty of harsher options if we need 'em. I love you kids, and I promise I won't let nothing happen to either of you."

CHAPTER 55

*L*exi pulled the Jeep into Todd's driveway. She walked around to open his door and helped him out, ignoring the churning dread in her gut.

He smiled and handed the crutches to her as he positioned himself to slide out with only one leg. "You know I can do this on my own, Lexi. It's only a cut on my leg. Growing into a teenager resulted in more devastating injuries." He winked at her, trying to pull her out of the weird mood she had been in since she arrived at the hospital.

She smiled weakly. "Somehow, I doubt that."

His heart lightened as he stepped into his own kitchen. There was a time, back in the Tandy's cellar, when he wasn't sure if he would ever see his house again. It brought back the rush of love he felt for the perplexing woman a step behind him. He whirled around, grabbing her by the waist, heat in his eyes. Pulling her close, countering her weight by leaning against the couch, he pressed his firm lips against hers. He let his tongue search curiously, then more recklessly, until she pulled away.

Running her hands through her hair, she walked toward the kitchen. "Can I get you anything? Maybe something to drink?"

Bewildered, Todd grabbed her hand and pulled her back to him.

"Lexi, what the hell is going on with you? You've been acting weird since I woke up in the hospital. What aren't you telling me?"

"Are you kidding me?" she said, exasperated. "I dropped a huge emotional bomb on you and just left town, and less than a week after, you almost died."

"I had a long time to think about that, and it doesn't change anything about my feelings for you. I love you, but I feel like everyone around me is talking behind my back, and I have no idea what is going on. Honestly, when I look into your eyes lately, I have no idea who I'm looking at. I feel like we've gone back to the first week we met. Jesus, Lexi, please tell me what is going on in that head of yours."

"You need some rest. We can talk about it tomorrow."

"No, we fucking can't! I am not going to bed until you tell me exactly what is going on. Have I ever kept anything from you? Even when I was terrified of your reaction, I was still honest with you. I thought after you told me about your suicidal thoughts, the secrets and lies were over. Spill it."

She looked into his eyes, sighed, and led him to sit on the couch. She cleared her throat, hesitating because she didn't know where to start. "This," she said flatly, lightly running a finger across the bandage on his leg, "is all my fault."

"What are you talking about? What would ever make you—"

"Her name is Crystal."

"Who?"

"The girl who hurt you."

"How do you know that? Did the cops find her and nobody told me?"

"No, she's still out there. They think she may have run back to Cincinnati."

"Cincinnati?"

"Yeah, she was here because of me. As I said, I'm the reason all of this happened to you." She stood back up, grabbing two beers from the refrigerator. "Here, this is a long story, and you're probably gonna need this."

Todd took the drink and settled back into his couch, a wrinkle of confusion forming on his forehead. "So, are you telling me you know this girl?"

Lexi paced from the couch to the back window, picking at the label on her bottle. "I know who she is," she started. "We were never friends or anything, but years ago, we worked at the same company for several months. Crystal was in customer service, so we didn't really work together very often. We'd been in a couple of training classes together, and she shadowed me one day to learn more about my daily job activities. They let her go after only a couple of months for attendance or something. As I said, we didn't work together, so I didn't know she was gone until she started working at the coffee shop across the street from my apartment. I didn't even remember who she was at first." She huffed and shook her head, staring out the back door.

"Okay, I'm confused. Why do you think she was here for you if you didn't know her very well?"

"Somehow, in the last couple of years, I hadn't realized how involved she'd become with my life. Her job at the coffee shop just seemed like a coincidence. Fuck, I even casually bitched to her about my life." She sat back down and looked into Todd's eyes. "Apparently, she has been stalking me for well over a year and I didn't even notice. Remember how I told you I felt like my life was falling apart, and I hadn't felt comfortable in my own skin for the last couple of years?"

He nodded, taking her hands. "Lexi."

She stopped him. "She'd been in my apartment, Todd. She had my email password. She was canceling appointments, stealing my mail; I thought I was losing my mind." A wave of indignation ran through her body, and her hands were shaking. "She had pictures of me. Pictures she'd taken of me at home without my knowledge. I'd unknowingly been completely stripped of my privacy," she said, wiping a tear from her face.

"When? How did you find all of this out?"

"When I went home to pack. I hadn't heard from you, which wasn't too alarming. Then I met a friend from work to pick up the box from my office."

She proceeded to explain everything she had found out in Cincinnati, including her trip to Crystal's house and the stuff from the computer. She told him about seeing Crystal's car in the bank parking lot before she left town, and the security footage Abby found at the grocery. As Lexi spoke, she paced the living room floor, wringing her hands and frequently stopping to keep her emotions in check.

Todd listened quietly, trying not to interrupt as she relayed the events from the past several days.

When she finished, she sat next to him on the couch, staring at the floor.

"Damn," was all Todd could say.

"Yeah," she sighed. "So now you understand why I have to leave."

"Wait, what? What do you mean leave?"

"I can't be here with you; not while she's still out there. None of this would have happened to you if we hadn't met. I wouldn't have been able to live with myself if we hadn't found you. And I'm not willing to take that chance again, not knowing what I know now. The best way for me to keep you safe is to go back to Ohio for a while. It's me that she wants, me that she'll follow."

"No," he said flatly.

"This really isn't your decision to make. It's my mess, I'm the one who needs to clean it up. Besides, the plans have already been made."

"No," he said again, more force in his voice.

Avoiding his eyes, Lexi shook her head and stood up. When she started to walk into the bedroom, he grabbed her arm.

"Sit down," he said sharply. "We're not finished with this conversation."

"There is no..."

"I said sit down, Lexi."

She tried pulling her arm away.

Todd pulled her back to the couch with him. "I let you talk, now it's your turn to sit here and listen."

Surprised by the aggression in his tone, she sat next to him and nodded.

He took her chin and pulled her focus to his face. "I want to look at you while I talk." When he was sure he had her undivided attention, he continued. "Let me start by saying there is no way in hell I am letting you leave my sight."

She started to interrupt, but he reminded her, "You've said your piece; it's my turn now. I spent two days in a dark basement afraid I would never see you again. Nothing that girl did to me —hell, nothing she could have possibly done—could hurt me more than the fear of not having you in my life. Lexi, I know what that kind of loss feels like. I wouldn't let her take you from me then, and I damn sure won't let you take that from me now just because you're scared."

"That's just it, Todd! If you knew there was something you could have done to ensure Caleb was still here, wouldn't you have sacrificed anything to make that happen? Well, I do know what I can do to keep anything else from happening."

"This wasn't your fault."

"How can you say that? If not for me, none of this would have happened," she shouted, swatting at the hot tears on her cheeks.

He pulled her head to his chest, even as she tried to pull away. "Okay, that may be true, but that doesn't mean any of this was your fault. How were you supposed to know some random girl you barely knew was going to do any of this? You're as much of a victim of this situation as I am. And it sounds to me like she's hurt you a hell of a lot more than she hurt me."

Despite herself, Lexi sank into his chest, wrapping her arms around his warm body. The sheer velocity of exhaustion hit her like a wall. In his arms, her façade of strength began to slip. Even knowing she had to leave eventually, she couldn't force herself to let go.

"I'm here," he murmured, running his fingers through her hair. "I'm not going anywhere. I won't let that bitch anywhere near you ever again. God, I was so afraid she would get to you while I was trapped in that stupid room. If I had known what she'd done to you..." But instead of letting his temper flare, he lifted her face to his and kissed her.

"How do you do that?" Lexi said, letting herself ease into his embrace.

"Do what?"

"Disarm me so efficiently. I'm supposed to be taking care of you, keeping you safe, not the other way around."

"You *are* keeping me safe. We're keeping each other safe. I won't let her win by pulling us apart. If we give in to our fears, she will have accomplished what she set out to do. She thought the temptation of sex would be enough to cause a rift in our relationship, and when she realized that wasn't going to work, she got desperate. She underestimated our love, and that will be her demise. Trust me, that girl does *not* have her shit together. She's erratic, controlled by emotion and compulsion. People like her are sloppy, which makes them easier to catch."

"How could I have missed all of this? It's humiliating knowing she had interjected herself into my life for so long, and I hadn't even noticed. She had cameras in my house, Todd; complete access to my world, and I was completely unaware."

"You weren't completely unaware. You knew something was wrong, which is why you ended up here. Crystal obviously didn't give you any reason to think she was anything more than a friendly acquaintance. Hell, she's been here for months and I didn't realize anything was wrong either. If I had listened to you the morning we found that dead cat on your deck, things may have ended differently. I even had a conversation with her, caught more than a glimpse of her crazy, and still managed to get drugged and kidnapped by the girl. We can't sit around blaming ourselves for any of this."

Lexi ran her fingers across the bandage on Todd's leg and the dam of emotions burst. She laid her head in his lap and allowed her body to shake violently with long, painful sobs. The anger and fear festering in her chest over the last few days released a bit.

He held her tight, knowing that the sooner she rid herself of that initial burden, the sooner she would be able to see the situation more clearly.

Eventually, her tight grasp around his waist eased and her breathing steadied itself.

While she slept, Todd processed everything she told him, feeling the knot of anger in his chest tighten.

CHAPTER 56

Todd and Abby left to run errands, so Lexi went back to Kate's to practice focusing her energy and intention.

Alva left her instructions on how to create a confusion doll.

Lexi dug through her laptop case until she found what she was looking for, pulling out a brush and the photoshopped picture of her and Crys she snagged when she'd rummaged through her place. She cut her stalker's face out of the picture and discarded the rest, then pulled just enough of the hair out of the brush to create the personal link, leaving plenty for DNA testing if the cops needed it.

Walking the property, she filled a bowl with red clay, and found two strong, similarly sized branches.

It turned out Kate knew the Tandys, so after the police swept the place, she got permission for her and Lexi to go through what was left of Crystal's stuff. There hadn't been much, but they did find a t-shirt Lexi recognized.

She cut the fabric into strips and added them to her workspace. Before she started, she created a circle of protection using a mixture of salt and brick dust around the kitchen table.

Getting down to work, she focused her intention as she prepared the herbs she'd be using. She mixed a generous amount of poppy and black mustard seed into the clay, letting her hate infuse into the ball she rolled in her palms. Before it dried, she plastered the picture of Crystal's face on so it looked like a doll's head, and pushed some of the hair into the scalp with the athame Alva gifted her at the start of her spiritual journey.

Setting the clay head aside, she focused on the body. Whittling the branches down to a practical size to keep on her person, she placed them in the shape of a cross. Black candle wax held the sticks together, and she pressed the remainder of the hair into the hot wax. Spanish moss and twitch grass were attached, transforming the cross into the beginning of the doll's body. As she wound the strips of fabric from her intended target's shirt, the body of the doll started to come into form.

As she traced the vertical bar of the cross with her right hand, she said aloud, "I name thee Lexi Greer." As she traced the horizontal bar of the cross, she said, "Thou art Crystal Lamothe."

In a small black cauldron on the table, she threw in the poppy seed, black mustard seed, and twitch grass, then lit confusion incense. Holding the doll over the smoke with her left hand, she focused on all the harm Crystal had done over the past years. The righteous rage and desire for justice was palpable. With the same intention, she allowed her words to flow into the doll.

"Inimicus Carpo!

Fazed and flustered

Vexed and addled

Lost in the smoke of delusion

I hold thee firm

Bewildered and bound

Cast into confusion

By word and will addressed to thee

Confusion to Crystal Lamothe be!"

Once the spell had been cast, she could activate the confusion doll at will.

Alva explained that the benefit of this particular poppet was it could be activated from afar, so when Lexi was outside of her warded spaces of protection, she could use the doll to disorient Crystal long enough to escape.

Lexi set the doll aside, closed her sacred circle, and started to return herbs back to Kate's apothecary cabinet. She brushed the remains of her work into the cauldron and disposed of them in the outdoor firepit. Her focus had been so singular and intense, she hadn't heard Kate's car pull up. She yelped as her friend walked into the kitchen from the backyard.

"I see you have been practicing," Kate said approvingly. "Do you have a plan for keeping the confusion doll on your person at all times?"

"I hadn't gotten that far yet."

"Wait here. I think I have just the thing." When she returned, she handed Lexi a small pouch. "Put it in here and tie it shut, then you can knot one of the ties and attach it to a carabiner. That way, you can hook the carabiner to your pants, purse, jacket, etc. Appalachian ingenuity meets modern application," she laughed.

"Genius," Lexi agreed, and clipped the poppet to her purse. She leaned in to hug her friend and jumped when their touch created a static shock.

"Girl, you might as well be glowing with all that power. It is truly a sight to behold. I can't wait to see you once you've learned to crank it up full tilt, and I feel blessed I get to be beside you for the journey." Kate beamed at the young root worker.

"That felt good. I feel powerful, although I didn't do anything major."

"Anytime you practice your craft, you *are* doing something major. You are connecting with your divine feminine and these ancient mountains. Do you know how old the Appalachian Mountains are? They are over a billion years old, the oldest mountain range in North America. Just think about that. Think of how many ancient secrets they hold; how long their power has been changing and building. And that magic chose you, Lexi. If that isn't major, I don't know what is."

"I didn't realize the Appalachian Mountains were that old. I would have thought the Rocky Mountains were older because they are so much bigger in scale."

"Time has worn them down. These magnificent mountains are older than trees, oceans, dinosaurs, limestone, and even bones. That's why you won't find many fossils except that of ocean life. Scientists even say that the emergence of the Appalachian Mountains may have triggered an ice age. It's insane if you think about time in a linear path. I encourage you to do your research and learn about the territory you have now claimed as home."

"Oh, I can assure you I'll be doing my research. That makes me love this place that much more. Is that why Alva told me to use the local clay to make the confusion doll?"

"Your magic is definitely stronger for it. One of the hallmarks of Appalachian Folk Magic is its diversity. Practices don't just vary from region to region and hill to holler, but each person in touch with the magics in these mountains has practices unique to their family lineage or their mentors. It's not a closed-door practice like many organized magical religions, so each healer or root worker may use the magic steeped in these mountains differently. The thing that ties us together, from each of the thirteen states these mountains call home, is the power we gain from them and the love and respect we give back in return."

"Wow. I mean, I knew this part of the world was special, and I could sense the depth of wisdom in the local energy, but I had no idea. How can we use that magic to eliminate Crystal? Between the three of us, I'm sure we could end her."

"Now, hold on a minute. Appalachian magic doesn't abide by the rule of three, as in many magical circles. Back when our ancestors settled in this area, the logistics of these mountains made life extremely hard. Often, our folk magic was the only power we had over the greedy with no morals, and they weren't averse to using it against someone wishing them harm, but Alva gave you the confusion doll to work for a reason. We want all paths that lead to our desired outcome to hurt as few as possible. This spell gives you protection without damning the intended to death. In our practice, elimination is the last resort. People who go down the dark side of the path tend to bring dark spirits into their world, and those spirits are not easy to work with, especially if you don't know what you're doing."

"This isn't a last resort? That crazy bitch tortured Todd, and I have no doubt she would have killed him if she'd gotten the chance. Don't you think she deserves the same?"

"What she deserves is a whole different matter. Have you ever intentionally ended someone's life?"

"Well, no, obviously not."

"That's a spiritual burden we hope to keep from anyone. Many people believe in an eye for an eye around these parts, but we have found taking a gentler route with our magic has kept the peace and brought more positive blessings into our community."

Lexi wasn't convinced, and it must have shown on her face.

"Don't worry, darlin'. If it ever comes down to a battle for life, we will pull out our full arsenal."

CHAPTER 57

*L*exi's parents showed up first thing in the morning. Todd enjoyed meeting everyone but wanted to give them some privacy with their daughter. Knowing Lexi would not be alone, he took the opportunity to talk to his sister about what really happened while he was locked in that damn room, and how he should play his next move.

Todd and Abby sat across from one another at Mama's.

"I don't know what to do, Abs. She's pulled back again and won't let me in."

"It's only been a couple of days. Lexi just had her world turned upside down again. I was there when she opened that computer file. She turned completely white. Did she show you the pictures?"

"No, and I haven't pushed. I figured she would show me when she was ready."

"I wouldn't expect her to show you any time soon. I don't know if I would share them with anyone. These weren't just pictures of her in the kitchen, Todd. These were pictures of her in very intimate and private situations. And I'm not talking just one or two either, I'm talking folders. Her in the bathtub, in her bed, you get what I'm saying?"

Todd's face dropped in shock. "Damn."

"Yeah, some heavy shit, dude. And what about when the cops catch this chick? All that shit will be evidence, won't it? How many people are going to be looking at those pictures? I don't know if they'll even be able to use any of it since it was illegally obtained. And if they can't use it, what physical proof do they have for the stalking charges?"

"They'll be able to make a case for the kidnapping. Maybe they won't need to use any of it."

"Even to get the conviction for kidnapping, don't they have to prove a motive? I don't know, but I know how I would feel about it if I were her. She's been raped of her privacy. Did she tell you the bitch was fucking her ex-boyfriend too?"

"She mentioned it, said that's how she found the house where she got the computer files."

"Apparently, every time he and Lexi would start to get close, Crystal would swoop in and mess things up. Lexi thought it was because she wasn't worth loving, I guess, that she wasn't good enough or something. And this was just one of the guys. If this has been going on for years, you know there have been other guys. It's a damn wonder she trusted you to begin with."

"I'm going to kill that crazy bitch," Todd hissed.

"Let the police handle that part of it. Trust me, I want to kill the bitch too, but it's your job to take care of Lexi, and you can't do both right now. Dad's got plenty of people working to find her, and we have your testimony, Lexi's testimony, and the tape from the grocery store. There's plenty to hang her with once we find her. Your woman needs you now, Todd, more than she's probably ever needed anything. Remember how hard it was after you found Caleb? It's going to take some time before she's able to talk about it."

Todd teared up and smiled weakly at his sister, nodding in agreement. His face was contorted in a mixture of temper and grief, which gashed a hole in his sister's heart.

She squeezed his hand. "How are you? You've been through some serious shit too."

"Frankly, I don't know. It all seems so surreal, you know? Waking up in that dark room, having no clue where I was or why I was there..." His voice trailed off momentarily, his pride stopping him from going any further. "She tried to seduce me, but I wasn't sure what she was trying to get out of me, so nothing I said appeased her. It was all so confusing. And she was really getting off on playing with that knife, let me tell ya. Not only on me, but she'd use it on herself too. Like it helped her direct her anger or something. Then, when she realized her plan wasn't going to work, she completely lost it, threatening Lexi. At that point, I knew my girl was in danger, so I did what I had to do to get to her." He absently rubbed the bandages on his wrists.

"You're lucky she didn't kill you!"

"I knew she would when she came back."

Abby shivered. "Thank god I was on that couch when she came to the house. I just wish I hadn't fallen over that stupid table. If I had gotten outside sooner, she wouldn't still be out there."

"I'm just glad you guys are safe. Did I tell you she admitted that she almost killed herself? It was the reason she ended up here."

"Shit, Todd. How do you feel about that?"

"When she first left, I wasn't sure I could take that kind of risk. I was hurt she'd kept it from me for so long, but after everything that happened, her love is worth it. Life is short and I've spent too much of it pushing people away."

The two were sitting in quiet thought when Mama walked up to the table. "Okay, I've let you two sit here wallowing in seriousness long enough. My late husband always used to tell me that focusing on the bad stuff when you have more than enough happiness was a waste of time and energy. I have some of my own magic brewing to handle Lexi's stalker. You kids have worried this old lady enough for a lifetime lately. Since you're all safe and only slightly damaged," she said, looking at Todd's battered body and snorting, "it's time to focus on the happy. Have you bought that girl an engagement ring yet?"

Todd pulled his friend into the booth with him and squeezed her until she squealed, laying a big kiss on her lips. "You know, once I put a ring on her finger, I'm off the market. And you won't be able to talk me into a torrid affair afterward either, so this is your last chance to steal me away!"

She pushed him off, straightened her apron, and whistled. "As temptin' as that is, honey, I am way more woman than you could ever handle!" Leaning over and kissing his head, she laughed. "I love you, kids!"

CHAPTER 58

Crystal was mindless with panic and anger as she drove around the curvy back roads to evade the cops, navigating the unfamiliar holler until the dirt road ran into the water, revealing a cove of the lake unseen from the roads above, which was, apparently, used as a dumping ground.

A local radio station informed her that her prisoner escaped his restraints and called for help. Apparently, someone had fed Lexi a bunch of bullshit about Crystal being a stalker, so both local and Cincinnati police were tracking her.

She switched the plates on her car and grabbed supplies from some shithole mom-and-pop bait shop before news of the event got around, but they still had the description of her car. That's how she found herself surrounded by old tires, broken appliances, and years of trash these hillbilly fuckers were too lazy to take to a real dump; or maybe that was the place to dump things you never wanted to be found again. Either way, the irony was not lost on her.

Her shoes sank into the mud as she stepped out to see the giant gully of red clay eroded by weather and the lapping lakeshore. The amount of trash was almost unimaginable—everything from old TV sets and a rusted-out car, to bags upon bags of human trash. Unsure which smell triggered her gag reflex more, the smell of dead fish or burnt rubber, she instinctively covered her nose and mouth. But it wasn't the revulsion of humanity's disregard for Mother Nature that troubled her the most. It was the shadows whispering words that she could almost understand. That was a place where the dead were neglected and the land was desecrated.

THE CAR'S headlights were her only source of light, clouds obstructing any celestial glow. The fuel leaking into the water created an opalescent film, which made movement detectable even a healthy distance from the shoreline. As she poked through other people's discarded lives with a stick, a cacophony of small scavengers erupted around her, and she found herself face-to-face with a giant raccoon.

It hissed and barked at her, so she moved closer. The snarling critter grabbed a chicken bone and chucked it at Crystal.

Its insolent attitude both amused and pissed her off, so she picked up a large rock and nailed it in the head, causing the thing to stumble backward into the water.

Immediately, the pressure around her increased, and as her ears popped, a sudden typhoon of emotion slammed into her all at once. Apart from rage and obsession, her emotional toolbox had always been dull, sometimes barely present at all.

Movement in the rotted vegetation alerted her to a large slithering creature. The unfamiliarity of terror filled her entire body with thousands of tiny electric shocks under her skin. An involuntary, ear-splitting scream released from somewhere deep within her.

What in the fuck is happening to me? she thought, trying unsuccessfully to regain control of herself. Every thought sparked another visceral emotion she'd never experienced before, leaving her squatting with her hands over her ears, rocking back and forth as she sobbed herself into hyperventilation.

Her focus on Lexi calmed her enough to semi-regulate her breathing. Once she got control of herself, Crystal ran back to the car and locked herself in.

Luckily, fall weather in the region couldn't make up its mind, so it was still warm well into October. Unshocked that her shit life had prepared her for no better option, she turned off the car engine and tried to settle in for a restless sleep until morning presented a better option.

She lay in the backseat with the windows rolled down when an eerie quiet rolled over her hideaway; the only thing she heard was her breathing. All of the scampering scavengers had fled, and the insects and frogs who sung her to sleep were completely silent.

She nearly jumped out of her skin when she heard three loud cracks. Sitting up, she saw a beautiful, anorexic, raven-haired woman wearing a white dress standing ankle-deep in the water. Crystal stared at the woman, perplexed at how she'd gotten there without making a soft footfall or even a gentle splash, then fear hit Crystal like a kick in the cunt.

Before she had time to speak to the woman, a wild hungry grin spread across her face, and the red car slipped into neutral, rolling toward the water. Just as the tires splashed into the lake, the woman flew at her, through the windshield, and wrapped her spindly arms and legs around Crystal, squeezing her into complete submission as water began seeping into the car. The bitch was like a boa constrictor, and every time Crystal tried to squirm free, the foul thing squeezed tighter.

"Your intention to take something beautiful and hollow it out until it is just a husk reminds me of the one who stole so many years of my own existence," she hissed, flicking her forked tongue at the girl's ear. "For such grievances, I have granted your worst fear, the full spectrum of emotion. As I slowly end your life, you'll endure all the pain and chaos you've created over that lifetime."

Crystal's scream remained silent in her gaping maw, as she had just enough air to barely breathe. Her face contorted as she was assaulted by memory after memory of her past sins triggering guilt, disgust, and fear. However, the further back she went into her childhood, the more she recognized sadness, loneliness, and loss. Remembering her mother's abandonment, the way her stepdad used her for his own greedy needs, and the fact she would never get her fairytale ending with Lexi sparked her strongest emotion, rage.

The car rolled, gaining momentum from the weight of the water, until the lake rushed in through the open car windows. As the car sank, the dark lady plunged her slimy black tongue down Crystal's throat. There were no screams as they slowly submerged.

Crystal writhed in pain, enveloped in claustrophobic terror as the lake swallowed the car. The mix of righteousness, untethered rage, and fear can be a dangerous combination.

CHAPTER 59

*L*exi walked back to the house, the weight of her board sinking her steps, causing gravel to dig into the bottom of her feet. Her family had gone back to their hotel, and she needed the solitude of the water. The sun was still high in the sky, but the pull toward late afternoon was pending.

Her mother had been adamant that Lexi stay with Todd at the lake, insisting she would be safer away from Cincinnati. She made some valid points. It was more than likely Crystal was headed away from town, and Todd had already called to have a true security system installed on both his and Kate's properties, not just a spiritual one.

It amazed her how quickly things got done when you threw a little money at it. Ultimately, she conceded, logic reigning over her initial knee-jerk reaction. But she felt much safer staying at Kate's place since it hadn't seemed to Todd that Crystal knew Lexi had moved there.

Lexi propped her board against the house, peeled off her wetsuit, and grabbed a water from the kitchen. After throwing on a pair of pajama pants and one of Todd's long-sleeve t-shirts, she plopped down to enjoy the sounds of the fall afternoon. Although she tried to relax, her nerves would not let the sense of anxious nausea settle. She could not keep from scanning the property line and the lakefront for unfamiliar shapes. The knife she refused to be without sat on the table beside her. The first thing they did when they got home was inspect the entire house for video or listening devices. She would have to talk to Todd about helping her get her conceal and carry license, wondering if she would ever feel safe again.

The fear of never seeing Todd again was replaced by a consuming anger over the atrocities done to him. This, coupled with the desecration of her privacy, left her cold, distant, and vindictive. She wanted to hunt the deranged stalker down and torture her, death seeming too easy a punishment. The emotions both frightened and disturbed her; she had never been a vengeful person. Still, the anger boiled inside her, and she feared it would permanently change her if they never found Crystal. She thought of all those people she had seen on the ID Channel, able to find forgiveness for their abductors or their children's murderers. The idea was unfathomable to her.

When the back door slammed shut, she jumped so hard she knocked her drink off the table and went straight for the knife. Whirling around, she saw Todd and Abby walking into the kitchen laughing, and she pushed down the pang of envy, followed quickly by irritation, and then shame.

"Hey Lexi, where's the family?" Todd asked casually.

"I wasn't much company, so they decided to head back to the hotel." She heard the snap in her voice and winced.

"Did you take the board out?"

"Yeah, you know it usually calms me down, but I still feel the storm raging inside me."

He settled into the seat beside her, pulling her closer to him. "I'm sorry, beautiful. How can I make it better?"

"Until that psychotic bitch is caught, I don't think it can be made better."

"Well, can't stop me from trying. Mama told me to tell you hi, and she sent you home some dinner. Do you want me to have Abs warm it up for you?"

"No. Besides, I need to shower anyway." She rose and walked silently past him, shutting the bathroom door.

Once Todd heard the shower running, he looked at his sister. "I don't know what to do. She's pushing me out."

"She probably is. Keep reminding yourself of how we were after Caleb left. She'll come around, it just takes time. She's probably terrified Crystal's coming back. You did notice the knife and the overturned drink, right? All you can do is be there when she needs to talk or be held. We need to find something to distract her. Maybe we should call Mom and invite Lexi's family out to the house for the weekend. I know Mom would love having everyone there for a big family dinner. They have plenty of room for everyone to stay, so we'll all get heavy on the booze and numb ourselves for the evening!"

"That's genius, Abs," he said, kissing his sister. "You call Mom and tell her what we want to do, and I'll go talk to Lexi." He stopped, grabbing her shoulders, face full of emotion. "I'm so glad you are home. You know how much I love you, right?"

She smirked. "Go sweet-talk your woman, dumbass. I love you too!"

It took an impressive amount of persuasion. Still, Todd convinced Lexi they all needed a night with their families, promising there would be no talk of recent events, and her parents had been called and were thrilled with the idea of the blended family evening. Addresses and directions were exchanged, and the excitement in her mother's voice warmed her heart. Maybe that was what they all needed.

CHAPTER 60

*T*odd's Jeep vibrated as they drove. Lexi was in the front seat while Abby sang in the back at the top of her lungs.

With the top down, music blaring, and the cheerful disposition of her companions, Lexi couldn't help but relax a little. Winding through the country roads, the crisp air reminded her how much she loved the summer and fall seasonal change. She breathed the clean, fragrant air and let herself enjoy the moment.

The playful banter between siblings amused her. It was the first time she'd seen them in their own element. Their ease with one another was an unmistakable expression of their closeness.

Abby was telling a story about Todd, his middle school girlfriend, and an unfortunate incident involving a snot bubble induced by laughter. Todd was swatting at his sister while her laughter sent her into tearful fits.

He noticed Lexi's smile and the vice grip choking his heart over the last couple of days loosened. He didn't care if Abby divulged all his embarrassing moments if it would keep that smile on her face, though he was not about to sit back without a little retaliation. "So, that's how you're gonna play this, huh?"

Abby giggled, scooting closer to the door and pulling her knees into her lap so her brother couldn't reach her. "Oh, that's just the beginning."

"In that case, let me tell you about the time Abby took her boyfriend, Bruce, to see the movie *30 Days of Night.*"

"You would not! That's not even on the same level of embarrassing, Todd."

"Don't forget you started this game, knowing all too well how formidable an opponent I am." He glanced over at Lexi. "So, Abs hadn't been dating this dude very long, but she had been crushing on him for months before he'd asked her out. She's kind of a chicken when it comes to horror movies, especially the ones with well-timed jump scares. That night she hadn't been feeling very well, but wanting to impress Mr. Dreamy, she agreed to go see the movie he'd chosen."

"You know payback is a bitch, right?" She groaned and covered her face with her hand, laughing despite herself.

"Well, there's this part in the movie where vampires jump from under the buildings to grab the humans, which made Abs jump. Unfortunately, she was in the process of swallowing some popcorn, and the scare caused a piece of popcorn to get stuck in the back of her throat."

"I hate you!"

"You love me. Now, here's where things go downhill fast." He had to stop talking for a minute to get his giggles under control. "Well, that cough caused an unmistakable fart to slip from my dear sister's ass."

"Oh no, Abby! You must have been mortified," Lexi said.

"Oh, that wasn't even the worst part." Todd's laughter was full blown, and he struggled to get the rest of the story out in between breaths. "Remember, our dear Abby hadn't been feeling well that night, so more than air escaped her body as she sat next to Mr. Dreamy."

"You can't even begin to imagine the panic that hit me. We were right in the middle of the aisle, so I had to waddle past 5 or 6 people to get out, and it took everything I had not to run out of the theater. Once I got to the bathroom, I didn't know what to do, so I stripped off my panties, tossed them in the trash, and tried to clean myself up. I couldn't face Bruce, who must have been completely horrified and unsure about what he had just seen."

"Or smelled!" Todd laughed harder.

"Ugh, or smelled. I called Todd and made him come and get me, leaving Bruce to fend for himself. Luckily, he left to go back to college a couple of weeks after I'd ditched him, so I didn't have to face him again. Seriously, I'm still traumatized. And can you imagine the stories he told his buddies when he got back to school? Thank god he went to college all the way on the west coast."

"The following Christmas, Dad got her a box of Depends. It was truly a classic moment."

Laughter filled the car as they pulled into the driveway. For a brief moment, the fear and worry were forgotten, and they just enjoyed the moment.

When Abby saw the couple holding hands in the front seat, she grinned at her brother in the rearview mirror. It may only be for the night, but she was happy "Operation Distraction" was off to a good start.

The smell of soup filled the kitchen while the mothers cleaned and chopped veggies.

Todd squeezed Lexi's hand before he let it go to wrap his arms around his mom's thin frame, causing her to sling water everywhere. Laughing, he kissed her and turned to Lexi's mom, "Good evening, Mrs. Greer."

"Please, call me Caroline. We're not big on formalities in our family."

"Perfect, neither are we. When did you guys get here?"

"Your mom called and invited us to come on over a couple of hours ago. Your dad wanted to take Mickey out on the boat, so he nearly pushed me out the door to get here," she laughed. "Your mom and I have been drinking her tasty, and rather potent, lemonade, enjoying the sunset from the pool area. The men should be back anytime."

Todd looked over at Lexi, both delighted with the way their

parents seemed to be warming up to each other. "Do you need our help with anything?"

"No, darling, why don't you kids go sit down and relax while we finish dinner and get to know each other a little better? The bar's stocked, and Dad ordered some finger foods from town, which are out there too. Besides, you don't need to be on that leg anyway. Abs, would you go pour Caroline and me another lemonade?"

Todd led Lexi to the back of the house. The large picture windows were propped open, and a fire was blazing in the fireplace of the outdoor patio. His mom had the music going, heat lamps lit at each outside corner of the space, making the atmosphere perfect. The sense of home wrapped him like a blanket, and he was thrilled to have both families together.

"What do you want to drink?"

"I think I want wine, actually." Lexi sat on the sofa, pulling her legs beneath her to get comfortable. She sighed and felt the tension in her muscles begin to soften, so she reached for the wine and took a drink. "This is great."

"Dad pulled out the big guns tonight. He must be aiming to impress your parents."

"Trust me, the house alone is more than impressive. I can't wait to hear what they have to say about tonight. Did you see how easy our moms seemed around each other? If I hadn't known better, I would have thought they'd been friends for years."

"I know. Your parents are great, though, so it only makes sense that they get along." He settled in next to her, his arm around her shoulder. When she snuggled close, relief washed over him.

"I'm sorry," she whispered.

"You have nothing to be sorry about, babe. I'm here whenever you need me, and I'll still be here even when you don't want me around. Healing isn't a cookie-cutter process, and it can't be rushed. I just need to know that you won't push me away or shut me out. I know I'm gonna need you around to pull me up when I fall. I hope you let me do the same for you."

"You already have." She turned his chin and lured him in for a soft kiss.

His arms wrapped around her waist, holding her close to him. He trailed a finger down her spine and smiled under her lips when he felt a shiver shoot through her.

"Eh, hum," a male voice said.

The couple froze, looking over simultaneously to find both of their fathers standing beside them. Todd fumbled to put a little distance between himself and Mickey's only daughter while Lexi simply buried her head in his chest, bursting into laughter.

"Smooth," smirked James, his eyebrows raised at his son.

"Um, hello, Mr. Greer. Lexi and I were just..."

"Calm down, son. I'm pretty sure my daughter is smart enough to take care of herself. Besides, I haven't heard that particular laugh in a very long time. You keep that laugh in my life, and I might even let you call me Mickey."

Lexi looked up sheepishly at her father. "Hi, Daddy. Hi, James. How was the boat?"

Her father's face lit up, and he launched into a story while Todd's father poured them both a whiskey.

"Did you know you can see the University of Tennessee's Neyland Stadium from the river? James was telling me that on home game weekends, hundreds of boats will all tie up together and tailgate before games. They call it the VOL Navy. He invited your mom and me to come down and go to a game. I know you aren't the biggest football fan, but you and Todd should go with us. There's a restaurant by the river with a big patio, so you could hang out there while the rest of us are at the game," said Mickey.

Right then, Abby burst out from the French doors, turning up the music, still singing at the top of her lungs. She pulled Lexi to her feet, swinging her around, giving her no choice but to dance along.

Todd and James shook their heads, accustomed to Abby's dance party antics.

Abby beamed when Mickey cut in, spinning her around the patio until she howled her delight into the night sky.

The conversation throughout dinner was natural and relaxed. There was no mention of malicious stalkers, pending investigations, or kidnapping. Parents told stories to embarrass their children, and children compared stories of parental guidance gone wrong. The food was delicious, and the libations flowed freely. Happiness was in abundance, and everyone appreciated its luxury.

CHAPTER 61

After dinner, everyone migrated back to the patio.

Abby lowered the lights and the music so they could enjoy the fire and hear the water lull in the distance. She was playing bartender, keeping Lexi engrossed in a conversation about the importance of sports-themed movies in contemporary society.

Mickey and James were lounging next to them, discussing a recent business venture.

Todd insisted on staying inside to help Caroline and Veronica clear the table, and although she had offered to help as well, Lexi was swiftly ushered back outside by Abby.

Lexi was no longer listening to Abby's ramblings, but still nodded in feigned interest, enjoying the harmony of the moment. She had been fighting to control her emotions for a lifetime, so when Lexi recognized the relief from her lifted anger, even if only for one evening, she felt silent tears fill her eyes. Nonchalantly wiping them away, she thought herself unnoticed by her slightly inebriated company. At least until she turned to find Todd staring, hands tucked carelessly in his pockets.

He didn't go to her, just leaned against the door frame and offered her a knowing look, lips tilted slightly upward and expression soft.

Taken by the tenderness and love on his face, everything else faded out, and her full attention was on him. She exhaled a soft laugh and shook her head at him.

From somewhere behind her, she heard Abby instructing the men to come with her to help the women finish up in the kitchen.

As the party migrated back into the house, Lexi's eyes never left Todd's.

Todd had been watching his enchanting soulmate as her focus slowly shifted from his sister's conversation to somewhere else. His first instinct was to worry she drifted back into the darkness she surrounded herself with lately, but the emotions he read on her face were relaxed and content. He watched her fear and anger slowly slip away, so when she finally noticed him standing there, he simply waited for her, and once everyone else left, she walked toward him, looking almost shy and embarrassed.

She had let her hair back down after their drive, and the dim lights reflected the blonde left from the summer's sun. Her cutoff shorts exposed tan skin, drawing his eyes over her bare legs and up to the long sleeve, pink t-shirt doing nothing to hide the chill of the evening. As his eyes surveyed her approvingly, she did not bother to stop the tears.

He grabbed her hand and pulled her toward the river. "Come with me."

She hesitated.

Before she could protest, he said, "Trust me, Lexi, Dad has so much security here tonight, a Navy Seal officer would be hard-pressed to surface without being noticed. We'll only go as far as you feel comfortable." He led her to a patio closer to the water.

The night sky was littered with stars, and the full moon twinkled off the moving river. A breeze plucked dead leaves from the trees overhead and delicately laid them on the damp stone at the couple's feet.

Lexi's grip on Todd's hand loosened, knowing they were clearly visible under the security lights.

"I was hoping I could steal a little of your attention without the watchful eyes of your dad. I'm not gonna lie, he's a little intimidating."

She laughed. "You have no idea how much he will relish in the fact that he made you feel uncomfortable. He usually doesn't get the opportunity. There's really not been many men in my life worth the introduction."

"I'm glad I made the cut."

She turned to him, her blue eyes shimmering in the light. "Thank you for tonight."

"Hey, you brought this family together the night you decided to trust me. Besides, that's what families do, they hold each other up. Then all we have to do is feed a little booze to Abs and watch the antics unfold."

"It's been so good watching you two together. That girl's a trip. Is there a shy bone in her body?"

"Nope, that's one of the things I love about my Abs; she wears her emotions on the outside for everyone to see. If she's ever quiet or subdued, it either means she's irate and ready to blow, or she's plotting something. She's like a toddler. When things get quiet, it's time to see what kind of trouble she's found. She fell instantly in love with you, you know."

"I can't imagine why. I've been a mess of nerves and raw emotion since she picked me up at the airport."

"In her eyes, you are the personification of strength. And the fact that your dad is not only a willing, but also skilled, dance partner doesn't hurt your cause."

"Those two could be dangerous together," she laughed.

Lexi shivered, and Todd pulled her into his embrace.

No matter how close she snuggled, it didn't seem enough. Desire, entwined with her need to feel his reassuring touch, nudged at her all evening. When he leaned in to kiss her, she let herself get lost in the moment. She needed him with parts of herself she never knew existed. Maybe that was what it meant to have a soulmate.

She pulled away, brushing her thumb across his temple. "I seriously don't know what I would have done if anything more had happened to you. You can't imagine how terrified I was or how help-less I felt."

"Trust me, I have an idea," he said.

"Yeah, I guess you do."

"Listen, I actually brought you out here for a reason. I need you to do something for me."

"What do you need? You know I'd do anything for you."

"That's what I'm counting on. After that little scare when we came home from the hospital, I need some reassurance that you're never going to try and run away from me again."

"I wasn't running away from *you*, Todd. I was doing the only thing I knew to do to keep you safe. My world was spinning, and it was the only thing I could do to regain some kind of control."

"I know you wanted to protect me, but the moment you told me you loved me was the moment *your* decisions became *our* decisions. So, I have something for you, a constant reminder of sorts, in case you try to make any other crazy decisions without me."

He pulled a small, navy velvet box from his pocket and opened it. Nestled inside was an antique Victorian engagement ring, centered with an exquisite emerald of impressive clarity and encircled in small diamonds.

Lexi looked at the ring, then back to Todd, in stunned silence.

"This was my great-grandmother's engagement ring. From the stories I've been told, she and my great-grandfather had quite the whirlwind love story as well. I mean, it didn't involve stalkers or kidnappings, but then again, ours is a love story beyond compare." He took the ring from the box and slipped it on her finger. "I've known I wanted to give you this ring since you left for Ohio. I was waiting to plan a wildly romantic and memorable situation to give it to you. It took a feisty old lady to remind me I would be an idiot to waste one more minute waiting for the right time. Every moment we are together is perfect, and I need reassurance that I will have a lifetime of those opportunities with you. Lexi Greer, will you marry me?"

She looked at her hand and tried to swallow the lump in her throat. She was swamped with emotions: love, hope, pride, longing, need. She needed him and knew, undoubtedly, her life would forever be a partnership with this perfect man. The waterworks, once again, flowed freely as she enveloped him within her embrace. "It's perfect! Leave it to you."

"You did the seducing, lady. I simply gave you a reminder of the promise I made you that first night we steamrolled over the friend zone," he said.

"This afternoon, before you and Abby got home, I was lost in my head again, jumping at shadows, afraid holding onto you was unfair of me, and spilling over with frustration and fury. Then, within hours, you've, once again, saved me from myself. This ring means a lot more to me than just a reminder. I don't know how I'll ever be able to give back as much as I seem to take."

"Sweetheart, you taught me to love again, to trust again. That's an irreplaceable gift. One I will forever be indebted to you for." He leaned over to kiss her, wanting more but knowing there was a room full of women upstairs dying to cause a scene. "How about we go upstairs and let everyone fuss over us, so I can finally have you all to myself for the night?"

CHAMPAGNE CORKS WERE POPPED, and tears of elation were shed. Hugs and laughter were in abundance.

Abby sang and forced everyone to dance, allowing herself to be merrily led around the makeshift dance floor by each man in attendance.

In the wake of devastation, the families chose to celebrate life, and Lexi sat on the sofa, smiling at her surroundings. She looked up when she felt a steady hand on her shoulder.

"Hey, baby girl."

"Hey, Daddy."

"I know I'm not supposed to ask, but how are you?"

"It's okay, you can ask. I'm glad everyone forced me to get out tonight. I think this is the first time I've been able to breathe in a week."

"Good. I have to say, when you came home talking about moving to Tennessee and telling us about the amazing guy you met, especially after we hadn't talked to you in months, I thought you'd lost your mind. But after seeing the way Todd looks at you, and meeting his family, I can see you've instead found everything you deserve."

"Crazy how that happened, isn't it? But you have always told me that once I quit looking for all the answers, they would find me."

He took her hand and squeezed it tight. "I'm sorry I didn't see how much you were hurting before you left. I guess I was just..." he paused, looking for the right words.

"Daddy, stop. You didn't see it because I didn't let you see. I was trapped in my own madness for a while, and it took stepping away from all I knew to find my way back. Luckily, I met a handsome man who was smart enough to let me uncover that path on my own. He was kinda like my flashlight, I guess."

"Well, I'm glad you finally had sense enough to use one," he said, laughing.

"Me too," she said.

Lexi leaned her head on her father's shoulder as he wrapped a warm arm around her, and she let herself sink into the bliss of the evening.

Todd looked over at Lexi and her dad, a warm smile enveloping his face. The night felt right; exactly where they all needed to be. When the song "Forever" by Ben Harper came over the sound system, he walked over to his beautiful bride-to-be and asked for a dance.

Her dad kissed the top of her head and let her go.

She reached for Todd's hand, nestling herself into him, carefully avoiding his injured leg. He whispered lyrics into her ear while they slowly swayed with the music. When the song ended, the couple said their goodnights, and he led her upstairs to his childhood bedroom.

He lay on the bed, watching her methodically remove her make-up. She wore nothing but a tiny tank top and panties, and his eyes lazily perused her body. The tension she had been wearing since he woke up in the hospital was gone. However, he still noticed the occasional sigh of worry she made when she didn't have complete control of a situation. As she finished brushing her teeth, his eyes fell on the ring on her finger, and he had a sudden, desperate hunger for her.

She gave him a side-eye. "You can get those naughty thoughts out of your head, Mr. Novak. You are in no shape for such activities."

His voice was low and determined. "I want to touch you."

She blushed, despite herself, and felt her body tense as she walked toward him.

His lids were heavy with desire, and as soon as she was close enough, he tugged her onto the bed, his hands firm and demanding. As she began to protest, he silenced her with his kiss and groaned with satisfaction at her surrender. His fingertips slid under her shirt, slowly and intentionally, until she stopped him.

He propped himself on his elbow and traced the contours of her body. "You are so tempting. How is a man expected to control himself around you?"

"Oh, I don't know, giant flesh wounds?"

"Oh yeah, that. Can't stop a man from admiring the woman he's going to marry. I just need to have you close so I'll know when I wake up that this wasn't all just a dream."

Lexi shifted as he spooned his body around hers, blanketing her bare skin with his, and she drifted to sleep with the whisper of his slumbering breath in her ear.

CHAPTER 62

*L*exi's eyes slowly peeled open, and she looked for Todd. As her eyes adjusted, the familiarity of her own house washed over her, and she settled back onto the couch. The quiet was only interrupted by the low hum from the refrigerator, trying desperately to lull her back into the peacefulness of sleep. But her mind was sluggish, and a tugging sense of dread descended on her like a shroud. As she sat up, a muffled murmur coming from the bedroom caught her attention.

The door was closed, casting a thin frame of light into the living room. Lexi stilled herself, listening closer, trying to determine if she had really heard a noise. She heard another and saw a shadow pass behind the door. Panic seized her even before she understood her alarm.

"Todd," she whispered, "is that you?"

No response.

"Todd?"

She slowly crept toward the door, and as she neared closer, she heard the click of the doorknob releasing the latch, and light slowly flooded into the room. The rustling of fabric and a soft moan came from inside, so she inched forward. As she rounded the corner, she immediately froze. The light in the bedroom spilled from the closet, and lying on the bed, she saw her fiancé, arms and legs bound with barbed wire, blood puddling on the sheets. He was gagged, his eyes swollen and full of fear. She peered through the shadows in the room, but Todd was alone. When she stepped inside, his eyes widened, and he tried to nod his head.

"I wouldn't do that if I were you," a taunting voice called from the closet. "It's your fault he's in this situation. Do you really want it to be your fault he dies?" Crystal stepped from the closet wearing one of Lexi's sundresses, holding a gun in one hand and a knife in the other.

"What's going on? Crystal, what are you doing here?"

"Come on, Lexi, you know why I'm here. Did you think I wouldn't know about your little trip back to Cincinnati? I mean, I did find you all the way here on Norris Lake, a trip you kept secret from everyone. In fact, there hasn't been a single decision made over the last few years that I haven't known about and discreetly guided you through. I'd honestly hoped it wouldn't come to this, but I'm tired of waiting for you to make the right decision. It's time you and I take this relation-ship to the next level, and the only way to do that is to eliminate all distractions."

She pulled the knife across Todd's arm, watching with satisfaction as the skin separated and blood began to flow. He cried out in pain beneath the gag, even as his eyes pleaded for Lexi to run. The barb-induced lacerations from his restraints opened further with every flinch his body made, tearing at the fabric of his mental clarity.

"Stop! Why did you bring him into this? I'm the one you want."

"And he's in the way. At least now he'll serve a purpose, a lesson you must learn." Her knife hand aimed at Todd's face.

"*Wait!*" Lexi screamed.

Before she had a chance to say anything more, Crystal sliced clean through his cheek.

Lexi's stomach sank as the fileted piece of skin fell away from his face, exposing the blood-smeared silhouette of his molars. Before she could stop herself, she lurched forward, trying to put herself between Todd and Crystal. The sound of his scream echoed in her head, dulling the burn of metal perforating her own skin. "Oh god, Todd, are you—" The cold muzzle of the gun against the nape of her neck cut off her words.

"Oh, Todd," Crystal mocked. "See, this is what I'm talking about. You need to learn exactly what will happen to the next person you try to use as my replacement. You are mine, and you will always be mine. I tried every fucking thing I could think of to get your attention without it having to come to this. All you had to do was lean on me, need me. But instead, you ran."

"I'm sorry. I know you love me now, and I promise I won't run anymore. Just let him go. Please." Her voice filled with sobs as she desperately tried to think of a way out of the situation. She reached her shaking hands behind her, hoping to calm Crystal with a touch, and as she ran her fingers across the fabric on Crystal's dress, she felt the pressure on the back of her head release a little. She stepped away from the bed, coaxing her stalker to follow with her gentle caress.

When she had put a satisfactory amount of distance between herself and Todd, she turned to face her captor. She forced a smile and kept her body close as she spoke, ignoring the gun pressed to her middle. "Tell me what you want from me, Crys. I know you say we are meant to be together, but until last weekend I had no idea you even had feelings for me. If this thing between us is going to work, I need to know how you see this ending."

Crystal stepped back and focused all her attention on Lexi. "I want it all. I've spent years waiting for this moment, dreaming about our future together. All that's left is to clean this mess up and go." She glanced at Todd, and then back to the object of her affection.

"Let's just go now. You don't need this gun anymore. I'll follow you anywhere you want to go." Resting her hand on top of the weapon, Crystal allowed her to lower the gun. Hoping to distract her even further, she leaned in and pressed their lips together, glancing to see if Todd was okay.

Crystal jerked away. "You have got to be fucking kidding me. Even as you kiss me, you look at him. I'm done with this bullshit. Just remember, you're the one who sealed his fate. Your selfishness will be his demise." She raised the gun again, and before another word was spoken, an ear-splitting pop filled the silence.

Lexi whirled around just in time to see Todd's lifeless body slump to the side of the bed. Her body went rigid, and the scream caught in her throat.

CHAPTER 63

"*L*exi, can you hear me? Wake up! Seriously, babe, you're starting to freak me out."

With a gasp, Lexi shot up. At first, she only looked at Todd in confusion until a tidal wave of relief washed over her, and she threw herself into his arms.

"You're okay? Oh thank god it was just a dream." She pushed herself away from him, grabbing his face for proof of its solidity, then pulled him back into her embrace. She could feel her body trembling and buried her tear-soaked cheeks into his shoulder.

"I'm perfectly fine, but you are trembling all over. That must have been one hell of a dream. Wanna talk about it?" He gently stroked her back until she looked up at him. "You scared the shit out of me."

"I scared you?" she questioned.

"Yes, you scared me. You were thrashing about in your sleep, and then suddenly, you sat straight up and let out a feral scream. When I went to touch you, you slapped at me and kept screaming no. I didn't realize you were still asleep at first because your eyes were wide open. It took me a good two or three minutes to get you to wake up."

Her breathing started to return to normal, but the intense fear of loss was still overwhelming. "It was her, and she had you, and I couldn't get to you."

"Enough said, enough said. I'm okay. Listen, it was just a dream. Come here," he said, cradling her as he laid back down. "We're both safe here, so relax. You know how tight the security Dad has on this place. She can't hurt us anymore. I won't let her have that power over us ever again."

Lexi let Todd hold her and tried to squash her fear, but despite his reassuring words, she could not shake the memory of his limp body from her mind. As much as she wanted things to be the way they were before she left for Cincinnati, she doubted that could ever be. Crystal had been inserting herself into Lexi's life for years, and followed her all the way to Tennessee, so she knew it was not over. She absently twirled the new ring on her finger, wishing it could actually fulfill the promises it offered.

"I don't know if I can do this, Todd," she said in a hushed voice. "She's already taken too much of me. I just don't know if there is enough left to make this work."

Ignoring his exasperation, he tightened his grasp. "Crystal hasn't taken anything you won't be able to get back in time. All the things I love about you are not capricious. Sure, they may change as life gets in your way, but your inherent makeup won't change. She will never be able to destroy who we are or what we have. Never."

A knock on the door interrupted their conversation, much to Lexi's relief.

Abby popped her head into the room, her hand comically covering her eyes. "Is everything okay in here? I heard screaming and wasn't sure. Are you guys decent?"

"Yes, Abs. Lexi had a nightmare, but everything's okay now."

"Thank goodness," she said as she crossed the room, throwing herself on the bed between the couple. She wiggled and pushed until she was situated comfortably between them, her hands propped behind her head. "So, what's the plan for today? I thought we could take the parents on a little getaway excursion. I was talking to Lexi's folks last night, and they don't have to be in any hurry to get back to

Ohio. I know Mom and Dad would be down for something, especially considering all that has happened."

"Come on in, Abby. Make yourself comfortable. Don't mind us," Todd joked, pushing playfully at his sister.

"I don't think I'm in the mood to be around a bunch of people right now," said Lexi.

"So, what are you going do instead, sit around and worry yourself to death? Besides, it seems to me like getting out of here for a while would not only be a good distraction, but a sensible strategic move, as well. With Crystal on the run or in hiding, it's not going to be easy for her to follow us any kind of distance, right?"

"She actually makes a good point, Lexi. Besides, I would enjoy spending some more time with your parents getting to know them better. I know my parents would love more time with you. The cops already have all the information we can give them and have alerted every station from here to Cincinnati to be on patrol. Don't get me wrong, I want to help find her more than anyone, but honestly, there is nothing more we can do."

"Well, we can't just up and run away from this. Trust me, I know better than anyone that running away doesn't work. It just ends up putting more people in danger." Without looking at them, Lexi got up, walked to the bathroom, and closed the door.

They both stared after her for a moment until Abby turned to her brother. "Why don't you go downstairs and give us a minute?"

"I don't know, Abs. That nightmare really shook her up."

"Trust me, dear brother, just go downstairs and get breakfast started. Let me talk to her alone."

Still unsure, he pulled on his pajama pants and hesitantly headed downstairs.

Abby sat up and waited quietly as the bathroom door opened, and Lexi peeked her head out, thinking everyone had left.

Her eyes were red from crying, and she let out a breath of frustration when she noticed she wasn't alone.

Starting to close the door, Abby stopped her. "Wait a minute, please."

"Listen, Abby, I'm not trying to be a jerk, but I told you I wasn't in the mood to be around people today."

"I know, but just hear me out. If you still feel the same way when I'm done, I'll let it go."

"Fair enough." Lexi walked into the room wiping the tears from her face and sat down on the bed facing her friend, forcing the impatience and fear back a notch.

"I'm not going to pretend I understand what you are feeling right now. I can see the appeal of pushing everyone away and hiding from the world. It's obvious you're feeling guilty for what happened to Todd, which is completely unfounded, but I get it. What Crystal has taken from you goes back to before we came into your life, and I'm not expecting, or asking, you to run away or act like it never happened. That kind of betrayal and defilement of trust will take years to process fully. But you need to remember you aren't going through this alone, Lexi. You aren't the only person who was violated this week."

"You don't think I realize that?" Lexi barked defensively.

"I'm sorry, I didn't mean it like that," Abby said. "What I am trying to say is that I know my brother, and I'm worried about him. I know he isn't ready to talk about what she did to him while he was in that basement because he doesn't want to add any more guilt or pressure on you. I know he's worried you're pulling away from him, so he's bottled up all his emotions in an attempt to be strong, but he can't deal with all this alone, any more than you can. Right now, I feel like Crystal has too much control over everyone's ability to move forward. Everyone's afraid of what's around the corner, terrified she'll return. I just want us all to be able to step away from that fear, even if it's just for a week or two, take away that control, and give the cops a chance to find her and put her away forever. I'm not trying to downplay your feelings, but Todd's my first responsibility, and I want to give him every opportunity to heal. He won't do that unless you're on board."

"I'm not the only obstacle to this plan. My parents can't afford to just pick up and go on an extended vacation. It's not fair of me to ask that from them."

"Trust me, money is not an issue."

Lexi laughed acrimoniously. "Of course money isn't an issue for you, but we don't live in the same world as your family."

"Hold up a minute. According to that ring on your finger, you're a part of this family now, which means your parents are also a part of this family. I understand we may have grown up in different financial situations, but our families aren't that different. I saw how you interacted with your parents last night, and your relationship is obviously built on love and respect. Are you telling me that if you invited your parents to come on a trip, they would say no because you wanted to pick up the tab? If you're marrying my brother, you need to find a way to get past that bullshit. Everyone will miss out on some incredible opportunities if you can't let go of that way of thinking."

"You don't understand."

It was Abby's turn to snap. "Stop. Do you think you're the first person in our lives who hasn't come from money? Listen, I respect that you don't want to feel like you're taking advantage of Todd's money. He's never made a habit of making money an issue. And trust me, if you were that kind of person, you wouldn't still be in the picture. Can you just do me a favor and at least give them the chance to make up their own minds on the subject? Will you please let go of your own insecurities, just a bit, and give Todd a little breathing room?"

Lexi fell back on the bed, kneading her temples with her fingers. She was torn between her heart and her instinct to run. A tangle in her hair was snagged by the unfamiliar ring on her hand, reminding her of the promise she made last night. How could she hurt him more than she already had? Deep down, she knew Abby was right. Her aversion to the idea of a trip had nothing to do with money, and everything to do with fear. Realizing it was finally time to take back control in her life, she sighed. "Okay, let's see what they say."

The two girls headed downstairs to the kitchen to meet up with the rest of the family for breakfast. Abby was still excited about her idea but promised to let Lexi talk to her parents before she said anything.

As they walked into the kitchen, the house phone began to ring, and Todd's dad answered, "Hello?"

Everyone stopped to look at James when his demeanor changed from comfortable and relaxed to rigid and alert in an instant. His answers were short and direct, and after a few minutes, he put down the receiver.

"That was Sheriff Whaley. He wants me to bring Todd and Lexi down to the station. He wouldn't give me any details, but it seems they have located Miss Lamothe."

Todd looked over at Lexi and back to his dad. "Are you serious, Dad?"

"Seems so." His dad smiled and embraced his son, throwing a knowing look at Lexi. "Go get dressed, you two. Let's go!"

CHAPTER 64

The next day was kind of a blur. People were coming and going, asking questions about Crystal's involvement in Lexi's life in Cincinnati, and confirming details of Todd's ordeal.

The morning before, the sheriff explained that a fisherman had found Crystal's body floating near an illegal dump site on the lake. Not long after, they found that the car had rolled into the lake, submerging Crystal inside. The body must have floated out of open windows after her death. The cops were perplexed at why she hadn't tried to escape, but they assumed the toxicology screen would come back positive for drugs. Whether her death was intentional or accidental, no one would ever be able to say. Lexi selfishly hoped she was awake for every minute of terror, and with that thought, a sinister chill hit her spine.

It turned out the police had gotten a warrant for Crystal's house, so they were in possession of the computer. Unfortunately, there was even more information than what Lexi had been able to retrieve.

Todd's dad called his lawyer in case there were any charges filed for Lexi's little excursion into Crystal's house. Plus, they wanted to know precisely how the evidence of the stalking would be handled and disposed of.

Everyone seemed to be in good spirits, and understandably more relaxed, since the immediate threat of physical danger was over.

Lexi's parents had gone back to their hotel, leaving her and Todd entirely alone for the first time in two days.

Todd plopped down on the couch and rubbed his eyes. The stress of the past week finally pulled him down, and exhaustion tugged at every part of his body. He looked at Lexi with eyes much older than those she had initially met, but the tenderness was still there.

She lay on the couch with her head in his lap, and within a few minutes, they were both asleep.

LEXI WOKE *to three thunderous cracks of a whip and found herself standing in the water near the lake's edge. Unfamiliar emotions consumed her: a wicked thirst for death, urged on by anger, and a need for completion. She was not in control of her body; she was just a visitor watching the scene unfold from the dark lady's perspective. Ahead of her, next to a shocking amount of discarded junk, was a red car slowly rolling toward her. She could sense the curiosity of the girl staring at her from the back seat. In a rush that stole her breath, the lady flew at the girl she recognized as Crystal. The lithe body wrapped around the stunned girl, claws sinking deep into her flesh. An instant later, she felt the death-laden tongue penetrate Crystal's lips, slithering down to engorge the girl's throat.*

She could taste Crystal's terror as her airway closed. Her fear was as delectable as anything Lexi had ever tasted. She felt the water quickly rising in the car, but she was enjoying this taste of death and revenge too much to be bothered. As the car completely submerged, Lexi felt the life leave Crystal, leaving her empty and slumped in the back seat.

The dark lady rose from the water and turned to leave.

Lexi could feel the lady's sense of completion at a job well done, but before she'd traveled far, an unearthly shriek stopped her. Turning, she watched the spirit of the young girl struggling to rise from the water, only to have tendrils of water wrap around her legs, keeping her spirit from moving on. Crystal raged against the land's trauma, but the connection with her own trauma held fast. All the obsession, hatred, lust, and need for control that consumed her life was amplified in her death state. Lexi felt the dark lady's surprise when Crystal's maddened spirit broke from the water's entanglement and came at her. The sting of Crystal scratching at the dark lady's eyes just before she broke free terrified Lexi.

Outraged by her circumstances, Crystal's spirit flew off, but the dark lady stayed on Crystal's trail, her dismay punching Lexi in the gut.

In spirit form, Crystal was no longer tied to earthly restraints, and she soared through the sky until she spotted Todd's house. As she dove toward the property, she slammed into an invisible barrier as solid and impenetrable as a concrete wall. Frustrated, she repeatedly threw herself against the wards to no avail. Realizing her efforts were futile, Crystal noticed a bright glow and curiously searched through the night for its source.

Lexi immediately recognized the property as Crystal circled, strategically testing her boundaries this time. Hearing Kate and Mama's conversation pulled Lexi from her vision.

Lexi woke from her sleep with a startle, but Todd's exhaustion had finally taken him all the way under, and he snored peacefully as she carefully rose from the couch, took the keys to the Jeep, and left the house.

CHAPTER 65

*C*rystal had lost control of her situation, and the murky lake water saturated her with coldness and hopelessness as the car started sinking more rapidly. Instinct to live took over. Slowly releasing her last breath, she realized she was going to drown. As the darkness closed in from all sides, she refused to let her life end on those terms. Desperation was suddenly replaced with hysterical indignation, and she screamed with all the fury of her newly awakened emotions.

As water filled her lungs, her corporeal body slipped away, and she frantically reached for the surface, suddenly aware she had no more need for oxygen. Her violent, unstable spirit burst into the fall night air, but she immediately felt an overwhelming, energetic soup of loneliness, abandonment, grief, righteousness, deceit, and fury grab at her from the depths of the lake. With each grasp, she felt jolts of memory from their forgotten lives, and the heaviness started pulling her back into the darkness of the watery cemetery.

Exhausted, she considered letting them take her. Her dream of the perfect life with Lexi had been stolen, so what else was there?

When the dark lady floated above her, expecting her soul to be trapped by the hopeless and discarded graveyard rotting and forgotten under hundreds of feet of water, she snapped free. Fuck these ass-backward mountain idiots. She had no tie to this land.

She was invincible and engulfed in her need for vengeance and retribution. Her first obstacle was this Reaper Goddess of Fate, who she learned was named Giltine.

An unhinged screech startled Giltine as Crystal flew at her with hate and death on her agenda.

Giltine's shock at the vapid young woman's determination and ability to escape the lake's grasp caught her off guard. Black blood from the gashes of Crystal's sudden attack blurred her vision, so she swooped beneath the water to heal her wounds and clean her face. She'd involved herself too much in the death of that evil human, but she hadn't considered the repercussions of her actions. Giltine underestimated the girl's venomous spirit, an experience she had only encountered once before, which had stolen youth, beauty, and time from her—ironically, the same reason she'd acted so capriciously in the first place.

As she trailed Crystal's erratic spirit, she found Lexi sleeping and tried to explain the result of her poor judgment.

LEXI'S HANDS shook as she fumbled to insert the key into the ignition. Wind blew through her hair as she hastily maneuvered the curvy back roads to get to Kate's. In retrospect, it would have been easier to go by water.

Fear, she'd learned, was a strong trigger for her magic, and still being an apprentice, she worried at the dark storm she knew her emotions were creating. At the moment of awareness, she unsuccessfully tried to ground herself and calm down.

A quick glimpse of what looked like a cloud of navy, crimson, and black alerted Lexi that Crystal knew she was on the move. The icy intention of her vision haunted her, and she was especially worried over the fact that the spirit had been able to attack the dark lady physically. Lexi was no expert on human spirits, but she assumed they were their weakest just after death. If that was Crystal weak, she didn't want to imagine her at full strength.

Just then, visual modality switched from physical to mental, filling her mind with Crystal's new noncorporeal state. Her body remained a dark, smoky semblance of her old form, stained in writhing red whisps. But it was the face that caused her to run off the road. Instead of the impish features and clear blue eyes Lexi remembered, Crystal's face was a melting vortex of flesh, bone, and blood. The only identifiable human feature was her tinted blue lips. The rest was a dreadful melody, shifting in and out of the wet blonde roots of her hair. A maelstrom of every adult's worst nightmare.

Lexi was frantically feeling around on the seat next to her for the confusion doll she'd put in the Jeep for protection when the front end of the vehicle slammed down into a ditch. At the same time, her mind cleared, and she could see where she was again. She found the doll, shoved it into her pocket, and took a moment to catch her breath.

Above her, where the road to Kate's house cut into the mountain, she heard a shrill scream. It sounded like a girl being attacked. Confused and slightly battered by the accident, she trudged up the rough terrain, quietly calling out to the unfamiliar voice.

Movement in the underbrush led her up the hill to a red fox sitting in the middle of the road. She was exquisite. Her fiery orange fur was brilliant, highlighted with a light blonde stripe down her back, in contrast to the long, dark legs she sat upon so gracefully. Her majestic, bushy tail was a luxurious burnt orange with grey streaks, tipped in white, and she whipped it around with authority. The well of wisdom was deep in her almond eyes, poised beneath a crescent of blonde framing her petite black nose.

Her erect ears twitched when Lexi stopped short and said, "Was that you screaming? I thought someone was being attacked."

"As if I would need a human to get *me* out of a bind," the fox jested.

Lexi stood dumbstruck for a moment, unsure how she was communicating with a fox, while a giant flash of lightning streaked through the sky, illuminating the still confused Crystal.

When the thunderclap echoed off the water, Lexi jumped and slid downhill on the damp vegetation. The fox stretched and flaunted her amazing tail as she turned towards Kate's house.

Lexi instinctively followed without hesitation.

"I've been watching you since you got here. Not like I could have avoided you. You really need to learn how to control your magic," said the fox, "and I ain't sure you got the time."

"Okay," mumbled Lexi, mostly to herself. "The stress of everything has broken my brain. I am having a conversation with a fox and running from a dead person through the Appalachian Mountains."

"Is a talking animal the crazy takeaway from this situation? Maybe Alva was wrong about you after all."

Lexi stopped again. "Alva can talk to animals?"

"We're a little short on time, so talk while we walk."

"Do you have a name?" asked Lexi, trying to keep up with her spry new friend.

"Alva calls me Foxy. Original, right? My true name doesn't translate into human."

"Foxy, how am I able to understand you right now? I can almost feel what you're gonna do before you actually do it. It's kind of freaking me out."

"Have you ever heard of witches having a familiar?"

"Like Salem from *Sabrina the Teenage Witch*?"

"I'm assuming that's a human pop culture reference. I live in the most glorious mountains in all the realms, I spend most of my time out here. A familiar is an animal that has a magical bond with a witch. Our job is to guide, protect, and assist in magical predicaments like this one," said Foxy.

"How have I not noticed you before?"

"You have. You've seen me plenty of times, but you hadn't opened yourself to your magic, so I couldn't connect to you. I've known Alva for a long time, so she explained your situation to me. I felt when your crazy stalker transitioned and broke free from the Reaper, so when you summoned this storm, I figured you needed me."

Girl and fox turned down the long gravel road leading to Kate's point.

"What's the deal with you and the dark Reaper anyway?" asked Foxy.

"I have no idea. I can't see her on this plane of existence, but she sends me visions and comes to me in dreams. She's the reason I knew Crystal was trying to attack everyone. Most of her previous communications were almost cryptic, but the last one seemed like a recent memory from her perspective. I was very close to ending my life, so maybe she felt death in my energy. What do you know about her?"

"I simply know her as 'the dark one,' and she is some kind of goddess of fate and death. Her people are from another part of the world. They called her to this area when the big floods came, but she never left. Lots of death in these mountains, I guess. She often takes the form of a snake, and usually hangs out alone near cemeteries or places where she can feed from the dead."

"I've seen her a couple of times, but she never speaks forthrightly. The last vision she sent me was pretty clear, though," said Lexi.

"She also has a sister most call the light one. She often shows up for births and is rumored to assign fates that will determine the newborn's future. She and Alva have a pretty good working relationship since Alva is the best midwife in East Tennessee. She's a Reaper too, but only for special deaths. Her animal form is a swan."

They reached the driveway of the white house on the point. The house was lit up, and you could feel Alva and Kate conjuring.

Lexi quickened her steps, following Foxy's lead.

Before they reached the door, Kate opened it and ushered them inside.

"Alva felt you coming," said Kate. "Hurry in so we can discuss what has your emotions on hypervigilance, summoning a literal storm. We thought after the confirmation of Crystal's death, you would be relieved and taking some much-needed rest."

"Hey there, Foxy. I see you've finally introduced yourself to Lexi," said Alva.

"Didn't have much choice in it, did I? She's gonna need us all tonight."

CHAPTER 66

"Well, then, let's start by interpreting the vision. Where's my baby boy?" Alva asked.

"He's fine, sleeping peacefully on the couch. I set all our protection wards as soon as we last spoke on the phone and witnessed their enforcement."

"What do you mean you witnessed their enforcement?"

"It's a long story, and I feel like we are running short on time. So, Kate, if you could make us some tea that opens us to the astral plane, I'll explain."

Mama took a seat at the table while Kate began rummaging through her apothecary for the right ingredients.

Lexi couldn't sit, so she paced back and forth, explaining her latest vision from the dark lady.

In the middle of Lexi's story, Kate interrupted. "Wait a minute, did you say Crystal's spirit didn't move on?"

"Yes, the lake water rose and wrapped around her like a rope. It was the craziest thing I have ever seen. It tried to pull her under, but she was too strong and broke free," said Lexi.

Mama nodded her head. "I've seen the water take untethered souls before. Just reaches out and pulls them under to add to the collective discontent. I ain't never seen one strong enough to pull free. That definitely ain't good."

"Well, not only did that bitch's spirit get free, it came at the dark lady. I felt the sting as Crystal clawed at her eyes. Then, she immediately went to Todd's house, banging against the invisible wards over and over again. Now, I assume she's back outside circling your property, strategically testing the boundaries, and looking for a way in. On my drive over here, she came at me, causing me to run Todd's Jeep into a ditch. I managed to activate the confusion doll, so it kept her off my trail long enough for me to meet Foxy and make our way here."

"During your vision, you say you saw all of this through the eyes of the dark lady?" asked Kate.

"Yes and no. I not only saw it through her point of view, but I could feel all the emotions. Not just hers, but Crystal's too, and I could distinguish their emotions from my own. It was fucked up. I sensed the dark lady is a Reaper of death, like that's her job, and she enjoys it. I simultaneously felt the dark lady's satisfaction with the malicious way she ended Crystal's life. Then came the terror, pain, confusion, and rage as Crystal processed her death. Crystal's face had lost all features but her dead lips. It was a swirling and indistinct mess of color because during life, she never had a true sense of self. She constantly shifted personalities and changed how she looked for the acceptance of others or to blend in."

"That sounds like a hard way to live," said Foxy.

"It felt like her facial vortex was more than confused rage. It was terror made real because of the despair she felt over not understanding who, or what, she is outside of her vengeance."

"Let's start with the positives. I think the omniscience is a good thing. I think the dark lady showed you her memory of the event. This conversation wasn't only in metaphors and pictures. I think she is trying to help you, especially since you said she felt satisfaction in the way she took Crystal's life. I think she is a harbinger of fate, but the way she ended that girl's life so callously seems like she shared a hatred for her."

As soon as the words left Alva's mouth, the lightbulb in the hallway burst.

"I don't know about you ladies, but I'm gonna take that as a yes," Alva said.

Kate sat down with the teapot and filled her ceremonial set of silver goblets with hot water over one of her spiritual tea blends. "Is it normal for a human spirit to be able to touch this elemental?"

Lexi covered her ears, flinching as the word *No* boomed in her mind. She shook her head, trying to silence the ferocity of the thought and find her way back to the conversation.

She sat down a little more than rattled. "Fucking hell, that was a very loud and adamant *no*. If Crystal's spirit is that strong, what can we do to get rid of it?"

The room temperature dropped 20 degrees, and the witches and fox were unexpectedly joined by Giltine and Laima.

Giltine lingered behind her sister, ashamed of her involvement in creating the mess.

Laima stepped forward, speaking directly to Alva because of their previous relationship. "Please, before any other actions are made, may I make introductions?" Laima asked.

Alva nodded.

"My name is Laima, and this is my sister Giltine. We were pulled here from the Baltic region by our people who came for work after the devastating floods. We fell in love with the energy from these ancient mountains, and grew to love the diversity, grit, perseverance, and loyalty of its people, so we stuck around to help.

My sister realizes her mistakes when transitioning this vengeful spirit into death. She let her emotions control her, and she has beckoned me to help rectify her error. I encourage each of you to act as a candle for this lost spirit. We are creatures of light, so it is our responsibility to find light in *all* people. We need to help this spirit reconnect with her humanity so she can pass over peacefully."

"I'm sorry. Did you just say we needed to *help* the bitch that stole my privacy, dignity, and desire to live? You do realize she also kidnapped and tortured the man I love and is now coming after me, right?" asked Lexi indignantly.

A hostile bolt of lightning streaked through the sky, turning night into a flash of daylight.

"I understand your animosity, Lexi, but the path of the cunning ones asks you to be the change you want to see in your world. Hurt people will continue to hurt people. Crystal led an agonizing human life during this incarnation, so the cycle needs to be broken, and we can mend a tiny bit of generational trauma."

Lexi walked out the back door, closely followed by witches, goddesses, and a fox. The whole situation seemed surreal, and she still hadn't completely wrapped her mind around how she came to be in that position. She flopped onto the grass, absorbing the earth's grounding energy. Ignoring everyone staring down at her, she wrestled with her ego and old thought patterns.

Foxy came to her, settling on her chest, and cupped Lexi's chin with her soft tail. No words were needed between the two as nature worked her magic.

Lexi's heartbeat slowed, and her tendency to overthink was balanced by the simplicity of Foxy's animal instinct.

The white tip of Foxy's tail directed Lexi's attention to the sky above them, where she saw Crystal's spirit slamming into the property's wards. The fox hopped off her soulmate's chest as Lexi sat up and understanding washed the anger from her body. She touched noses with Foxy to show her gratitude.

"Laima is right. We need to offer Crystal an opportunity to right her wrongs in the next life, but I don't want to communicate with her until I am as prepared as possible for all scenarios. So, Alva, what do we need to do?"

"Lexi, hon," Alva said, "you are a very powerful girl, and in a perfect world, we'd take steps to unlock that power, lettin' you learn to deal with it over time under our guidance. But it seems we've jumped from the frying pan right into the fire, and if these ancient elementals are worried, then we got no choice but to pull out the big guns. You're a strong girl, so I know you can handle it, but after tonight you are gonna need to spend much of your time here learning to control the repercussions of our actions tonight."

"What does that mean?" asked an apprehensive Lexi.

"We're going to do an unblocking ritual which will give you full access to your powers. With Kate's eidetic memory, my years of experience, the magnitude of your power, and Foxy's guidance, we should be a formidable team with the ability to eliminate that booger. Not to mention, our goddess friends seem more than willing to help, as well." The warmth that enveloped the oldest of the conjuring women reaffirmed her statement.

"Are you sure she is ready for that?" asked Kate.

"You know as well as I do that life never makes no promises. But I am sure that without it, she and Todd both might as well be sitting ducks anytime they leave either of the warded properties, and that ain't no way for two young people in love to live."

The women wasted no time getting the ritual space set up. Because most of their magic came from nature, it only made sense to do the ceremony outside, but within the property's bubble of protection.

First, Mama drew Lexi a road opening salt bath, explaining the properties of the ingredients: rock salt, crossroad dirt, dried sage, hyssop, and both orange and lemon essential oils, which Kate had processed. Along with the bath, Kate made Lexi a potent tea infused with mauve, lemon balm, and psilocybin caps intended to open her mind.

Mama gave her a full cup of tea to drink, then instructed her to soak in the hot water until the temperature had turned tepid, and try to clear her thoughts of any negative emotion or energy and open herself up. Afterward, she told Lexi to dry herself with the towel supplied and join them within the ceremonial circle of stones near the water's edge.

"Come in nothing but your birthday suit, hon. The less between you and nature, the easier it will be to release your blockages into the land."

"Is the nudity really necessary?" asked the modest girl.

"Not all the time, but for this ritual, it is. There won't be anyone around except us ladies, and we've got all the same parts you do. Shame is one of your big blocks, so let that go in the bath before you come out. You are a beautiful example of the divine feminine, so wear that with pride. Shame is societal; this is spiritual. Now, don't drain the bathwater. We'll dispose of it later." Mama recited a short incantation, kissed Lexi's head, and walked out of the room.

Lexi did her best to clear her mind, repeating the incantation until it was the only thought she was focused on. She felt a pressure she had never noticed release in her body, and she easily fell into a meditative trance. When the bath water was no longer warm, she stood to step out of the tub to dry off.

The world felt weird. Her journey to the sacred circle felt like she was walking on clouds, and she was unable to stop the giggle that bubbled out of her. When she took her position with her mentors, her affection for them was almost all-consuming.

"What was in that tea?" she asked in awe.

Both women laughed as Mama explained that psilocybin was a hallucinogenic mushroom used to open parts of the psyche not regularly active. She anointed Lexi's chakras with some kind of oil and asked her to hold hands in a circle around the iron firepit, which looked suspiciously like a cauldron to Lexi.

Mama tossed in an herb called Abre Camino she received from one of her friends who was a hoodoo conjure woman. She reconnected hands with her sisters and closed the circle and recited, "As the bonds of sisterhood unite us and make us stronger, use our energy to open Lexi Greer's path to magic fully and completely."

At that instant, the flames of the firepit leaped six or seven feet in the air, releasing a wave of power with such force that it tossed all three women and the fox out of the stone circle. The wave of power erupted with such force that it also shattered the property's protection magic.

The force had blown Kate clear onto the dock. When she shakily stood to her feet, her jaw dropped at the sight before her.

The magic surging through Lexi was palpable. The once-dark night was completely illuminated, and she could see everything. Spots of energy clung to the lake like fog. She could see the dark lady clearly, hovering just above the water next to Kate.

"Holy shit," said Lexi.

"Holy shit is right," said Mama, "come help an old lady up."

As Lexi walked over to help her friend to her feet, the magic lifted her before Lexi had time to reach out a hand. Both women were momentarily shocked into silence, but that moment didn't last long.

A guttural wail echoed off the mountains around them. Before anyone could move, Crystal's spirit tried to swoop in, but Laima intercepted. "You must make the offer now, Lexi."

"Crystal," Lexi shouted to get the confused spirit's attention. "We would like to help you release this emotion and pass through into your next stage of existence. I know you faced unimaginable suffering in this life, but this beautiful Goddess of Fate has decided to offer you another chance—a chance to move on and break the cycle of generational traumas your family has been stuck in for lifetimes."

The violent vortex within Crystal slowed. The grotesque facial shifts looked more curious and sadder. She shifted toward Laima and accepted the goddess's outstretched hand, opening a peek into the girl's next existence. Crystal slowly stepped one foot into the light, the child within desperate for the love and attention she never received the last time around, but at the sight of her mom, she hesitated.

Laima softly explained how Crystal's next life would give her the opportunity to mend things with her mother's soul, but the power dynamics in the relationship would be switched. All the abuse from their last life together would not exist, eliminating Crystal's obsessive traits and self-hatred.

As Laima tried to get Crystal to let go of the anger and pass over, Giltine left Kate's side and went about trying to determine the damage to the property's wards.

Lexi's magical awakening had, essentially, left them spiritually unprotected. Giltine did not have her sister's optimism about reasoning with that unhinged spirit, but she promised herself she would never intervene with human emotion again. She warned Alva and Foxy to be prepared to fight.

Laima was guiding Crystal's spirit further into the light, the last step of the transition.

As soon as Crystal's curious and hopeful spirit took that last step, she felt her mother's familiar, narcissistic energy. It triggered all her post-traumatic stressors, and she leaped back into Laima, knocking them both off balance.

Once Laima lost control of the situation, she knew it would not end peacefully. As she fought to hold the humiliated and enraged spirit, Crystal easily slipped away, diving at the weakest link.

She snatched Kate by the hair and plunged them under the still, dark water. As Crystal pulled the woman deeper into the lake, Lexi dove in after them to save her friend, but she could only watch the two women sink out of view as a swan-like entity pulled Lexi back to the surface.

When she emerged, Alva helped lift Lexi onto the dock. She screamed and fought but eventually realized she was being cradled by the breathtaking blonde goddess. Confused, she looked to Alva for an explanation.

Through tears, Alva said, "It wasn't your time, Lexi."

"We have to save Kate!" Lexi screamed, but the gentle blonde looked at her with tear-filled eyes and shook her head no.

Undeterred, Lexi stood, opening both arms wide, palms up. The turbulence in the water boiled as Lexi's magic pulled the women up, dropping them on the grass beside her. She immediately realized Kate was dead, and her emotions took over.

Lexi grabbed Crystal's corporeal body by the neck, bringing them nose to nose. "I am done with you. You are nothing. You have always been nothing to me. I am finished being manipulated and weak. I found my power and will never let another person take that from me. Even in death, you still manage to take from me. Not anymore. You are no longer tethered to this land or me. You no longer exist in any form, bitch."

Lexi's words were Crystal's undoing. Her spirit split into millions of dark flashes before vanishing altogether. Lexi crumpled to the ground in tears and exhaustion.

CHAPTER 67

*L*exi glanced toward Kate's broken body as sobs ripped out of her in jagged spurts. She held her face in her hands with the weight of guilt threatening to take her completely under.

A coolness fell upon her back, shocking Lexi back into the present when she heard Kate's voice speak plainly, "Lexi, this wasn't your fault."

She looked up, but Kate's lifeless body still lay on the grass. She turned to find Kate standing between the dark lady and the lovely blonde who had pulled Lexi from the water.

Alva walked over, eyes spilling over with love and loss, and took Lexi's hand and squeezed.

The three spirits floated just above the shoreline.

Giltine stepped forward, cocking her head of long black hair to one side.

Kate continued, "Giltine wants you to know that she took notice of you on the water the afternoon you arrived at the lake. She was fascinated by the complex relationship you had with death, so she started keeping an eye on you. She said she tried to warn you against the danger you were facing, but she could not speak the language of the living. Giltine is merely an agent of fate. When it is someone's time to pass, death is inevitable; she can only try to keep them from suffering too much. In special cases, her sister comes to help her. Laima is a goddess of fate and destiny, which is why Alva and I have seen her at so many births.

Giltine wants you to know that my death was predestined, so there was no way it could have been prevented. She doesn't want you to wear any of the blame. In fact, she wants to thank you for being one of the first people in a very long time to value her. Most people fear death, which is why everyone avoids her. Your trust allowed her to be the hero for once, and even though she had no idea what she was releasing, she enjoyed making Crystal's death feel like the punishment she deserved. Sadly, life needs evil for good to exist, just as we could not have dark without light. She says you understand both sides of the stone better than most, which is why she would like to help you in your journey to enlightenment. She promises to not interfere with your ancestral team's guidance, but she wants you to know you have a friend in death, anytime you need her."

"Is there nothing we can do to bring Kate back? How do we know Crystal is really gone?" asked Lexi.

Kate listened for a moment, then spoke. "Sadly, Lexi, my time in this life has come full circle. My soul is headed to the next step in my journey. Giltine assured me Crystal would not be back on this plane, so you no longer need to fear her. She did say I would be able to pop in and say hi from time to time, so you ladies are not permanently rid of me. In fact, Alva, would you help Lexi with all the paperwork to ensure this property and the business is transferred into her name." Looking at Lexi's ring finger, she said, "Consider it a wedding present. Know I will love you from wherever I am." Then she turned toward her mentor and best friend. "I love you, Alva. Take care of our protégé. I'll tell my mom how much you miss her. I can't wait to finally get to know my own mother," she giggled.

Before another word was spoken, all three ethereal women faded away, leaving Alva and Lexi alone on the cool grass. They held each other and cried, overwhelmed by relief, love, and longing.

EPILOGUE

The women gathered on the frigid November evening. It was the one-year anniversary of Kate's death.

Mama had taken a lock of Kate's hair, and along with a lock of her own, she braided the three women's hair into a lock at the base of Lexi's neck. Mama explained to her that braided hair was an ancient Irish symbol of feminine power and luck. She instructed Lexi never to remove the braid, which interwove the bond and power the three women would always share.

Lexi had no idea how, but she Alva also managed to obtain a lock of Crystal's hair. The night's ceremony was about forgiveness, healing, and release.

The women braided the hair from the three witches with that of Lexi's nemesis, Crystal.

Mama held the braid over the ceremonial fire and recited, "As with creation, we entwine both light and dark, hard and easy, good and evil. Let this fire burn away the anger, hatred, and fear created by Crystal Lamothe." She dropped the braided hair into the fire.

The three cracks of the whip alerted them that Giltine arrived for the release ceremony.

"We offer forgiveness to Crystal. We hope her darkness does not follow her into her next journey. I release you from my heart, my mind, and my life. May happiness find you," said Lexi.

Lexi and Mama stood at the warm fire holding hands, spirits mingling with the ether.

After what seemed like a lifetime, they broke their connection and headed back into the house.

Todd stood at the stove, putting the last touches on that night's dinner. He turned to face his wife, laying his hand on her bulging pregnant belly. "Hey, old lady," he shouted at Mama. "You ready to be a great-grandma?"

"I can't wait to meet our little Miss Katherine and teach her everything we know."

The End

ABOUT THE AUTHOR

A kid of the Southeastern Kentucky mountains, Rachel Coffman learned about Appalachian folklore and the art of storytelling from her Granny O'Boyle. She writes about strong women, mountain magic, and overcoming trauma in ways that recognize generational horrors and empower her readers to face their fears and take back their power. Reverberations, Norris Lake Witches Book One, is her debut novel and the first in the series.